A Debt Redeemed

A Debt Redeemed

Andrew Clark

First published in Great Britain in 2024 by
Pen & Sword Crime
An imprint of
Pen & Sword Books Ltd
Yorkshire - Philadelphia

Copyright © Andrew Clark, 2024

ISBN 978 1 03610 536 5

The right of Andrew Clark to be identified as the Author of this work has been asserted by her in accordance with the Copyright, Designs and Patents Act 1988.

A CIP catalogue record for this book is available from the British Library

All rights reserved. No part of this book may be reproduced or transmitted in any form or by any means, electronic or mechanical including photocopying, recording or by any information storage and retrieval system, without permission from the Publisher in writing.

Typeset in INDIA by IMPEC eSolutions
Printed and bound in the UK by CPI Group (UK) Ltd, Croydon, CR0 4YY

Pen & Sword Books Limited incorporates the imprints of Atlas, Archaeology, Aviation, Discovery, Family History, Fiction, History, Maritime, Military, Military Classics, Politics, Select, Transport, True Crime, Air World, Frontline Publishing, Leo Cooper, Remember When, Seaforth Publishing, The Praetorian Press, Wharncliffe Local History, Wharncliffe Transport, Wharncliffe True Crime and White Owl.

For a complete list of Pen & Sword titles please contact

PEN & SWORD BOOKS LIMITED
47 Church Street, Barnsley, South Yorkshire S70 2AS, United Kingdom
E-mail: enquiries@pen-and-sword.co.uk
Website: www.pen-and-sword.co.uk

or

PEN AND SWORD BOOKS
1950 Lawrence Rd, Havertown, PA 19083, USA
E-mail: Uspen-and-sword@casematepublishers.com
Website: www.penandswordbooks.com

Chapter 1

John checked his appearance in the rear view mirror, unaware that his pupils would soon be fixed and dilated, with sclera shattered by scarlet webs.

He sat in his car staring towards the calm stretch of water north of the falls with daylight starting to fade, the warmth of the day still permeating the air. Midges danced frenetically by the slow flowing water, their bites clouding the air in the stillness of the riverbank. His thoughts were grim. This had been a venture which was always going to cause him issues, but energised with the vigour of youth, it had been financially irresistible. High risk, high reward, with little chance of failure. He had been impregnable in his twenties, his armour of youth bulletproof, his personal mantra 'no one's gonna mess with me', and they didn't.

***

Rosie stood transfixed, poised ready, straight as a dart with tail extended as her black nose twitched, scenting her prey. Her sleek frame frozen in time, in the unmistakable posture of an English Pointer having sighted its target. Her short white and orange coat glistened in the last sultry embrace of a summer sun descending towards the tree's crowns, as it bowed farewell to the day. To Rosie's right, the riverbank sloped towards the gently winding waters of the River Stern, travelling serenely past, whispering its tales. In the distance, a dull rumbling kneaded her senses, an indication of a more energetic river upstream. She stood unmoved. Nothing would deviate her from her prey as she focussed intently and tensed her muscles ready to pounce. It moved, she moved, diving into a swathe of Yorkshire fog grass, disappearing below the tufted purple heads, as she missed the butterfly who elegantly carried on with its business, unperturbed by her actions.

"Rosie, Rosie," a woman's voice called out. The dog froze recognising the timbre of the voice.

Kate looked ahead into the velvet grass where she had last seen Rosie from a distance. A black nose, followed by intelligent brown eyes and orange and white mottled ears, poked through the purple canopy looking back towards her, the dog's pink tongue lolling from the side of its mouth in a drunken grin.

"Come here, girl," Rosie's head tilted to one side, her ears alert. "Come on."

Kate watched as Rosie gave a bark and turned towards her, pouncing up in the air and disappearing again as she landed, the long grass enveloping her. Her progress to Kate was measured by a series of leaps and concealments as she charged her chosen route. Ears flying up and down as she moved as if to assist her in her propulsion through the riverbank meadow, excited yelps pierced the air as she closed on Kate. Now out of the tall grasses she stretched out, her claws gripping the earth, her haunches powering her forward. Kate laughed as Rosie charged towards her and overshot, almost tumbling over in a tangle of legs as she adjusted and turned back towards Kate.

"Good girl, good girl," said Kate, squatting down to pat Rosie's head. "Now leave the wildlife alone." She put Rosie on a lead, in preparation for nearing the falls and both then followed the riverside track.

Kate strolled along, camera suspended around her neck, ready to take a photograph of anything of interest. She had always had a passion for nature and particularly enjoyed the tranquillity and seductiveness that she felt that North Yorkshire provided. The diversity of town, dale, moor and sea was not captured in all of England's counties but was particular to this area, for which she felt blessed. She'd had a pleasant day off from working in one of the town's coffee shops and had spent her time relaxing and enjoying the summer sun. At twenty years old, she was young and carefree, working full time and sharing a house in the town with some friends. Raised by grandparents, who lived in a nearby village, she was now enjoying independent living. Hearing the "keey ya" call of a bird, she looked up to see a buzzard circling the thermals as a pair of rooks approached, their "cawing" unheard at this distance.

"Sit." Rosie responded immediately, looking quizzically at her owner, waiting for her next instruction.

Kate crouched and, using her walking stick as an ad-hoc tripod, quickly trained her camera to the sky. Panning out, she observed the rooks approach and dive at the predator. No contact made, their target veered away chased by the attacking birds. With the distance too far, she lowered the camera to watch the aggressive birds with their continued mobbing in fierce defence of their territory and possibly their young. Neither buzzard or rook would wish to collide, as the chance of injury was high, and though at an advantage with weaponry and agility, the buzzard would make a hasty retreat rather than risk a full-scale attack from a larger number of birds. The buzzard made a sharp turn and dive, distancing itself from its assailants and headed away from the oncoming pursuit. *Birds could teach humans a lot*, thought Kate, slowly stroking Rosie behind an ear and causing her tail to drum on the ground rhythmically. Kate stood up followed by Rosie and both headed towards the thrumming noise of the waterfalls of the river Stern.

***

John had worked hard, taken risks and made money - lots of money. Now living in luxury, he had a beautiful house, a beautiful wife and no kids. He had aged and he had matured. 'Retired' at fifty he now enjoyed his days playing golf, having meals out, taking holidays abroad (whenever he felt like it), and he lived in a beautiful village outside of Sterndale. His wife knew little of his history. They had been married for ten years and she was just happy that he could support her and that they could enjoy their time together. She didn't know he was here now. She would just presume that he was finishing a round of golf and having a swift pint before driving home for a late tea and a glass of red. Well, here he was, and he was here to attend to some unfinished business. Business from years gone by, business that should have been laid to rest back then, but he was still no pushover; he was wiser and still bulletproof. John looked at the picture of his wife on his phone and then switched it off. Opening the glove compartment, he placed the phone inside and, reaching further in, pulled out a cloth-wrapped item. Placing it on his lap, he unravelled it, revealing a small handgun, and checking the safety was on, he released the chamber lock revealing the rounds. Tipping them out and clicking the chamber back in, he placed the bullets in his jacket pocket. The gun was safe, nothing in the barrel. He gently depressed the trigger with an audible click as the hammer struck home. He smiled to himself. If they thought he was a pushover they were in for a shock. Handgun placed in his right hand jacket pocket, he opened the car door. The meeting was soon, and he was ready.

John gently closed the door to his vehicle and walked away hearing the click of the locks fastening. He placed the keys in his inside pocket then fastened the lower buttons of his brown leather jacket. The sparsely wooded area to his left climbed steeply towards a walkway which navigated the ruins of a castle wall, the trees guarding the embankment against the encroachment of any further developments in the area. The sloped ground was foreboding and in itself must have provided a substantial barrier to any attacking marauders in days long past. A tarmacked road had been built at the base of the embankment mirroring the path of the river and

John followed this at a slow pace, his stomach fluttering as adrenaline and nerves took effect. The river's speed increased as it navigated its banks and the clumps of rocks and trees within the watercourse. Canoeists often attempted the Stern as it headed to the waterfalls. The water level was low at this time of year, hence the river was devoid of kayaks today. He checked his right pocket once more, just to be sure, then turned off the road onto a track which would keep him out of sight but would give him a clear view of the car park and fall as he approached. The man that he was meeting would be nearby, possibly with some associates, and would be waiting. The meeting had been arranged two days ago and John had chosen the location. A location that was safe, quiet at this time of evening and with no security cameras. A good meeting place where the sound of the fall would mask conversation, where the police were unlikely to patrol, and where two men together admiring the area would look natural. Now at the riverbank, John paused. Here the river curved left from view and opened up to a pebbled area with calm waters preceding the limestone rocks forming the dramatic fall. The sonorous tones of the cascading water enveloped the air. John took a deep breath and slowly crept forward, assessing the area. A lone male stood on the pebbled area wearing a T-shirt and jeans, skimming stones across the subdued water as they skipped their way to the far bank. He kept glancing around but appeared calm. His gaze regularly checked the fall car park where a dark-coloured Mercedes sat with the motor running. *Right*, thought John, *that means there is at least one other person in the car*. He checked his watch and gave it one more minute. He hadn't brought anyone as his back up; he wouldn't know who to bring, all of his friends were honest. He'd wing it. He took a deep breath and, with no one else about, he squared his shoulders and stepped from hiding, moving confidently towards the male, his weight crushing some pebbles as others skittered away under the soles of his shoes, as if in avoidance of the forthcoming encounter.

***

Kate stood admiring the limestone waterfall in the dimming light, the current low level belying the mighty force that the water could produce in full flow. Outcrops of rock stood resolutely, pillars of dry stone walls placed by behemoths, funnelling the water which coursed over three lower tiers, white frothy caps pounding the river bed below. She loved this area and drank in its beauty. At the weekends families would gather here, younger children paddling in the quieter waters above the fall and older ones daring each other to leap from the platforms into the plunge pools below. Framing the top of the fall was a weathered concrete jetty, which protected the calm pond beyond, directing the water towards a narrower gap, where it increased speed prior to its sprint to the fall. Kate lifted her camera capturing the fall of dusk as daylight seeped away, Rosie lapping at the water beside her with front paws sinking into the mud of the riverbank.

"Oh, hello," said Kate to herself, as two men appeared on the stone pier and began walking out, one in a brown jacket and one in a T-shirt. The man wearing the T-shirt strode confidently out whilst the male in the brown jacket scuttled behind looking as if he was shouting to be heard. Rosie turned at Kate's voice, head tilted to one side, tail wagging slowly, and quickly flicked her head towards the sound of the shouting male. 'Click' - photograph taken, the men continued walking, oblivious of Kate's presence. She lowered the camera and continued towards the falls where a path would lead her left in the direction of a field where she would eventually meet the main road leading her home. She'd also get a better view of the drama from there. Reaching a small rise Kate saw the men, now closer to each other. It looked like an argument with both in deep conversation and 'brown jacket' gesticulating irritably with his hands. Faint raised voices could be heard combined with aggressive arm movements.

She felt uncomfortable, an intruder upon someone's privacy. This was obviously a private conversation between two grown men and nothing to do with her, yet she remained transfixed as she watched the showdown, "Rosie, here." Kate took Rosie's lead, harnessing her as she watched.

'T-shirt' held the other by his jacket front, both faces almost nose to nose and suddenly, with one hand whipped back, 'T-shirt' slapped 'brown jacket' across his face. Kate's hand raised to her cheek in parody as the echoed slap faintly reached her ears. She reached for her camera, raising it and, with shaking hands, attempted to focus towards the falls. Unable to, she looked to the side to watch 'brown jacket' being headbutted in the face as he reached into his right pocket, before being hauled forward again as 'T-shirt' screamed into his face. A car horn sounded from the car park. 'Brown jacket' pulled an item from his pocket, raising it. The sun clipped Kate's lens as a beam momentarily blinded her. 'T-shirt' looked right, straight at her, the reflection from her lens triggering his senses. She instinctively crouched. Rosie growled. 'T-shirt's' arm blocked 'brown jacket's' and he punched this time, 'brown jacket's' head rocking back, body lowering as his legs gave way. 'T-shirt' gave a final push. 'Brown jacket' fell, his head hitting a protrusion of limestone rock on his descent. The deadweight body tumbled down further to crunch onto the paving below. Kate screamed, Rosie barked, 'T-shirt' looked down. The body didn't move. Kate could see a red pool of blood colouring the rock where a shoulder and arm hung twisted unnaturally. She remained crouched and grabbed Rosie as if a shield, as 'T-shirt' looked towards the sound of the dog barking and then straight at Kate. Kate shrank, held her breath, and froze. She watched as his right arm rose, finger pointing directly at her. He had seen her. The male turned and ran towards the falls' car park. The body remained motionless.

*＊＊

"Oh my God, Oh my God" said Kate. She was shaking. She grasped Rosie desperately pulling her close in an attempt to comfort herself, still crouched low with her mind racing, Rosie whimpering in response to her owner's feelings. *I need to ring the police, ambulance or someone. That man looked in a bad way, blood seeping onto the rocks from his body.* She rose slowly and looked, the body hadn't moved. *I can't get to him from here, I'm on the wrong side of the river to help and I've been seen by 'T-shirt'. Oh my God, I've been seen. I need to move and move quickly. What if he comes looking for me?*

Kate took a deep breath, forcing her panicked thoughts to quieten so she could make sense of what she had just seen, and what she was supposed to do now. The track ahead would take her on a steep incline to the road where she could head back to town and her house, or she could head out of town to the farmhouse on the hillside and get help. That would take too long though. She fumbled in her pocket pulling out her phone, whimpering to herself, failing to suppress the panic. The phone fell to the ground from her shaking hands. She quickly retrieved it as she took further deep breaths. Trembling fingers navigated the keypad as 999 was punched in and the receiving phone line rang out. Glancing around, like a fugitive in flight, Rachel scanned for signs of anyone else. There was no one else around. She didn't want to be involved in this. Terrified and vulnerable she started to move forwards.

"999, which service?" a male's voice sounded in Kate's ear.

"There's been a fight at Sterndale Falls. A man's fallen off, he's bleeding, he's not moving, he needs help."

"OK, calm down, madam. When did this happen?"

"Just now, just now, I saw it."

"Right, ambulance." The call was diverted.

"Ambulance Service. Is the patient breathing?" asked a female's voice.

"I don't know. A man was pushed at the falls. I don't think he's moving." replied Kate.

"What address are you calling from?"

"Sterndale Falls, Sterndale Falls. You need to get here." Kate's voice was rising in panic as she tried to hold back tears. "I can't be here. I have to move," she mumbled to herself.

"What was that?" asked the female.

"Nothing" Kate replied "I need to go now. Send someone quick."

"What number are you calling from?"

Kate hung up the call. They weren't getting her details, definitely not, she'd done enough to help and needed to get out of here. She turned, pulling Rosie with her, the dog lead giving way and dropping from the collar. Rosie took off, barking in excitement.

"Here!" screamed Kate, realising that she couldn't have attached it correctly before. Rosie's ears pinned back and with her body dipped low, she slunk back to Kate who clipped her to the lead again. They set off at a jog, heading uphill to the road. The distant sound of sirens piercing the running noise of the river. Behind and unnoticed, a silver disc lay in the grass.

Kate ran up the hill, keeping low as if a deserter escaping from pursuit, Rosie tugging on the lead, scouting the way ahead. Kate tripped in her haste, fell on the path, scuffing her palms as they scraped the soil, preventing further injury to the rest of her body. She was terrified, panicking. *What if the man recognises me? What if he is driving round to me now to hurt, injure or kill me?* Rosie stopped, ears poised. She heard something. Kate froze, ears straining, but the throb of her pulse in her head drowned out everything.

"What is it, Rosie?" she asked. Rosie gave no response except to return to Kate and lick her hand. "We need to get off this track, girl," Kate told the dog, "This way." She tugged the lead as she approached a dry stone wall. The tall grass was shorter in the lea of the wall and Kate turned right from the path, crouched low, using the wall for cover and headed for a tree lined hedge not far away. This would give her concealment and take her to a wheat field next to the main road. Trusting Rosie's sense of hearing, she picked up her pace as daylight was fading, relying on the sanctuary of the hedge. A thrum in the air loudened as Kate recognised a throaty engine being pushed to its limits, then a sudden squeal as brakes were applied harshly. She dived to the hedge line, landing chest down, a piercing pain erupted in her chest. Her camera had jolted against her and her sternum was compressed. She couldn't make a sound, couldn't breathe as she lay stunned. Rosie moved her head towards Kate's face, her pink tongue dripping saliva before she smeared a comforting lick to Kate's cheek. Kate groaned and rolled clutching her chest in agony then sucked in sweet air. The pain was excruciating, but she'd made cover. She pulled Rosie close, Kate's nervousness in temporary abeyance as she dealt with her pain. Turning to face the path she had run from she squinted in the dimming light as a male in dark clothing climbed a stile from the adjoining field. He turned to talk and was followed by 'T-shirt'. *Oh shit, he's definitely looking for me.* Her breathing quickened, pulse increased, she felt hot. They were looking for her and had found the path that should take her to the road. She couldn't move, shouldn't move. She pulled Rosie close and placed a hand round her muzzle, a signal telling her to be quiet. Rosie had learnt this as a pup so complied, though her body trembled with nervous energy. Kate sat still watching, waiting to see what they would do. They had passed the area where she had left the path and now approached where she had stood near the river. Now looking at the ground as though trying to determine her tracks, though the hard soil and stones would reveal nothing. Kate grabbed her camera and on checking the lens saw it was undamaged. This time hooding the lens she looked towards the males in time to see 'T-shirt' squat and pick something up. *What was that? Had she dropped some money?* she thought. 'T-shirt' flipped the item, as if a coin, and smiling at the other male, clapped him on the back and indicated for him to follow the path back. On approaching the stile both males glanced back to the far side of the river where blue lights could be seen flickering at the falls' car park. Kate watched the males climb and disappear from view and held still until she could hear an engine start and a car speed away.

She was safe. Exhaling a breath she didn't know she'd held, she stood up, the lactic acid in her muscles aching as her body relaxed. She released Rosie's muzzle, who immediately gave a doggy sneeze as if in disgust. *Now I need to move. Be cautious, but move.* Kate tracked up the tree line heading for the wheat field and the road. Her brain now kicking into gear she needed safety for the night. She didn't know who the men were but did know that they were looking for her, a witness to 'T-shirt's' act of violence. She hoped that the other bloke was OK and that the paramedics had arrived to find him breathing and treatable. She needed home, she needed friends and she needed help. She didn't want to be a police witness, didn't want the involvement, and she wasn't going to go to them. They could certainly sort this without her. They'd done nothing last year when she'd reported her bike stolen, so they weren't in good favour anyway.

Reaching the road, she listened and looked for cars, of which there were none. Climbing over a gate with Rosie squeezing under, Kate quickly crossed to an adjacent field. She cut down its side to a forested path, where she could negotiate the route to her rented house.

* * *

The ambulance slowed as it headed into the falls' car park, its full beam headlights illuminating the area which was devoid of any cars or people. The driver switched off the flashing blue lights and came to a halt, facing the river. The passenger was immediately out in her green overalls and fluorescent jacket with 'Paramedic' emblazoned across the back. The driver, having radioed in his arrival to the control room, climbed out of the vehicle and called to his colleague.

"Dragon lights, mate." She nodded and they both went to the rear of the vehicle, opening its doors. The interior lights remained illuminated, showing all the equipment tightly strapped in position. The female paramedic reached for her green grab bag, containing all the initial equipment required to save and preserve life, and unclipped a large hand torch with her other hand, flicking the beam on and pointing it towards the river. The driver grabbed a further bag and torch and with the doors secured, both headed towards the water and its falls.

The light from the torch cut through the darkening gloom leading the way, with the only sound of drumming water over rock hanging in the air, the crescendo rising as the crew neared. They walked the footpath to a public viewing area of the waterfall to optimise their chances in the search. Flicking the beam left and right, Helen scanned the area looking for a person. Jim was close behind her, ready to transmit on the radio airwaves should they locate anyone.

"There," Jim pointed to the left, an area where the beam had just clipped. Helen flicked the light back and highlighted a body lying still on a rock outcropping, near the base of the waterfall. The rock had a darkened shadow near the head and upper torso area and the body's limbs protruded abnormally.

"Looks like one for the police too, Jim," said Helen as she turned towards the man-made steps leading to the bottom of the falls. Jim transmitted their find and requirements to ambulance control and followed Helen, halting her at the top of the steps.

"Right, let's take stock of what we've got. He doesn't look like he's going anywhere," he said, indicating to the body. "There's no use two of us messing around in a potential crime scene. One of us needs to go down there and check if he's alive."

"Agreed," replied Helen, expectantly. She briefly assessed the climb down and nodded confidently.

"Off you go then" said Jim, in his Welsh accent, a smile on his face. A portly, ageing medic, squeezed into his overalls. He was not going to make a fool of himself clambering over the rocks unnecessarily. "You're younger and fitter than I am, and what's more I did the last one." He held out an arm, inviting Helen to begin the descent, and was grateful to be partnered with a paramedic eager to prove her commitment. She smiled and with a torch and bag headed gingerly down the steps. Jim trained his torch on the unmoving body to assist her, and taking out a pad and pen commenced recording the scene and route, in case it was required later.

Reaching the bottom step Helen eyed the best way forward and with the bag on her back, began her clamber. The aggressive spray from the falls moistened the rocks and started wetting her hair as the droplets clung to the dry strands, the sound of the torrents dominating her senses as she negotiated slippery footholds in her effort to reach the male. The torchlight cast shadows outside its beam where darkness enticed her into its embrace. She stopped and turned to look for Jim but was blinded by the beam from his torch. Turning back, she closed her eyes, the torch light emblazoned on her retinas, her body rocked as dizziness took hold. Helen opened her eyes and focussed on the rocks ahead as her body responded to the stimulus and righted itself.

She steadied herself and, refusing to fall or fail, she edged forward. She approached the figure. One area of the skull appeared to sink inwards with blood congealing in the area. The eyes stared at her vacantly, the mouth slack with tongue to the side. She reached forward towards the neck to check for a pulse she knew she would not find. This guy was dead. She turned towards Jim, shielding her eyes, and gave a hand signal with thumb pointing downwards. He would know what she meant. *Nothing she could do here, this was one for the police,* thought Helen. She looked the body up and down, committing the area to memory, as she would probably need to give a statement to the police officers later.

"Poor sod," she said, turning away and reaching into her bag for a yellow crayon marker which she carried. Checking the route back, Helen flexed her shoulders, readjusting the pack, and set off. On the return journey she marked rocks intermittently with the wax crayon so that the police could clearly see the route she had used.

Jim watched Helen's progress as she returned, noticing the apparent ease with which she negotiated the rocks. Had he undertaken the task he was confident that he would have landed on his backside, in the river, making a complete fool of himself. Helen arrived at the platformed area at the base of the steps and he yelled down,

"The police have just landed and are just getting their kit out of their cars."

Helen gave him a thumbs up and ascended the stone steps to the viewing platform.

"Well?" asked Jim.

"Dead." she replied. "Looks like he has fallen, and cracked his skull open on the rocks when he did. Fallen or pushed, if someone else was here? I've marked my route for the bobbies and I'll go and brief them. Wasn't so bad, Jim. You'll be fine to do the next one. Good luck with that." She winked and walked away. Jim chuckled to himself. He liked working with Helen. She was a good laugh and always got stuck in. Her humour was needed in this line of work. She returned after ten minutes.

"Right, that's us, matey," she said jovially. "Cops have control of the scene now. Handover completed. So, if you're not too scared, we'll get back out on the road and wait for the next call." She smiled and walked back to the ambulance to deposit her equipment. Jim followed, waving goodbye to the police as he went.

* * *

Police Sergeant French looked at the scene in front of him, his dragon light highlighting the route from the viewing platform to the body. *What a place to try and cordon off!* he thought, blue police tape in his hands. *At least there are no members of the public to deal with.* The control room operative had already called for the Criminal Investigation Department, due to the nature of the call to the ambulance service, and had dispatched another uniformed car. Night shift would be on duty at ten o'clock and they'd have to secure the scene all night. Control room could sort out all of the staffing, get hold of the coroner and update the duty superintendent. French's job was to secure the scene and protect any evidence. He started by taping off the viewing platform and stairs and then directed one officer down-stream and one up. They would keep a close watch in those areas and stop anyone from entering the area, using police tape to cordon off as best they could. CID would arrive shortly, and they could go out to the body for an immediate scene assessment. If the Scene of Crime Officer got here with them, then that would make everyone's life easier.

"Sal," he called his last free officer over, "can you commence the scene log please." Sally grabbed her pocketbook and recorded a couple of details before commencing the log. Police vehicles stood parked with engines running, their headlights illuminating the area. French was conscious that the scene may extend to the car park as well but, with an ambulance and two cop cars having raced into the area, there was little he could do.

"Sal," he called, "I'm just gonna move my car to the car park entrance to prevent anyone else coming in." Sally waved in acknowledgment that she had heard him.

Thirty minutes later Detective Jamal Kaur watched as the SOCO, dressed in a white protective suit, carefully negotiated the area, photographing the body in situ. He had managed to get to the other side of the body, photographed it and then raised his hand to Jamal for attention. The sound of the falls and the distance made talking ineffective. Jamal watched as the SOCO lowered his camera and then using his right hand shaped it into a child's symbolism of a gun. Jamal looked at him and cast his arms aside, shrugging his shoulders. *What's he on about,* he thought. The SOCO repeated his action, this time clasping his right hand with his left as if cradling the handle of a gun, and stood in a shooting position. The penny dropped as Jamal imitated the SOCO's movement, both men now standing, pointing make-believe guns at each other. The SOCO nodded, gave a thumbs up and continued photographing. *Bloody hell,* thought Jamal, reaching for his radio and lifting it to his mouth.

"DS426 to control."

"Go ahead, J," came a friendly response.

"Can I have a firearms unit here asap please. We have located a firearm and I need it to be made safe."

"On its way, J. They'll be with you as soon as they can."

"Further," Jamal continued. "Can you call out the duty detective superintendent? We're going to need her here."

Chapter 2

Wetted stones at Loch Creagan lay impassive, the loch's salty waters gently bathing them, cleansing the shoreline. Wind skirting the water climbed the banks, halted and was dispersed by a thin rank of trees, offering scant protection to the three motorhomes parked in their designated bays beyond. The vehicles sat motionless, as dawn cast its rays on a glorious morning in Scotland, in sharp contrast to the squally showers of the previous night.

One rear window blind slowly raised on the right most vehicle, followed by the creak of a side window opening, and the resonant belch of an unsettled stomach. The birds' chorus interrupted for five seconds before resuming their welcome chorale to the day. The home rocked as a person moved within, before the side door was gently opened, and a remorseful Matthew Forster exited wearing boxer shorts, a T-shirt and sunglasses. *Bloody hell, my head hurts*, he thought, touching his scalp gently, as if examining it for injury. However, any injuries sustained were internal and self-inflicted from last night, caused by his inability to say 'No'. A night on which he was encouraged to sample the malt whiskies of the West Coast. Matthew had now stayed in this area for two days and was due to move on today, for which his head was relieved.

Matthew recalled the previous day. He had driven up to Fort William and parked at the Glen Nevis Visitor Centre. Donning his walking shoes, he negotiated a small footbridge and took a gentle stroll towards the Ben Nevis Inn, where he relaxed, absorbing the intoxicating views of Glen Nevis. The morning had been clear and the walk comfortable, but clouds in the distance hinted at possible rain later in the day. Lunch had been great at the Inn and was definitely a place that he'd have to return to at a later date. *I'll have to bring Rachel,* he thought hopefully, *she may manage this walk.* Climbing back into his vehicle, he started the engine and set off back on the Glen Nevis Road towards Fort William and onwards to Creagan.

The day was fine and the roads were busy with tourists enjoying the beauty of Scotland. Unwittingly, Matthew seemed to have been indoctrinated into the motorhome's drivers' clan. Having dropped Rachel at a spa and convalescent care hotel near Edinburgh a week ago, he'd collected his pre-booked van and headed off to explore. Setting off on day one he had been surprised when, on passing a motorhome going in the opposite direction, the driver had raised his hand in acknowledgement. *Was that someone he knew? Was he doing something wrong?* After two or three further waves from motorhome owners, it clicked. He was now one of them, accepted in the club, one of the team. *Ridiculous,* thought Matt, though he always waved in reply. There was no point in being impolite, and what's more you may end up parked up next to one of them at the end of the day. He'd only ever noticed a familiar phenomenon with motorbike riders, who appeared to acknowledge other riders with a tilt of their heads. Only bike riders though, as it seemed that moped riders weren't in 'the gang' and were subsequently staunchly ignored. Clearly a different class of rider who, despite riding a petrol powered two-wheeled machine, were deemed lowly members of the riding fraternity. Matt wondered whether there were different classes in the motorhome world. *Did a 6 berth have seniority over a 2 berth? Were caravan owners included? Was waving a quintessentially British thing?* Irrespective, Matt had been drawn in and now towed the line. He'd arrived at his pre-booked site and having parked the van, decided to walk the ten minutes to the local pub for dinner and a pint. A pre-meal pint had led to two more, a snack at the bar and dinner forgotten. Before long, Matt had been cajoled into taking a seat on the outside decking with a couple of locals. They sat and watched the sun set on the loch, birdlife setting at dusk and the occasional seal's head popping up in the distance, before their curling backs took them below the water. It was bliss, despite the bites of midges, held in quiescence by a log burner. The burn of whisky in his throat warmed him sufficiently, combined with the good company.

Now, the following morning, Matt was suffering. The weather had turned in the night, with a wind picking up and rain lashing down, though Matt had been oblivious to it in his comatose state. Another glorious morning, now that the rain had cleared, and time for breakfast. He turned and climbed back into his small haven. He was enjoying his time travelling but though practical, he would never say that life on the road was comfortable.

"Give me a hotel anyday," he said, wincing as he stretched his stiff neck, his head throbbing. The entrance to the motorhome opened into a small kitchen with a little dining area. The main bedroom, toilet and shower were at the rear of the vehicle. The bed was too small for Matt and, though purporting to be a double, it would be really cramped if he shared it with Rachel. The toilet was serviceable; he'd coped with the intricacies of its technology, though he didn't relish emptying time. He pulled the interior curtain open, which provided privacy from the windscreen, and noted the moisture gathered on the interior of the screen. It would clear in time and definitely by the time he was ready to go. Kettle on for a coffee, Matt wrestled himself like a contortionist into clean clothes and squeezing into the toilet, checked himself in the mirror. With a damp smell unpleasantly pervading his nostrils, he noted dark rings under his eyes, unkempt hair, and the need to tidy his beard. It would have to wait. The kettle sang out loud and with a coffee made, Matt sat in the doorway of the van enjoying the view, contemplating his trip. Van life wasn't for him. Too small, too much time on the road, and too untidy. The sights and scenery were beautiful, but you could get that by staying in hotels and hiring cars.

No other people stirred in the vans nearby and Matt relaxed in the solitude of the sun bathing the loch, the bitter taste of black coffee stimulating his senses. He stood up to check the windscreen, which was beginning to clear. Time to look at getting packed up. He had a long drive today via Oban and Inverary before landing back to Edinburgh to meet up with Rachel.

***

Rachel exited the changing rooms in her swimming costume, leaning heavily on a handrail which would lead her to the therapy pool. Steam rose languidly from the clear water enticing her towards it. With the pool currently empty, Rachel was saved from embarrassment as she hobbled along, her scars to her hip and shoulder clearly showing her sustained injuries from the attempt on her life last year. The physical scars she wore, though looking horrific in her view, were minor compared to the psychological trauma which she still experienced. Eight months had passed since the devastating day when Brown had deliberately pushed her in front of a moving vehicle in an attempt to murder her. Eight months and still she struggled. Six months off work following the surgery and now two months back on duty, she had come north for further treatment and recuperation. The job had been great to her. She had not been forced back into work too early, and welfare had been supportive throughout, giving her a desk job in the Witness Protection Unit. While not an easy job, it was empathetic to her physical condition and was also mentally stimulating. Ultimately, it wasn't detective work though, and she felt unhappy. She pushed her thoughts away and lowered herself down near the entry steps by the pool into the water. Rachel felt like a child, taking her first tentative steps into the water. *No mum or dad to help me though, I'm on my own,* she thought. She sat herself down and shuffled forwards to the pool, right leg extended and, with an audible sigh, allowed the water to cover her body. She relaxed and couldn't deny that the water felt terrific. She would get about ten minutes to herself before the others would join her, ready for the scheduled pool therapy session, when a trainer would take them through a programme of exercises designed to increase mobility and strength. Rachel tipped her head back and closed her eyes, enjoying her weightlessness and pushed her worries from her. As a silent calm spread across her body, a sudden dread overrode her senses. Darkness encroached her mind as a face looked down at her, beaming in delight, the face of Geoff Brown! Her eyes shot open, her arms floundering, her lower body sinking, pulling her down as water covered her face. She panicked and sank, her right leg hitting the bottom of the pool and with a jolt of pain she pushed, propelling her face up and out of the water. *For Christ's sake*, she thought, *I know how to swim*. A chortle came from the far side of the pool.

"You nod off there, hen?" said a male, in a deep resonant Scottish voice.

"Must have," she replied, forcing a smile as she stretched an arm to the side of the pool to hold on.

"Too much juice from last night?" he replied, raising his arm as if downing a pint.

"If only."

The male walked along the poolside to the steps, sporting some green luminescent swim shorts, the colour doing little for his pallid skin and hairy beer bellied torso. He slowly sank into the water, dunked his body and as his bald head resurfaced, he smiled at Rachel.

"I'm Bruce," he said, in introduction.

"Rachel," she replied.

Two other people now entered, one lady wearing a polo shirt and shorts, with an athletic figure and hair tied back, and the other was older and wearing a swimming costume. The costumed lady gingerly walked into the pool and sank into the water with a sigh. *Oh, the joys of middle age,* thought Rachel, *what a sight we must all look,* though if the trainer had any concerns she didn't show it. The session started with the captives trying hard, as they were taken through a series of exercises, by a cheerful and exuberant trainer.

※ ※ ※

Rachel folded her towel and placed it in her backpack, which she hooked over the back of her chair. Even after a few months, any exercise took it out of her. She lowered herself into her chair, released the brakes and with arm muscles braced, wheeled herself out of the changing rooms and into the wide corridor. With her room on the ground floor, the way was easily navigable for her. *Who'd have thought I'd end up like this,* she thought, still with an edge of bitterness, as she eased her chair forwards. The 'accident', as she referred to it, had altered her life drastically. Severe damage to her right side had disfigured her leg and hip. The contusion to her head had caused a cerebral haemorrhage, resulting in a temporary paralysis. She'd worked hard over the past months and as the paralysis diminished, she had become more mobile. Life had been hard though and she doubted that she would have done so well without Matthew's strength and support. She hoped to not always be reliant on a wheelchair but still found that following physical exercise, or at times of extreme tiredness, she required its support. Arriving at her bedroom door she placed on the brakes, stood with her bag and walking stick and entered, placing the bag down and lowering herself to the bed. *Last day here.* She lay back looking at the ceiling.

There would be further exercise to do this afternoon, where she would be taken through her set routine in the gym followed by a relaxing massage to loosen her muscles. The facilities and food here were great, she couldn't praise it enough, but she was ready to go.

She was looking forward to seeing Matthew later, when he arrived to collect her and take her on the next leg of their trip. They needed to have a good talk with each other. She'd been thinking a lot about Matthew, her life, her career. *Decisions need to be made,* and she felt strong enough to make them.

Following a light lunch, Rachel used the corridor handrail for support as she steadily walked towards the gym. Conscious of her gait, she walked with head down looking at the carpet, avoiding the glances she was sure were being fired towards her. Looks of pity. She felt them everywhere, even when there wasn't a soul in sight. Upon reaching the gym door, she peered through the glass. There were five or six people in the room using various pieces of equipment, grimacing in pain in their attempts to overcome their physical and psychological demons.

Lycra was abundant with maximum effort being applied by people who were confident they would win. Nevertheless, Rachel hid her body beneath a baggy T-shirt and jogging bottoms, feeling saddened by her own scars and disability, robbed of her health by anger and cruelty. A male, using a treadmill, spotted Rachel at the door and raised a hand in greeting. Then, overenthusiastically pressing buttons on the machine, increased its speed, stumbling before hitting his stride. Rachel smiled. *I suppose we all have our obstacles along the way.* She entered the gym for her thirty minutes of torture, to be followed by an hour of bliss. *The pain is worth it.*

***

Kate ascended the steep soil bank towards the road, darkness masking the creeping roots which grasped blindly, slowing her progress. The trees, like sentinels, judging her route as she desperately sought the sanctuary of home. Rosie led the way, dog lead taut, as she pulled Kate forward. Kate's mind was spinning. *Of course I've done the right thing. I rang for help and I know it will be there. I've got to look after myself now.* She stopped, her breathing quickening, panic rising from the pit of her stomach. Rosie turned back, angled her head and padded back to Kate, circled around her, and began nudging her legs.

"Good girl," said Kate, gently stroking the dog's head. Kate's breathing slowed, calmed by the naive joy of Rosie's affection.

"What do we do now, girl?" Rosie looked up the bank to the road as if saying, "We move on. We move quickly." Rosie's imagined words gave Kate solace. *The men at the falls have found something, something they are happy about. I have to assume that they were still looking for me. I'll need to be careful.* Standing tall with determined focus, Kate began to move.

"Come on girl," both strode forwards up the hill. Walking the hedge line of the field adjoining the road, Kate had seen little traffic. The few vehicles that had passed appeared to have been travelling at normal speeds and she'd seen nothing that she thought suspicious. She moved to the kissing gate, checked the road was clear and with a swift movement wiggled herself and Rosie through, over the road and into the entrance of a darkened driveway. Adrenaline pumping, Kate took a deep breath and moved along the path, ducking into driveways for cover where she could. She would hear any approaching cars but did not want to be silhouetted in their headlights. She stopped and planned her next moves. *If I take The Avenue I can head towards the school grounds. Before the school entrance I can turn left down a back lane where I can get to the back garden of my house, and in the back door to the safety of my housemates.* The Avenue was well lit with street lighting so she'd just have to be careful.

Anyone looking out of their window that evening would have seen the farcical sight of a young woman flitting between driveways, desperately trying to pull her dog along, as it casually attempted to check and mark territory. Kate was conscious of this, but she was making her best effort at being discreet. *It all seems so easy in books and on TV.* Approaching the school gates, Kate entered the lane and walked cautiously towards her back garden, her hand on Rosie's muzzle. The dog knew that this was her signal to keep quiet. Kate cracked the garden gate and peered through. The house was in darkness with only the back outside light on. *Shit,* she'd forgotten. *They were all going out tonight and wouldn't be back till late.* Kate moved forward, letting Rosie off her lead. Rosie trotted forward casually, now that Kate's game appeared to be over, as Kate walked swiftly forward to the door. She stopped and squatted down as she reached under the third plant pot to the right of the door. Retrieving a key, she placed it in the lock, turned it slowly and entered the kitchen. Rosie followed, then in the darkness Kate could hear the noisy lapping of Rosie's tongue as she drank from her water bowl.

Keeping the lights off, Kate closed the back door and went through to the lounge. The front curtains were open and with no lighting on, she closed the door behind her. She moved towards the left side of the front window where she could check the street, from its optimum view. Using the open curtain as cover, she slowly stood and looked out to the street-lit area. No movement. The usual cars parked on their driveways and one on the road three houses up, which was also normally there. Kate's shoulders dropped, relaxing, her body uncoiling in relief. Moving to flick on the lights, she heard a car engine and froze, her finger resting on the switch. Turning her head, the rest of her body rigid with fright, she looked out of the window and watched a pair of headlights slowly moving down the road. Unnaturally slowly, looking, seeking as a car crawled past her house. Her hand moved from the switch to her mouth, muffling her voice, "Oh my God," tripping from her lips. A whimper and a claw scratched at the kitchen door. Rosie's senses detected something wrong. Kate stood still, terrified, praying she was wrong. The engine faded, then returned as Kate watched a black Mercedes cruise past her house and park three doors down, beyond the parked vehicle. *They're here!*

Kate squatted back down, her legs almost betraying her as she held her balance. *Am I being paranoid? Was it really them? How could they have found me?* Now on hands and knees Kate crawled to the hall door, which was already open, and ran up the stairs towards her room. With no lights on, she switched on the torch on her phone and entered her bedroom, which overlooked the back of the house. *Think, think, think! Right, I have to get out. Get somewhere safe and take Rosie with me.* She grabbed a daysack and started shoving clothes randomly into it, followed by make up, toiletries, phone charger and her laptop. Already wearing leggings Kate quickly shoved a hoodie over her shirt. Turning to her desk, she scribbled a quick note and left it prominently outside of her bedroom door as she left. Gently opening one of the front bedroom doors, she then covered the torch and approached the window. The car remained in place, but this time the headlights were off. It was late but she needed help. *Let's hope that he's up.* Back in the hall she texted.

Grandad, I can't speak but I need you to come and collect me now. Head to the school lane junction with the main road x

Pressing send Kate put on the backpack, placed her phone in her pocket and went quickly downstairs, dropping to a crouch on entering the living room. Crawling to the kitchen door she opened it and received a wet nose in her face, accompanied by frantic tail wagging and whimpering. Anticipating the inevitable slobber from Rosie's tongue, she clamped her hand around Rosie's muzzle, knowing that she would accept the command. Rosie went still as Kate entered the kitchen, shutting the door behind her.

"Right, girl. We're off". She grabbed the dog lead and fumbled trying to clip it on Rosie's collar, the process feeling different in the dark. With her hand placed again on Rosie's muzzle, she headed towards the back door. The garden remained lit, but was empty.

Hoping that the people were still in their car, she raised her hood, took a deep breath, and stepped outside with Rosie. No sound or apparent concern from Rosie, so it was probably clear. Kate locked the door and on doing so heard a car door shut. Rosie's ears moved with the sound. A quiet growl reverberated in her throat. Kate moved.

"This way," she whispered to the dog.

They moved as one, across the garden and into the rear alley towards the school entrance. Kate approached the end of the lane cautiously, but the alley was hard to find if you didn't know of it. The road beyond looked clear. Stepping out, Kate moved into the school grounds, a security light triggering on the school wall as she did so. She heard a loud knocking at a door behind. *Was that my house door?* Kate wasn't waiting to see. She ran.

The school grounds encompassed the building itself but also contained hockey, football and rugby pitches to the rear. A country lane split a nearby housing estate from the grounds. Now, throwing caution to the wind, Kate set off, running straight across the fields to the lane end, to her grandad, to safety. Her phone pinged, she checked it,

On my way love x

Kate smiled, kissed her phone and ran on, her pursuers none the wiser.

* * *

With no reply at the front door and no lights on in the house, the male decided to check around the back of the premises. George walked confidently down the path to see if he could find a back way in. Broad-shouldered and tall, he walked with an air of calmness about him, a man who knew his own abilities, who feared little, and ignited fear in others. He had now been working for his employer for five years, was well looked after and, more importantly, well paid. With his military background, he felt he could deal with most situations, and tonight was a prime example. Chris had got 'a bit frisky' with that idiot at the falls and the idiot had paid for it, possibly with his life. It was the fool's own fault, after all, a debt was a debt, and a debt needed to be paid. He'd ignored his warnings, and that meant George and Chris had been called in to 'resolve the matter'. George was unphased if that meant someone got hurt, he was paid to cause pain, when necessary. The issue tonight was the girl. Chris had been seen, or may have been seen. Either way it mattered. She was a loose end that they needed to find and tie off.

Reaching the end of the path, he was confronted by a sign for a school, with a fence line running down its side between the school and the houses. He checked the end of the fence and spotted a worn track which looked like it went behind the rear of the houses. Checking left and right, he nipped in the gap, right hand resting on the small of his back where he had a knife secreted. Chris had only given him a basic description of the girl, but if a woman came down this track, he'd grab her and deal with the situation. Walking slowly along he checked the roof line, estimating the location of the house in which he was interested. He pressed his hand to a wooden gate which was locked, glimpsed up, and checked the roof again. *The next one*, he thought, and smiled as he saw an open gate within a leylandii hedge. He moved forward, sneaked a peek, to see an empty garden and the back door illuminated by a security light. *Why is the gate open?* Looking again he checked the back of the building for private CCTV cameras, of which there were none, and stealthily moved around the perimeter of the garden to the door. Stone flags divided the building from the garden and drying on the path, outside of the back door, were the damp, fading paw prints of a large dog. *Just missed her*, he thought exasperatingly, letting his knife hand drop to his side. *Damn*! Plant pots stood in a row below the kitchen window, with one slightly out of place. Reaching down George lifted it, his sleeve covering his hand.

Resting underneath the pot was a keyring holding two keys. George smiled, *Silly, silly woman.* The keys looked identical. He gently retrieved them and placed one in the rear Yale lock of the back door. It slipped in with ease. He removed it, deftly took one of the keys off the key ring, and replaced the other back as he'd found it. *Pushed my luck enough, time to go.* Retracing his steps George appeared back on the street and looked out towards the school and its fields, observing the darkness for any hint of movement. *You out there woman? Running scared? You should be.* He turned and walked calmly back to the car where he climbed in as the driver. He turned to Chris,

"She's not here mate, but I've got her house key," he stated, holding up the key.

"Nice one," replied Chris in a Liverpudlian accent.

* * *

Kate and Rosie had made it across the fields and now traversed the uneven ground of the lane. Hedges lined either side with the occasional tree towering over. It was dark now, so Kate had to risk her full torch to prevent a trip and fall. The main road wasn't too far ahead and hopefully her grandad would be waiting. If not, she'd have to hunker down and wait. He was her only hope tonight, the only person she could really trust to get her. He'd have left Gran at home and told her to put the kettle on and not to worry. Of course she'd worry but she'd keep herself busy.

Approaching the head of the track, Kate was suddenly blinded by headlights. She froze, Rosie growled. Fight or flight? *Shall I run?* The driver's door opened.

"Katie, it's me. Grandad. What the hell's going on?" shouted a grizzled elderly voice.

Rosie barked and bounded, pulling her lead from Kate's hand, heading towards a voice that she recognised. She sprinted at the figure, claws grasping for hold as she careened beyond her target, her body twisting to halt her movement. Kate's grandad reached his arms down, and with a bark Rosie returned, tail still wagging, and accepted her pats.

Kate stood watching, tears on her face, and ran to him grasping him in a fierce embrace.

"There, there, Katie. I'm here now. You're fine. You're safe," he said. She held him at arm's length.

"No, Grandad, I'm not. I'm being followed. We need to move now. Get away from here." She opened the boot and Rosie immediately leapt in, tail wagging, clearly enjoying herself. Boot closed, they both got in the car.

"I'll take you to Gran, Katie. She'll have the kettle on and we can have a cup of tea." He smiled at her, relieved that his Katie wasn't injured, and confident in his Britishness that 'a good old cup of tea' would resolve the issue.

Chapter 3

Steel rods driven into the riverbed held a rope handrail, now indicating the route to the deceased body which was about to be removed from its location at the falls. All the photographs required had been taken by the SOCO, and they would be produced for the Senior Investigative Officer who was running the enquiry. Jamal stood on the viewing platform surveying the scene in front of him, ticking off his actions in his head, double checking that he hadn't missed anything. The superintendent would land soon, and she'd expect a concise report from him. The search team stood ready to be deployed to the river to harness any evidence which they could. Luckily, he'd got UWSU, who were used to working in this type of environment, and he was confident that they would do a good job for him. The night was warm with no rain anticipated, but the window of opportunity to search would be limited due to the terrain and the unpredictability of the river. Temporary lighting had been set up to cast light across the area to assist the searching officers. Although not ideal, they may not get the luxury of a daylight search. It would only take some rain here, or further upriver, for the watercourse to change, thereby obliterating evidential opportunities. Jamal watched as the body was manhandled onto a stretcher and transported to the riverbank, where an undertaker's car waited to transport it to the mortuary. A firearms officer climbed the steps carrying three filled exhibit bags.

"Hi J, how are you doing?" asked the officer.

"Been better, mate. The boss will be here soon. What have you got?" The officer held up the bags.

"9mm pistol. It's been made safe. There were no rounds in it. The second bag has five rounds of 9mm ammunition in it, which were loose in the right pocket of his jacket. The third, his wallet, which may help you to identify him. All the exhibit bags are signed. I've spoken to the exhibits officer, so I'll take the weapon and rounds to be stored securely, and the wallet is all yours." The officer checked his watch and noted the exact time when he physically handed the third bag over. Jamal signed the bag, his years of training in maintaining the continuity of the evidential chain etched into his behaviour.

"Cheers mate," said Jamal, and as the officers parted company, he turned and observed Detective Superintendent Andrea Finch approaching.

"DS Kaur," Finch approached him, "where are we at?" There hadn't been much progress since an earlier call where Finch was given a verbal briefing on the scene.

"Body has just been removed, Boss. The Home Office pathologist is aware and will attend. UWSU are ready to commence their search of the scene. We've lit it up as best we can. SOCO are still out there doing their stuff. The firearm and ammunition were recovered, and also the bloke's wallet. I've also got some officers looking around the area in case he came by car." He held the wallet up for Finch to see.

"Witnesses?" she asked.

"No one so far, Boss. The area isn't overlooked by any houses. It's quiet down here. No sign of the woman who called it in. We have the call on tape, but nothing much else. We don't know who the deceased is yet, but hopefully, when we take a look at this," he indicated to the wallet, "we will."

"So, all we know about the witness is that she is female and that she claimed to see whatever took place here?"

"Yes, Boss. She could have seen it from anywhere, even here, where we are standing. All units have used the same route to approach the scene. I have uniform, upstream and downstream, in an attempt to secure the area. We're going to have to review the full area in daylight and make a further assessment."

"You've done well DS Kaur."

"Thanks, Boss. Oh, and the latest update."

"Yes."

"The firearm that was found had no rounds in it. Looks like the rounds were in the deceased's coat pocket."

"OK. Unusual, but let's face it, a firearm found in Sterndale is unusual. Let's get back to the office with that wallet and find out who our dead man is."

* * *

Sterndale Police Station stood within small, mature gardens on the outskirts of the town. A listed building, far surpassed by the needs of modern policing and a relic of times past, it was still the hub of policing within the town. A fingerboard on the roadside outside, illuminated by the car headlights, indicated its presence, and on entering the small car park the public were directed towards the main entrance and reception. Jamal and Andrea had both driven to the rear of the station, an area signed 'Police Vehicles Only', where they parked their vehicles and approached the back door. Using the digital lock, Jamal entered the code and opened the door, holding it in place for his superintendent to enter.

"Thanks," said Andrea, "let's head to my office. We can get a SOCO to deal with the wallet there."

"OK, Boss." Both detectives negotiated the quiet station.

All the other stationed officers were down at the scene and the front counter wasn't manned during the night. Jamal passed the old cell area, which was currently being used for storage. Any detainees were now transported to a larger custody suite, 'in the interests of efficiency', where a central hub of officers could deal with them. The cells at Sterndale had only ever been used as a temporary holding area. The room contained two cells only, both with barred cage walls, reminding Jamal of old Westerns that he used to watch on TV as a kid. There were no sheriffs here though.

Superintendent Finch glanced at the intricately tiled floor which could barely be seen beneath the files and equipment as she passed. In its day it would have looked outstanding; the room, reminiscent of policing in a different era. Her fleeting thought of a period, when the police held respect and criminals knew where they stood. Not necessarily a fairer time of policing but possibly a less complicated time.

The officers walked past the parade room, where a desk radio transmitted the voices of officers communicating with the control room, and climbed some narrow stairs to the next floor of the building. A small CID office was located there and next to it, the superintendent's office. Andrea entered and switched the kettle on for them both.

"Coffee?"

"Yes, please, Boss," Jamal replied.

"Jamal, Andrea is fine. Let's ditch the formalities. It's been a long night already and we've got lots to do."

"Cheers, Andrea. Black coffee for me." Both heard the tread of footsteps on the weary stairs. "That'll be SOCO" said Jamal, as a white suited figure appeared in the doorway.

"Hi there," said the suited female, "you needed a SOCO to deal with an exhibit."

"Yes, please," replied Andrea, indicating to the exhibit bag which Jamal had placed on her desk.

"The deceased's wallet. I thought it would be better for you to deal with the contents. We need identification, so driving licence, bank cards, anything with a name on would be a great start."

"No problem" replied the SOCO, picking up the exhibit, "The room next door's empty so I'll set up there. I'll let you know what I find and get it all back to you when I'm done."

"Great. Give us a shout the minute you find a name so we can start doing some intelligence checks."

"OK," the SOCO nodded confidently and left Andrea's office to commence work.

Andrea stood up and walked to a cabinet. Opening a drawer, she took out some fresh green Major Incident books, handing one to Jamal.

"We'd better get started on these," she said, also taking out a new policy book from the same drawer.

"I've already got the control room looking at staffing levels for today. They're bringing in extra uniformed staff to take over the scene cordon. UWSU is on a call out, so they'll keep working until they've finished the search. Control room is busy securing all the council town centre CCTV that may have been recording. Detectives, intelligence staff, and analysts are getting organised for the day shift. Gold command is briefed."

"Press officer?" asked Jamal.

"Nice one, I haven't sorted that yet. Can you ring control and see who is on call? It would be better to brief them tonight. It's early, but they won't want to walk into it cold, at eight o'clock."

"I'll get on with it," he replied.

"J," called a voice from the adjoining office.

Jamal stood up, "Excuse me," he said to Andrea, leaving the room.

He walked into the room where SOCO had the wallet placed on a large sheet of paper, its contents spread out in a meticulous row.

"I'm just going to start photographing it all for you J, so please don't touch anything. The name you need is John Duffield. That's his driver's licence with his photo on," she pointed to the pink card on the table.

"Can I just take his address and date of birth?" asked Jamal.

"Sure," the SOCO officer read both out to Jamal, who wrote them down in his green book.

"I'll crack on here," she said, "I should have everything emailed to you in about an hour. I'll itemise and exhibit each item for you and place everything in the exhibits store myself."

"Thanks, much appreciated," said Jamal leaving the room and returning to Andrea.

"We've got a name, address and date of birth" he started, "John Duffield, born 1965, from Howeskelf."

"Good, let's take a look at him," said Andrea, nodding towards the desktop computer.

Jamal sat down at the desk, logged into the computer and intelligence system and typed in the name.

"Nothing," he stated, "not recorded on our systems." He turned to Andrea with a confused look on his face. "Not a complainant, not a victim, no lost property or road accidents recorded and, probably most pertinently, no firearms licence recorded."

"So, we have an unknown dead male, in possession of an illegally held firearm, and a witness, of whom we have no details, who has reported a fight at the falls. Not a lot to go on," said Andrea. "That's what we are here for though, Jamal. We have a violent offender out there and we are going to catch him," she concluded with a determined look on her face. "You sort out the press officer. I'm going to sort out a uniformed officer to go to the home address and see if anyone is in. The guy had a wedding ring on, so if the wife's home they can pass the death message. We'll have her brought in to do the formal identification first, then we'll sort out the critical witness statement. I'll ring gold and update them. Clear your calendar Jamal, we're staying on this one as long as it takes."

***

A marked police vehicle drove slowly into the village of Howeskelf, its diesel engine disturbing the silence as it cruised through the main street, the officers on board looking for an address. Headlights illuminated the sleeping houses, whose outlines were becoming more substantive as dawn approached.

"I'll pass the message, Fiona," said Sergeant Wilson. "I wouldn't land you with that job on your first night patrol." Fiona was a probationary constable on her first night tour of duty and was thankful that her Sergeant was taking the lead. She'd never told anyone that their loved one had died and didn't relish the prospect of doing so. She was grateful to Sergeant Wilson for shouldering this burden.

"It's a crap job, but we often have to do it. The key is to be sensitive, but also to be clear. The last thing you want to do is get into a confusing conversation where, in this case, the wife doesn't understand what you mean." said Wilson.

"Doesn't understand?" asked Fiona, wondering how the news of death could ever be misconstrued. Wilson stopped the car.

"You know," he turned to look at her, "if you tell her 'he's no longer with us' or that 'he's left us', it can lead to confusion like, 'Where is he then? Where's he gone?'. Likewise, we can't be glib, such as, 'he's popped his clogs' or 'he's kicked the bucket'. You see what I mean?"

"Yes, got you. So what's the right way to tell her?"

"Watch and learn, Fiona, watch and learn. Sensitivity is the key." Sergeant Wilson resumed driving and turned into a small cul-de-sac, at the bottom of which sat a handsome detached house.

"Here we are," said Wilson, stopping the car directly outside. "No lights on, so it looks like we'll be waking her up. Let me do the talking Fiona and have your pocket notebook ready. Write down any comments that you think are relevant and we'll review it all after we've taken Mrs Duffield to the station."

Both the officers stepped out of the vehicle and headed towards the front door, Wilson leading the way. He reached out, pressed the doorbell, and turned to Fiona giving her a reassuring smile. He rang the bell again and stepped back, observing an upper floor light switch on.

"She's on her way," he said confidently.

After a short wait, they heard the front door key turn, and the door was opened revealing a small lady, wrapped in a dressing gown. Her brown hair was held off her forehead by a sleeping mask, her hand trembling slightly as she held the door ajar.

"Can I help you, officers?" she asked nervously.

"Yes ma'am" started Wilson. "Can you confirm that you are Mrs Duffield?"

"Yes, that's me, Vera Duffield."

"Do you mind if we come in, Mrs Duffield? Nothing to worry about. We just need a moment of your time, and it would be better inside. Sorry for disturbing you this early in the day."

"Yes, of course you can. I'm on my own though, officer. James, my husband, isn't here."

"That's OK, love." Wilson and Fiona entered the house as Vera opened the door fully for them.

"I'll put the kettle on," she said, walking to the kitchen.

"That's great, Mrs Duffield. It's been a long night," said Wilson, as both officers entered the living room. Wilson lowered his voice and spoke to Fiona.

"You see, lass? Gently in, no fuss. She'll need that cup of tea. Sensitive and gentle." He winked at Fiona, knowledgeably.

After two to three minutes, Vera returned carrying a tray holding three mugs and a plate of digestives. She offered them round and sat down holding her mug in a shaky hand.

"How can I help?" she asked.

"Well," started Wilson, "there's no easy way to say this." Vera leant forward in anticipation of a question, and Fiona took a sip of her tea. "Your husband's dead," finished Wilson. Fiona spluttered on her mouthful, spraying it back into her cup. Vera looked at Wilson in confusion.

"What did you say?" she asked.

"Your husband is dead," repeated Wilson.

"What do you mean?" asked Vera, placing her cup down on a side table and nearly missing.

"I'm sorry to say, it's bad news, James is dead. We've found his body."

Subtle as a brick, thought Fiona, placing her own cup on the side table and sitting down next to Vera. Fiona handed her notebook to Wilson and took one of Vera's hands.

"I'm really sorry Vera, but an incident has been reported and we've found James' body. He was dead when we found him and there was nothing that could have been done to save him. My boss has sent us here to let you know about it as soon as possible. I know that this is a big shock, is there anybody that you want me to contact?" Vera looked at Fiona's face with vacant eyes, shock hitting her hard. "Vera, can I contact anyone?" Tears welled in Vera's eyes.

"No…no, dear." Vera took off her sleeping mask and started wiping her face.

"Let's go upstairs, Vera," continued Fiona, "you can get dressed and we can pick up anything you might need for the day. We'll need to go to the station where we'll look after you." Veraa stood, allowing herself to be led to the hallway and out of the room. Wilson stood in their wake, oblivious to his ignorance, and helped himself to a digestive.

* * *

"There you go love. A nice cup of tea to settle you down," said Anne, handing her granddaughter a red mug with 'Yorkshire Tea' emblazoned on its side. "There's nothing that a cup of tea can't sort out." She smiled and sat down next to Kate on the green leather sofa, which gently creaked with the pressure of the weight, and placed an arm across Kate's shoulders to comfort her. Anne smiled over at Bill who gently patted Rosie's head, which extended forwards as she enjoyed the attention. Bill stopped patting, to pick up his own tea, and Rosie immediately pawed the air towards him, asking him to continue.

"All right, girl, steady down, I know you are there." He resumed patting with his free hand, and looked worriedly towards Anne, his concerns reflected in her expression. Kate took a sip from her tea, enjoying its comforting warmth, mug clasped tightly in both hands to control their shaking. *Where do I begin? Should I really be dragging my grandparents into this?*

"In your own time Katie, there's no rush here. You are safe," said Bill, intuitively.

She smiled at them both, her gran swaddled in her pink towelling dressing gown, smiling patiently. Grandad sat in his green slacks, green and white Rydale shirt and brown brogues, with his white thinning hair parted neatly to the right. They were both calm, caring and unflappable.

"OK," she started, taking a measured breath. "This is going to sound bizarre, but hear me out, and please believe me."

"Of course," they replied in unison.

"I saw two men fighting down by the falls. It was horrible. I think one of them is really hurt. He fell. He didn't move. He might be dead!" She blurted out her voice rising in panic. Anne sat silently, a look of shock on her face, and Bill's hand had halted on Rosie's head.

"OK, love. We hear you," he said, his hand unconsciously closing round Rosie's muzzle causing her to sit still. "Did you ring the police? Ambulance?"

"Yes, they'll be there now. But it gets worse, Grandad." Her voice began cracking, her words laced with terror. "The man who did it saw me, and he's trying to find me!"

Bill leaned forwards, "How, pet? What do you mean? How do you know?"

Kate then recounted everything that had befallen her that evening as her grandparents tried to take it all in.

Bill looked at Anne, as he paced in front of the fire. Kate had excused herself to catch her breath and calm herself. Anne had put Rosie in the kitchen, having removed her collar, which she clasped tightly in her hands.

"This is a right bloody mess, Anne. She's safe here, bless her, but what are we going to do?"

"Thank God Rosie was with her. Maybe she put him off."

"Pass that collar love," said Bill, squinting at it. Anne passed the collar and Bill took a look at it as Kate entered the room.

"Where's Rosie's name tag, Katie?" he asked, holding up the collar for her to view.

"It was there earlier, I never take it off."

"Well, it's not there now," he exclaimed. Kate walked over, took the collar and double checked it. Her mind replayed an image of the male stooping down at the river bank, picking something up, and flipping it in the air.

"It must have fallen off at the river," she spoke out loud to herself, eyes staring blankly at the wall above the fireplace. "That's how they found me. My address was on the tag." Kate then explained how she'd hidden and watched both men. Bill sat down, hands on his head, desperately trying to find a quick solution to Kate's problem. *Where to go from here?*

"Right," said Anne, "let's have another cup of tea." She smiled at them both, patting her thigh and turning towards the kitchen. Often the solid backbone to the family, Anne looked unflustered, prepared and ready.

"Why are you so cheerful?" asked Bill. "What are we going to do?"

"We're going to come up with a plan, Bill. Come on, we can sort this out. 'We're from Yorkshire', lad," she said, voice raised.

"But, what are we going to do?" he repeated.

"We're going to ring Matthew. That's what we're going to do." She smiled, turned and walked into the kitchen.

* * *

Matthew had taken the motorhome back last night and had collected Rach from her retreat. She looked better for a bit of recuperation, but she had seemed pensive and distant. They had enjoyed a beautiful drive eastward along the coastal road taking them to North Berwick. Matthew had learned not to intrude too much on Rachel's thoughts when she was in a contemplative mood. She would eventually speak with him and tell him what was on her mind. He'd kept the conversation light and they drove to their pre-booked accommodation, which was situated on the outskirts of the town.

Matthew had risen early, letting Rachel sleep in, and had treated himself to a 5K run through the green countryside estate that they were staying on. Arriving back at the small cottage, on opening the door, he could hear the radio playing in the bedroom. Rachel must be up and getting ready. He smiled and walked into the small kitchen to put the kettle on.

The house and location were unique; set within a private estate, the cottage was ideal for them both. The owners had completed a wonderful renovation of an old stone farm building, which historically had been used for fodder storage on the land. It sat detached from a row of private residences, which had originally housed farm hands and their families. The kitchen boasted an oil-fired Aga, which managed to provide heat throughout the house. Matthew intended to cook breakfast on its top plates, though he had never used one before. *It's just a hotplate. I can manage that*, he thought, bending down to have a look at the oven controls and doors. *Now, the ovens are a different matter.* With no knobs and dials that he recognised, he thought that it was unlikely that he would make a success of a meal on the first attempt. Kettle on, he strolled through to the hall and the double glass doors through to the lounge.

The room had two comfortable leather sofas sat at either side of the large fireplace, separated by a square wooden coffee table. The mantle of the fire was a cracked oak beam, darkened in the central area, demonstrating the age of the building. Wooden framed, tall windows interspersed the surrounding wall, with glazed patio doors leading out to an old red sandstone patio and the large garden. The room was surprisingly large and held a dining table, chairs and an upright piano. Already warmed up by the Aga, Matthew opened the patio doors, allowing the fresh Scottish air to permeate the room. The sun had risen, its warmth having dried the dew on the patio furniture. Matthew stepped out, taking a deep breath of refreshing air.

"Beautiful," he heard, turning to see Rachel smiling at him, dust motes dancing around her damp hair.

"Just out of the shower?"

"Yes. The ensuite is amazing."

"It's a special house all right," replied Matthew, walking to Rachel and encompassing her in his arms. "I love you."

"You too," she replied. They separated. Hearing the kettle whistling in the kitchen.

"Cup of coffee?"

"Yes please, hon."

Rachel walked slowly out to the patio, her stick supporting her. Her muscles and bones were aching following the last couple of days of exercises. She steadied herself on a garden chair back and worked her way around it, before gingerly sitting in it, leg extended. Matthew watched silently from the living room doorway, his face creased in empathy with her pain. Two minutes later, he walked out to the patio with a tray carrying two mugs and a cafetière full of freshly brewed coffee.

"There we go." He sat down opposite Rachel and poured them both a cup. "OK then, out with it," he stated. "Something's on your mind. You've had long enough to dwell on it, and I can tell you have something to tell me."

"It's nothing to worry about."

"I hope not, but it's worrying you, and that's worrying me. So out with it, we can discuss it and then move forwards."

"Right then," Rachel took a deep breath, grimaced, and stated, "I want to leave the police force." She squinted at him, waiting for his riposte. However, it didn't come. Matthew sat looking at her contemplatively.

"OK, no problem," he replied, taking a sip of his coffee, silence acquiring the air. Matthew sat back, smiling at Rachel.

"Is that it?" she asked, "OK, no problem," she mimicked his voice.

"Yep."

"You're not going to try to convince me to stay?"

"Nope."

"Why not?"

"You're your own person, Rach. You know your own mind and I have no right to make any judgement on your decision. I can tell you've been dwelling on it, and I know you'll have put a lot of thought into it."

"What about money?" she asked.

"We'll work something out."

Rachel could feel tears welling in her eyes. "I love the job, but I just can't do it. Look at me," her arm indicating towards her leg. "I'm a mess. I'm disabled and I'm scared, Matt. I can't do the job that I want to do. My mind is all over the place. I'm a liability." Rachel sobbed. Matthew moved around to her and took her in his arms.

"You're strong, Rach. Stronger than you know. I'm amazed at the progress that you've already made. You don't have to be a cop, you could do anything. Half of them are a bunch of idiots anyway. Just think what you could do without them holding you back." She held him tightly, her life raft in stormy waters, and let the tears flow.

Half an hour later, mascara restored, Rachel returned to the patio. The sun continued to warm the area and she looked out on a flourishing garden. A gunnera towered on the right side of the garden, its expansive leaves offering shelter to a small area of grass. At the bottom of the garden, a bench sat within a pebble-stoned sanctuary, the stones raked in concentric circles around a solitary large rock, a Japanese stone lantern perched singularly on top. Cut bamboo lengths framed the rear of the bench, which was accessed along a raised wooden path. Designed for relaxation, the area exuding serenity. Influenced no doubt by Ella Christie, Rachel thought to herself, remembering the brochure of the newly reopened Japanese Garden at Cowden placed next to the visitor's book.

The hot plate now mastered, Matthew jubilantly brought out a plate holding toast spread with avocado, poached eggs wobbling precariously on top, and placed it in front of Rachel for them both to enjoy.

"A light breakfast, then let's pack and head into town. Enjoy the calm, we can chat on the way in." Both savoured the morning in their private sanctuary.

* * *

The drive to town was only a couple of miles. Having packed their car, they drove through the estate towards the gate house which would lead them to the main road. With trees in full foliage and the surrounding fields burgeoned with crops, summer was in full swing. The air temperature towards town would drop slightly, with the effect of a welcoming sea breeze. Towering in the distance was Berwick Law, a natural land mass formed of phonolite. Tourists generally made a point of walking up to the top of it, but this was another aspect of Rachel's life that she felt had been stolen from her.

"There's a race up that hill held every year," said Matthew, starting a conversation. "Starts from the harbour. It's only a three miler, but not easy on those slopes. The same guy has held the record for the fastest time to complete it since 1989!"

"Are you up for challenging him?"

"No, not for me. Flat racing is fine for me."

As they drove towards the sea, the Bass Rock stood formidably out beyond the coast, its white surface reflecting the sun's rays. Historically, it was originally home to a hermit, before standing as a castle. It was then used as a prison, and it was now uninhabited apart from the large colony of gannets which crowned its top. The sea around the rock washed its sides, the quieter coastal beach sands disguising the vigour of the waters pummelling against the sentinel. Driving in towards the town, they passed tennis courts and verdant putting greens where visitors challenged each other for the winner's place within their family competitions.

The town was busy with visitors sporting shorts, t-shirts and various sunhats. The queue outside the ice cream shop snaked from its doors, and the smell of chip fat wafted through the air as the fryers from the next door chippy warmed up for the lunch time frenzy. Matthew slowly navigated the streets and managed to wend his way to the town centre car park, where he miraculously managed to claim a parking space.

"Can we head to the West Bay, Matt? Get a look at the sea. The paths are fairly flat when we get there. It'll have to be the chair for me on the way though." Rachel smiled apologetically, "I'll struggle to cope in any crowded street."

"Of course. I'll get your wheels out if you want to climb out." Rachel loved Matthew for his acceptance. No criticism of her, no mollycoddling of her. He gave her the freedom that she needed to cope for herself, and just made sure that he was available if needed. She opened the car door, hauled herself out and, begrudgingly, sat in her wheelchair. Matthew gently pushed her away from the cars to a pedestrian crossing which led to High Street. Checking over his shoulder for traffic, he took Rachel down the centre of the street before cutting right towards Forth Street and the sea.

"A bit quieter here. Away from the crowds."

"Yes, love. Let's find a bench. I hate this chair. I feel that I'm on show, and if I have to be faced with another half-exposed beer belly, I think I'll go mad." Matthew laughed and pushed forward to the West Bay. Approaching the beach, a footpath cut left towards the West side putting greens. A gentle onshore breeze cooled the air and the tourists who were occupying their claimed areas on the beach. Children ran from the gentle incoming waves, or jumped each set, with loud laughs and screams as they played. A vacant bench in sight, Matthew accelerated, claiming the throne with a self-satisfied grin on his face.

"Here we go, Rach, how's this one?"

"Lovely." Brakes applied, she stood and then sat down on the bench.

"I'll dump our bag here," said Matthew, placing it on the bench. "That'll stop anyone else intruding upon our space, and I'm going to grab us a coffee from that shack over there," he continued, pointing to a coffee shack near the beach. He wandered off, leaving Rachel to her thoughts.

Striding out, Matthew could see the first hole of the golf club, the fairways and greens tracking along the coastline. *I haven't played for ages*, he thought. *What a beautiful little town though. Could I see Rach and I here? I dunno. It's all going to depend on what she wants to do.* He looked back towards her, noting her contemplative look and gave her a wave, receiving a raised hand in reply.

Coffee ordered and collected, he walked back towards her, attempting not to scald his hands on the cardboard cups.

"There you go. Why the worried look?"

"Just thinking things over. Thinking about what my next move will be. A month ago, the force medical doctor put a report to the Chief Constable recommending that I be medically retired from the force. He didn't think that I could fulfil the full role of a police officer. I didn't want to tell you, or worry you, and it's not definite that the Chief will agree. The Chief makes the final decision, we just have to wait and see what he decides."

"OK," replied Matthew, "but that's what you want, right?"

"Yes, it is, but that leaves me with nothing. Obviously, I have us, I understand and treasure that but, I also need something for me, Matt. Something to focus on. A purpose."

"A change in career then. A change in direction. You'll work something out." Matthew's mobile phone buzzed in his pocket, and he reached for it. "Sorry, love."

"Hello, Matt speaking." Rachel watched as Matthew's smile dropped and the colour drained from his cheeks. "I'm with her now. We're away but coming back today." Matthew listened as the caller talked with Rachel trying to decipher their words through the muffled slur coming from the mouthpiece. "You've got her safe, Bill?" he took hold of Rachel's hand, grasping tightly. Matthew nodded. "Keep her there. We're setting off now. Don't worry, we'll help and we'll be with you as soon as we can. North Berwick, so travelling time to you. Ring me if you need me." Matthew terminated the call.

"What is it? What's wrong?"

"We need to go. It's Kate. She's in trouble and needs our help. Come on, I'll explain what I know as we travel."

Chapter 4

Chris sat within the rear of a white transit van looking at the front gate of their target's house. George had parked the van up about thirty minutes ago, locked the doors and, dressed as a workman, had wandered off towards the main road. He would not come back and collect Chris until the job was done. Their white van had replaced a dark box van that had been deployed by other members of their team earlier in the day. That crew had managed to get some photographic images of two young women leaving the house at around eight-thirty. They had seen no one else, and now Chris sat with their photographs in his hands. He was confident that neither woman was the one he'd seen at the falls. He couldn't afford to let his face be seen, hence his position in the rear of the van, with its mirrored back windows. He was the only one who could identify the woman they needed to locate.

After George had found the house keys last night, they had left Sterndale in the Mercedes and contacted base. The boss had been informed of the fight with Duffield and the likely outcome, and although displeased, he always looked after the team. They had been told to head to a location just off the A1 motorway and to get their heads down. A team would be up with a replacement vehicle and they would arrange disposal of the Mercedes. There they would get any further instructions. So, they headed on and waited, trying to get some sleep.

Three hours later they were met by a couple of their colleagues and given the transit. The boss had sent three men from Liverpool up and back and the intelligence cell members had been ousted from their beds and sent to the office to begin their work. The lads delivering the van had brought some false registration plates for the

Merc. The old ones were removed and new ones placed on. The Merc was then driven off and would be taken to a safe location where the car, all contents, and all sets of plates would be set on fire, making forensic retrieval almost impossible. The car was nicked anyway, so it was no great loss to Chris.

Almost in replication of police methods, the organised crime group had their own structure, their own professional means of working to achieve their aims. Though not hindered by red tape, they didn't have access to police computer systems and resources, and so were reliant on the internet, social media, and on the recruitment or placement of 'criminal assets within useful organisations'. Chris and George never questioned where these people were placed but assumed them to be within phone companies, council offices, government and such like. If the crime group were lucky, even within the police service itself. None of this was personal to the group, it was just business, and for business to thrive, strong and robust structures needed to be in place.

So, Chris and George had ended up here on the afternoon shift. They'd got some rest and George was adamant that he was going to enter the house today. They needed to search it, to get something about this girl, so that intelligence could work their wonders. Chris watched a post person approach the address with a large parcel in her arms. *She'd have to knock to deliver that,* he thought.

"Chris to George," Chris transmitted on a small walkie talkie and heard in reply in his earpiece,

"Go ahead."

"Postie has approached the house carrying a large parcel."

"Let me know if it gets delivered."

"Will do."

Chris watched studiously, unable to hear any knocking from inside his van. One minute later, the postie reappeared with the parcel still in her arms. *Great, we're on.*

"She's walked away, mate," he transmitted "parcel in her arms. Looks like no one's in."

"I'm going for it," replied George, "let me know if anyone approaches the house."

"Sound, mate."

George reappeared on the road leading up to the rear access of the house. He now wore a black T-shirt and jeans, having taken off his outer work clothes and stashing them in a small wooded area nearby. The clothes were hidden in some undergrowth and he would return later to collect them. Now focussed on the job in hand, he checked the small of his back, confirming that his knife was there, and from the right pocket of his jeans took out the house key. He had his cover story ready. Should he meet a neighbour at the back of the row of houses, he would just tell them that he was a friend of one of the girls from the house, who had asked him to check that they had locked the back door. As he had the key in hand and could show it, he felt that he would get away with that. If anyone was actually in the house when he entered, well he was more than a match for dealing with them.

Approaching the school and sighting the alley, George entered. He walked with confidence, as if he had the right to be there. There was no point sneaking about in the daytime as that would look suspicious to anyone watching him. He strolled into the alley, eyes sweeping the area, ears alert to any changes in the environment. The day was warm and with adrenaline pumping, sweat beaded his hairline. He loved the feeling, the feeling of danger and the risk that he put himself in. Nothing like his military days, but still a thrill and a damned sight safer. His ears heard the sound of music coming from one of the houses and the scream of kids playing in a garden. He strolled beyond that house and was now in sight of the gate that he entered last night, now closed, that sat within the leylandii hedge. He walked straight to it, listened and heard nothing. Quickly slipping on neoprene gloves, he reached forward, took a deep breath, and raised the latch and walked straight in. The garden was empty, all rear windows closed. It looked empty, as Chris had suggested.

"Approaching the back door," he transmitted quietly.

"Still clear," replied Chris.

George inserted the key and turned it, feeling the mechanism shifting. Trying the handle, the door opened silently and he entered, a smile on his face. *Silly, silly women,* he thought once more. The kitchen was empty. Some dirty cups and bowls on the side next to the sink, presumably left to wash following breakfast. *Only two of each,* he mentally noted. Opposite the sink stood a white fridge freezer, with the upper fridge door covered in photographs. George took his phone out and scanned the photographs, taking a copy photo of any that he thought would help. *There's the dog,* he thought, snapping a photo of a white and orange spotted mutt. He moved to the living room, which again was empty. The area was tidy, curtains open, with a soft dog bed sat neatly to the side of the fire. Conscious of time, he moved to the hall and crept stealthily upstairs. Experience told him that the house was empty; he could just feel it, the quiet presence of the house silently watching but no person breathing within. Bathroom empty, he now faced three doors. "Eenie, meany, minie, mo" he said quietly to himself, enjoying the game and the challenge. Reaching for a door handle he looked to his left where, opposite the door which would lead to the rear bedroom, a small piece of paper rested against the wooden stair spindles. He bent down to retrieve it and read in a hastily written script

Had to go to my grandad's for a bit. Have got Rosie with me.
I'll be in touch.

Kate xx

George pocketed the note and now chose to open the back bedroom door and entered, closing it gently behind him. He knew he was right straight away. Sat upon the bedside table was a photo of a young woman cuddling her orange and white dog. George took the framed photo.

"Got ya, young Kate" he said to himself.

Chris's voice spoke in his ear piece. "George, George! The two women are back towards the house. Just going towards the front door. George, can you hear me?" said Chris, his voice rising in panic.

"Yes, heard you" replied George calmly. *What a dickhead,* he thought, *the bloody idiot can't have been watching closely. All he had to do was give me enough notice to get out!* George opened the bedside drawer. Neatly within lay a small diary and a small address book. *Achieve as much as you can in the time given to you,* he thought, taking the books. Now moving back towards the bedroom door, he quietly eased the door open, and hearing the front door lock turn, smoothly closed it again. Stuck inside the room, he blocked the bottom of the door with his foot. *Only two ways out, the window or this door and through the house.* He heard the front door open and female voices speaking.

"Let's see how this one plays out," he said quietly to himself, reaching to his lumbar region and taking the knife from its sheath. The quiet calmness of a professional enveloped his body as he waited.

Chris sat in the rear of the van worrying. He'd been busy playing a quick game of tetris on his phone and when he looked up, the women were approaching their front door. He'd quickly transmitted it over the radio but he knew that George wouldn't be happy. *What can I do to help?* Placing a baseball cap on his head, and checking the back windows, he slid open the side van door and stepped out. *George needs a distraction.*

In the bedroom, George heard the front door closing and the women's voices continuing their conversation. He'd checked the bedroom window and it was a non-starter. It was locked, which meant the only way through was by smashing the glass. Footsteps sounded, ascending the stairs.

"I wonder where Kate got to?" a voice asked, from the landing.

"I dunno," yelled a reply from downstairs. "I'm sure she'll text or ring us."

"I'm just gonna ring me mam" said the woman, from the other side of George's door. He then heard a bedroom door open and close, as this woman entered another bedroom to make her call.

"And I'm gonna jump in the shower," said the second female, her voice increasing in volume as she climbed the stairs. "I'm knackered, so that should wake me up." She started singing and another bedroom door opened but didn't close. "You in there, Kate?" a voice boomed from the other side of George's door. She knocked. George stepped back, foot now removed, poised with knife in hand. The door opened. "Kate, you there?" A woman's blonde-haired head came into view. George pressed his back to the wall. If she entered he would take her, hand to mouth to stifle noise, knife to throat 'ready', and body weight to take her to ground.

"She's not slept in her bed, Em," said the female, head turning as if to leave. She pulled the door to but didn't close it. George slowly exhaled. *So close. She doesn't know how lucky she is,* he thought, moving quietly to look through the gap left between the door and frame. The sound of a shower started and he watched the blonde haired woman, shirt unbuttoned, walk from the bathroom towards the third bedroom, removing her shirt as she walked. The sound of the other female speaking on the phone could just about be heard. George waited. The blonde girl walked back across the hall, now in white bra and knickers, carrying a towel and entered the bathroom, closing the door behind her. *Perks of the job,* he thought, sheathing the knife, *but time to move.* Gently opening the door he stepped out, easing it back behind him, but not closing it. The sound of the shower and phone chatter masking any noise he made. At the head of the stairs he descended, feet pressed to either side of each stair to reduce the sound of any potential creaking. Now in the front room, he looked left out of the window. *Was that Chris approaching the house? What the hell was he doing?*

"Chris, I'm coming out," transmitted George. "Get back in the van." No answer. *He's a bloody liability.* George moved to the kitchen and on approaching the exit, heard a knock at the front door. *He's gonna get me caught,* thought George, his temper simmering. He moved to the kitchen and straight towards the back door. A dog bowl holding water stood to the side of the door. He picked it up and slowly poured it on the floor. He didn't have time to clean any footmarks that he may have left, but now, with the bowl placed on its side, hopefully the woman would blame the dog and wipe the floor over for him.

"Wait a minute" shouted a voice from upstairs, in response to Chris's constant knocking.

George eased out the back door, gently closing and locking it. Key placed under the same plant pot, he edged around the garden and out through the back gate, which he closed behind him. He wouldn't need to come back here again. Adrenaline pumping, he forced his breathing to calm, slowed his pace and walked nonchalantly down the back of the houses towards the road and his stashed work clothes. *Chris can sort out whatever mess he's creating for himself.*

"Answer the door, answer the door," a sweaty faced Chris said to himself. He wanted to give George a chance to get out, having given him the late call of the women getting home. An upstairs window opened and a dark haired woman looked out.

"Can I help you?" she shouted down, taking a mobile phone away from her ear. Chris put his hand to his ear, as if he couldn't hear her. He pointed to the door.

"Hang on mam, I'll ring you back. There's some bloke at the door." Emma terminated her call and walked through the hall and down the stairs to the front door, which she opened. "Can I help you?"

"Sorry, love, I'm just looking for a house number …," the male mumbled unintelligibly, in a Liverpudlian accent, head tipped down as if talking to the floor.

"What number?" replied, Emma confusedly.

"Twenty-nine," he replied hastily.

"Well, this is number ten," replied Emma, indicating the clearly marked ten on the door. "Somewhere down there," she pointed in the general direction.

"Thanks, love." The male turned and walked away. *Weirdo*, thought Emma, walking into the living room and looking out of the window. The male turned and walked in the opposite direction from which she had pointed and went out of sight. Emma shrugged her shoulders and dialled her mum's number to resume her call.

Chris walked away from the house and back towards the van. Hopefully, that had given George the chance that he needed to get out. He walked back to the side of the van and climbed in. Unbeknown to him, he was being watched by an elderly neighbour, who stood behind net curtains wondering why the van was parked outside her house. Five minutes later George, back in his work clothes, returned to the van and drove it away towards the town. *He'd better be in the back*, thought George. *Another close call caused by this idiot. I'm getting sick of him.*

His clandestine observer wrote down the car registration of the van as it left the area.

***

Vera Duffield walked away from the chapel of rest, within the cottage hospital, in a daze. Her world fragmented, she had just identified John as being the person who lay within the chapel. Life had drained from him. A cold, empty feeling exuded from his cheek as she brushed her lips against his face in farewell. The pain in her chest was crushing, suffocating her responses and her mind. She was numb, and walked supported by the lovely police officer, Fiona.

"Right, Vera, we're going to go up to the police station now. I'll get you a drink there and then we just need to ask you a couple of routine questions. Then I'll get you home and see if a friend of yours will come round and sit with you."

"OK, dear," replied Vera automatically "whatever you think."

Fiona placed Vera in the rear of her police vehicle, closing the door gently and climbed into the driver's seat. Sergeant Wilson had remained at Vera's house, waiting for a CID officer to attend and take over control of any enquiries there. Vera looked vacantly out of the window as the car pulled away from the hospital, the passing scenery blurred in her vision.

* * *

Jamal sat with Andrea in her office as they updated each other with the ongoing enquiries.

"We found Duffield's car, Andrea. Locked up securely in a small parking area at the bottom of the castle walls. I'm sorting a full recovery of it, then we will get it properly searched with SOCO in attendance too. The UWSU team is still searching the scene and it looks like the weather is going to hold for us."

"CCTV?" asked Andrea.

"There's none down at the river, but any council CCTV has been saved for the last twenty-four hours. Door to door enquiries have started on the residential road that leads down to the river. They've been instructed to identify any private CCTV cameras and to ask the owners to save any recorded footage that they can."

"Press?"

"Press officer was briefed early as requested and they will deal with everything. I've told them no press conference at this time and not to release too much. They realise that we are at the very early stages here and will do their best to keep the press off our backs." Andrea sat scribing in her green book as Jamal updated her.

"The wife?"

"On her way back from the hospital. She's identified his body. She's very shaken up, as you can imagine. There's a young PC with her, from what I've heard she is doing a terrific job."

Andrea smiled, "Good. Make sure that we get her details please, so that I can email her inspector about her good work"

"Will do." Jamal liked Andrea, he liked her style. She looked after the small details, the details that could make a difference to both careers and investigations.

"We know that the pathologist will deal with our victim next," she continued. "What about our witness? She is key."

"Nothing," replied Jamal. "We've got the recording of the call, but the phone was switched off when they tried to ring back. An officer has submitted a subscriber request to the telephone company, but I reckon it's been swallowed up in a load of red tape. I've asked for it to be resubmitted, so it should be back this afternoon. Nine times out of ten enquiries go smoothly, but when you really need a result, it's the one time it goes wrong."

"Keep pushing for it, Jamal. We need to speak to that witness."

"I'll let you know as soon as we have any details. I'm going to oversee the initial interview with the wife, if that's OK? See if that gives us anything."

"Just make sure that your detectives tread carefully there. We have no suspect yet and we don't know her involvement, if she has any. You can listen in, but I don't want you interviewing her. Keep yourself one step removed Jamal, don't get personally drawn in. It'll help you to make clearer objective decisions. Let's just concentrate on their relationship and lifestyle first. If they interview at the video suite, you can sit next door and watch and hear it all live. Trust your detectives to do a good job for you." Andrea dipped her head and started writing in her policy book which Jamal took as his cue to leave. Vera Duffield would be at the suite by now, so he'd head over there and see what he could glean from the interview.

* * *

Vera sat down on a comfortable sofa in the room which was similar to a small lounge. A coffee table stood to the left of her and a couple of armchairs opposite. Fiona had gone to make a cup of tea and said that she would be back with another officer shortly. Vera was on autopilot, bouncing between tears and silence as she tried to comprehend how this had all happened. She last saw John alive this morning, kissed him goodbye at the door and waved him off at the living room window. Now he lay flat, on a hospital trolley, beaten and bruised and gone forever. *How, could this happen to me?* The door to the room opened and the lovely police lady, who had consoled her earlier, walked in carrying a tray with mugs on. She had removed her fluorescent vest and equipment and looked less formal in her uniform top and trousers.

"Here we go, Vera. A cup of tea and a biscuit. This is Karen. She's a detective and a family liaison officer. She's lovely and she will be the officer looking after you."

"Will you stay with me, Fiona?" asked Vera. Fiona looked towards Karen who gave an imperceptible nod.

"Yes, of course I will," replied Fiona. The officers each sat in an armchair. Karen introduced herself.

"Hi Vera, I'm really sorry for your loss. I realise that it's been a great shock to you. I'm here to do everything I can to support you, to keep you informed, and to be your contact officer with the local police." Vera nodded, looking to Fiona for reassurance. Fiona smiled. Drawing her attention back, Karen continued. "I'm an experienced detective Vera, so part of my role is to build up a picture of John, what he was like, how his relationship was with you, who his friends were, what his work was. Those kinds of things. Is that OK?"

"Yes" replied Vera, her shaking hands raising her mug to her lips.

"We'll just take things slowly and cover some necessary stuff today. I may take some notes, but, just so you are aware, this is a video suite so everything is recorded. That just means that we can talk freely and I can get everything I need from the video afterwards. Is that OK with you?"

"Yes"

In the adjoining room Jamal listened patiently to a frightened, middle-aged lady whose world had collapsed around her, his determination to capture the offender solidifying in empathy with her loss.

***

Matthew took the offslip on the A1 motorway and, negotiating a roundabout, took the exit towards Sterndale. Rachel had just got off the phone from Barnston nick.

"Looks like they are going to declare it a murder" she told Matthew.

"Bloody hell, Kate will be bricking it." He replied.

"I've got the details of the detective running the enquiry. Let's just see what we have first before we go jumping in. I haven't told them anything. By the way, the rumour mill is working hard. No one thinks I'm gonna get early retirement from the Chief."

"It's not always right, love. How do they know anyway?"

"It's the police force. They've got almost as many leaks as parliament does." He laughed. "I'm leaving anyway, Matt. I've made my mind up."

"Good for you. I'm proud of you. So, what are we going to do about Kate?"

"Let's get there, assess what's going on, and take it from there."

"Can you flick Bill a text and let him know we'll be there in five?" asked Matt.

Rachel sent the message then looked out of the window, *Now I can give Kate all my attention.* She felt at peace, a sense of calm descending, now that she had made her decision to leave the force.

Green and yellow blanketed fields retained by grey dry stone walls passed by on either side of the road. The green being grazed by Swaledales and Friesians, whilst the yellow corn basked in the summer warmth, brushed by nature's palm in the summer breeze. The road towards Sterndale wound through copses of trees with similar dry stone walls, interspersed by hedgerow and fence, ushering it through the countryside.

"Idiot," Matthew said out loud, "get on your own side." Rachel looked forward, seeing a white transit van heading towards them on their side of the road, having taken a corner too wide and too quickly.

"He needs to slow down." Matthew hit his horn in exasperation. The van repositioned correctly on the road as it approached Matthew, and he looked into the cab of the vehicle. A dark-haired male looked directly back at him, face cold, expressionless, and the vehicle continued past.

"Doesn't look like someone you'd want to mess with." stated Rachel, clocking part of the registration.

"Bloody right," said Matthew "he can have as much of the road as he likes!"

They both laughed and continued on their journey. Though Matthew was still in touch with his goddaughter, Kate, and regularly spoke to Bill and Anne, he couldn't remember the last time he had visited their home. High Harton didn't look like it had changed much since his last visit. Ahead on the road a horse slowly walked, its rider in fluorescent vest, peering back and spotting their car. Now on a single track road, Matt slowed his vehicle and held back, trusting that the rider would indicate to him when it was clear to pass. Sure enough, the rider guided the horse to the grass verge and waved Matthew through, raising a hand in thanks as she did so. He drove slowly past the horse and in the foreground spotted the white sign set within an old mill stone indicating that they were entering High Harton. Only a small village, High Harton still managed to support a village pub, "The Crown", a shop and a village hall, behind which also stood a tennis court. A small notice board stood outside the hall, presumably providing updates to the villagers, and a large banner outside the hall proclaimed proudly that 'The Village Produce Show' would be held at the weekend. As they drove through the main street, Rachel saw an elderly lady finish off sweeping the pavement in front of her house. Clearly taking pride in her own home, she next began washing her front doorstep with gusto, soapy water sploshing over the sides of her well-used washing up bowl. The activity made Rachel smile fondly, reminding her of her grandmother. The houses on the main road were made of local stone and, as with many villages, the village looked like it had stepped back a few decades in time. An old gentleman wearing beige trousers, a white-collared short-sleeved shirt, and a cream fedora tipped his hat to the lady washing the step as he stopped to have a conversation. Rachel smiled again, for a moment forgetting her own worries.

Matthew took a right turn and drove to the front of an old farmhouse, set back from the road. Bill stood there, immaculately dressed, raising his hand in greeting as the car pulled to a stop. Rosie stood next to him, barking a warning to the house that someone had arrived.

"I'll manage with my stick," said Rachel to Matt.

"OK, love." Matt climbed out of the car.

"Bill, it's good to see you." He walked up to Bill and shook his hand. Rosie sniffed around his legs.

Chapter 4

"Thank goodness you're here, lad. We've got her inside. She's terrified. We didn't know what to do, but Anne said to ring you." Matt could hear the stress in Bill's voice, as he sounded his words in rapid succession.

"Don't worry. We're here now." Matt placed a hand on Bill's shoulder. "Rach will sort this out." Rachel walked up to Bill, supported by her walking stick. Bill's arms opened wide and he gently cuddled her.

"Boy, am I glad to see you lass." He held her back, looking at her. "You are looking terrific." Rachel smiled.

"You're not so bad yourself." she replied.

"Right, let's get in the house. Our Katie's up in her old room, Anne's got the kettle on. Leave your bags, we'll fettle them in a bit."

Matthew, Rachel and Bill entered the house where he took them into the large farmhouse kitchen. Anne had tea already poured.

"I'll go and get Katie," said Bill, leaving the room.

"Thanks for coming to see us. We didn't know what else to do and thought that you'd know, Rachel," said Anne.

"You've done the right thing," Rachel propped her stick against the table as she sat down. "I just need to speak with Kate, get her account, and we'll go from there. Can I have some paper and a pen?"

"Yes, of course"

"And Anne …."

"Yes"

"I'm not trying to be rude, but I'll need to speak to her without Bill or you being present. The police may need to take a statement from you both at some time, so it will be better if I get her version of events directly from her, with no other influences."

"That's fine, dear. You know best."

"Matt can sit with you and update you on what's going on with our lives." Matthew looked at Rachel, surprised that she was cutting him out of the loop. Rachel saw the disappointment in his face.

"I'll give you the full update afterwards." He nodded accepting her decision. This was Rachel in work mode and he had to respect the seriousness of the situation.

"We'll go into the garden, Matt." said Anne.

Bill walked into the room bringing Kate with him. Rosie immediately went to Kate's side. Matthew gave her a comforting greeting and sat her down with Rachel, explaining that they would be in the garden and the reason why.

"Come on, Bill," said Anne, ushering both Bill and Matthew through to the living room and out of the patio doors to the garden.

Rachel looked at Kate, took her hand and smiled.

"Everything's going to be alright, Kate. Let's just start at the beginning"

One hour later, Rachel appeared at the patio doors in the lounge.

"That's us done for now." she said.

"How is she?" asked Matthew.

"She's good. She just nipped upstairs to get her camera and her bag. She'll be down in a minute."

They all entered the house, returning to the kitchen.

"What's happening?" asked Bill protectively.

"I'm going to ring the officer in charge of the investigation. He needs to know that Kate is a witness. She'll need to speak to his team, but not until we have her at a safe location." Kate walked into the room and Anne placed an arm around her.

"Are you OK, bairn?" she asked.

"I am now," replied Kate. She handed the camera to Rachel, a digital image portrayed on its screen.

"I just need to make a call," said Rachel walking into the living room with Matthew. She checked the image, then handed the camera to Matthew to view. Taking out her mobile phone, she typed in a number and waited for the man at the other end to answer.

"Jamal Kaur speaking."

"DS Kaur it's DI Rachel Barnes from the Witness Protection Unit."

"Can I help you, inspector?" he replied, clearly surprised.

"Can I just check that you are the lead investigator on the Sterndale Falls murder?"

"Yes, ma'am"

"DS Kaur, I have your witness and, believe it or not, I also have a photograph of your suspect."

Chapter 5

Jamal put his mobile phone down on a desk and checked his notes. *A break so early in the case; just what we need.* Andrea was currently at headquarters, finishing her day with a briefing to Gold and she'd want the update. However it could wait whilst he put things in place. Barnes had advised him that she needed to move the witness from the area. He'd have to trust her judgement with this. Although he'd never worked with Rachel before, her name was well known throughout the force following the attempt on her life a few months ago. He'd accept her advice, she was respected and now looked after witness protection for the force. Barnes wanted to move the witness to a safe location where she could be properly interviewed, and Jamal needed to sort out the transport. Resources were always the issue. His detectives were still doing house to house enquiries and uniform officers were dedicated to the scene, although the search was nearly complete. He called the control room and asked for one of the traffic officers to complete the transport detail. Barnes could brief them with what she wanted when they got to her. Barnes had advised him that she would sort out the interview with the witness and keep him updated. She knew that a car would be with her as soon as possible.

Jamal was happy. The first witness interview was vital and would be completed by an experienced officer, uninfluenced by the investigation. It would ensure that the first account was 'clean', no words suggested to her, nothing inadvertently given away by the interviewing officer. His phone rang again.

"Jamal Kaur"

"Hi Sarge, just to update you from a search of the car we found."

"Yes"

"It's pretty tidy, Sarge. Nothing much was found, but we do have a mobile phone. It's switched off and bagged. It'd be best to tell Andrea. Where do you want it?"

"Straight to HQ cyber unit, mate. I'll ring them and tell them to expect it. Great work."

"Cheers. Will do." Jamal terminated the call. *This day just keeps getting better. It'd be best to tell Andrea now during her meeting so that she can update Gold directly.*

* * *

Rachel sat outside on the patio with Matthew whilst Bill and Anne said their goodbyes to Kate. Understandably, the family were all pretty shaken up by the situation in which they found themselves. The camera sat on the table in front of them, now switched off, pending it being handed over to the investigation team.

"So, Matt, I'm going to take Kate, and you are going to stay here with Bill and Anne. They're pretty jumpy, though they're hiding it well. Bill can take you over to Kate's tomorrow to fetch some of her things. I'll put her somewhere safe and then we can organise getting her stuff to her."

"Changed your thoughts about staying in the job? You know, now that you're in the thick of it?" he asked.

"No, love. I'll see what the Chief has said, but my notice is going in either way." The doorbell rang.

"That'll be the cops." said Matthew standing up. "I'll bring them through." He walked into the house towards the front door. Rachel stood slowly and entered the living room, where Kate and her grandparents now waited.

"We'll look after her," said Bill, as Kate squatted down to give Rosie a cuddle.

"I know. I'll be fine too. Rachel will look after me." replied Kate.

"Yes, I will." Rachel reassured them. "It won't be for long. You'll feel safer away from here, Kate. We can get to the bottom of all this, you'll be back before you know it." Matt and the traffic officer walked into the room.

"Ma'am, I'm providing your transport. Where to?"

"I'll let you know when we set off." replied Rachel. Bill and Anne hadn't been told where Kate would be going. For everyone's safety, only Matt and herself knew.

They walked to the front door, where goodbyes were said to Anne and Bill. Matt had already put Rachel's gear in the police car for her.

"Let's go in for a cuppa," said Matt, his arms around Anne and Bill, gently steering them back into the kitchen. He reappeared in the hall and gave Rachel a cuddle.

"Look after each other," he said, "I'll ring you later." She reciprocated the cuddle and stepped out the front door. Standing on the driveway was an immaculately clean marked traffic car. *Not ideal*, she thought. The village telegraph would be red hot. Lowering herself into the passenger seat, with the digital camera now in an exhibit bag, Rachel texted DS Kaur to inform him that they were on the move.

"Where to?" asked her driver.

"Let's head east," replied Rachel. "I've arranged for one of my team members to meet us. They'll meet up with us and you can take this camera to DS Kaur, if that's OK?"

"Fine by me ma'am." The car set off moving slowly through the village, the traffic officer clearly cognisant of the speed limits.

Rachel's mind whirred. She'd been in contact with her team, who were putting the required measures in place. No one within the organisation, apart from her staff, needed to know where the witness was going. She would update the investigating superintendent personally once they arrived. It was important to keep things tight.

The fewer people who knew that Kate would be secreted at Barnston, the better.

***

Joe Marsden was sitting behind the counter at Forsetti's. It was nearly closing time and he'd been left to shut up the shop by himself. His life had taken a turn for the better since the incident with Brown. It had caused him to take stock of himself and had made him realise that, if he didn't get a grip, then he'd have a short and wasted life. Matt had given him an opportunity at the shop, which he'd grasped with both hands. It was the first time that someone had trusted him and he knew what a gift Matt had given him. Drugs still featured in his life, but not the illegal ones. He'd engaged with his GP and social care and was on a drugs rehabilitation programme. He could never just have gone cold turkey, but was now on a reduced prescription of methadone. He was determined to follow the programme through, until he required none. He'd had to cut ties with his old friends, as most were likely to drag him down the wrong path. He called them friends, but in reality they were a means to an end. People to club money together with in order to buy the next fix. Heroin did that to you, stripped you of morals, self worth, and honesty. His only friend used to be heroin, a succubus which drained his heart and soul. The door to the shop sounded as an elderly lady entered. He looked up and smiled.

"Good afternoon love, how are you doing?"

"Fine, thank you, dear. I've just nipped in to see whether the book I've ordered has arrived." She walked up to the counter.

"Surname, love?"

"Murray," said the lady, "as in the mint."

"Here we go, Mrs Murray. Jane Eyre, in a lovely clothbound cover." Joe smiled and showed her the copy.

"That's correct, it's a present for my niece."

"She'll love that," said Joe, scanning it through the till. "Haven't read it myself, a bit too high brow looking for me. I'm more of a crime reader. I've got a bit more knowledge about that subject. Do you want it wrapped if it's a gift?"

"Ooh, that would be lovely." replied the customer.

Joe walked around the counter to the sheets of wrapping paper and chose one to match the book. Now, back behind the counter, he showed it to the lady.

"Will this one do? Complements the cover."

"Yes, that would be great."

Joe rolled the sheet of paper up in a tube and secured it with an elastic band. "That'll be another three pounds for the paper," he smiled, "I'd wrap it myself but to be honest, I'm not very good at wrapping presents and you'll probably do a better job yourself."

"Oh, OK! I thought you were wrapping it, but never mind."

"Trust me, it would look a right mess." He beamed his smile, and the lady responded in kind, won over by his charm. Goods paid for, she headed to the door.

"Let me get the door for you, love," said Joe walking briskly to the door and opening it for her. She stepped onto the street, turned and smiled walking off. *What a lovely young man,* she thought, *very polite.* Joe locked the door behind his last customer of the day. Cashing up, a quick tidy, then he could leave work and head home.

Twenty minutes later and jobs complete Joe set the alarm and wandered into town heading for something to snack on to tide him over. Home for Joe, for the moment, meant his mother's. He still had a room there, and having given up his council-funded flat and his old life, it was the safest place for him to be. He paid his mum a little rent, though she claimed she didn't want it, and he also contributed to the food bills. His mum took care of all the other household bills and for now the situation suited him. He earned minimum wages at the shop, working there five days a week, and he got on fine with Matt's university mate, who was running the shop. Matt had spent a lot of time supporting Rachel during the past few months, but had also kept a weather eye on Joe to make sure that he was coping. Matt and Rach were up in Scotland at the moment and Joe was unsure when they would return.

Up ahead, the local McDonald's called to him. His own culinary skills limited and his mum's not being that much better, he entered and stood in the queue. As usual, the place was busy with school kids standing in clusters, letting off steam following a day spent in the classroom. Young staff in the back kitchen called across the grills as each performed their specific task in the formation of the meals. Joe hit the front of the queue, and made his order of two cheeseburgers and a coke to a staff member on the till who looked harassed and tired. He felt for the staff here. It wasn't the best job in the world, was nearly always busy, noisy and he was sure that they'd have to put up with a lot from the kids or disgruntled customers. However, at least they had a job and were willing to work. That was more than Joe could do when he was stuck on brown. Brown and white, heroin and coke, now replaced by burgers and cola. *At least McDonald's won't kill me*, he thought, *not as far as I know anyway*.

He walked up town towards the railway station passing a big issue seller as he went. He gave the guy a nod, but steered well clear, and was given a nod in reply. Joe knew that he didn't begrudge anyone trying to kick the drugs and doubted his old 'friends' did. They all knew how hard it was to do and would admire anyone who managed it. Joe couldn't say he didn't still crave it at times, but it was now about self control. He ditched his McDonald's rubbish and pulled a pack of Golden Virginia from his pocket and commenced deftly rolling a tab, one handed, before flipping it to his mouth and lighting. Enjoying the aroma, he knew that this was one bad habit that he couldn't give up. His bus was waiting at the station and Joe picked up his pace. This was a deliberate element in his life that he had changed. The bus fare was cheap, but more importantly, it got him off the streets, forced him into a routine, and he used that routine to discipline himself.

Joe approached the stop, stubbed out his cigarette and climbed on the bus, showing the driver his ticket. The bus was busy with the back seats crammed with lively school kids, loud and energetic following a day cooped up in the classroom. Older adults sat towards the front, some grumpily putting up with the kids' behaviour, forgetting that they once were young too. Joe grabbed a seat next to a woman who his Mum knew, *Mary*, if he remembered right. She shuffled her body closer to the window to make room for him.

"Hi Joe, how's your mam?"

"Fine thanks love, just the usual."

"Good on her. She must like having you back home. Less worry for her."

"Yeah, I think so, though she never needed to worry."

"And how are you?" asked Mary, placing a concerned hand on his forearm, "Everything going OK with you?"

"Yeah, I'm good. Busy working in town. Keeping me head down."

"Good man. I always thought you'd be OK. I told your mam that you'd be fine, eventually. She'll be glad to have you around. Since my Barry left, I have been a bit lonely at home. Kids have moved away. Oh, they call me, but it's not the same. Not the same as having them at home."

"Right," said Joe looking out of the bus windows. His stop would be soon.

"You get lonely, Joe? You got a woman?" Joe glimpsed at Mary warily.

"No, Mary, I'm good on me own, thanks."

"No one should be on their own love," she replied, gently squeezing his arm and looking at him. "It's not good for you."

"It's probably best for me at the moment. I've got enough on me plate." Joe gently pulled his arm away from Mary's hand. "Anyway, next stop's mine, I'd better be going. See ya." He stood up.

"Well, you know where my house is, love." Joe checked out of the window, pressed the passenger stop button, and flinched as his backside was pinched. He moved, turned and smiled at Mary, making a quick retreat towards the front of the bus. The vehicle pulled to a halt and Joe jumped off, relighting the stub of his cigarette where he stood. *It's like getting chatted up by me gran*, he thought. *I'm sure she's a lovely woman, but maybe she should be hunting for someone her own age.* A few months ago he'd probably gone round to hers for a cup of tea, with no other intention than to see if he could steal anything from her house. He strolled towards home enjoying the warmth of an evening sun. *Full time job, a safe home to live in, money in me pocket, and propositions from women. Life was good.*

* * *

Positioned in a small terrace of shops, within a suburb of Liverpool, Phone Solutions was open for business. The ground floor to the shop displayed phone cases, charging cables, screen protectors and numerous phone accessories, all at reasonable prices. Two cabinets displayed refurbished phones and a lurid flashing display in the shop window, advising prospective customers of the owners ability to fix anything. The business looked to be successful. A pokey room, accessed from behind the sales counter, acted as an office and also led to an interior staircase leading to an upper floor flat.

A front for organised crime, the team had arrived at midday and had now occupied the rooms upstairs. The owner of the shop was paid in cash for supplying the flat whenever it was required, which was one of a few premises in which the group used to set up their intelligence cell. The cell was always mobile. Though they may spend the afternoon at Phone Solutions, they would move to another location this evening, or tomorrow. Keeping mobile meant keeping covert. Less detectable by the police. Members of the cell had been recruited for their technical skills and, as with all pivotal members of the OCG, the pay was good.

A coded message had been sent out early this morning to their personal phones, waking three of them up, all of them knowing to switch on their burner phones. A new burner phone was used by each individual for each operation, with a hub phone used to direct them. When their task was complete, the hub and burner phones were disposed of and new ones purchased. Not a foolproof system but difficult for the police to keep track of. Recruiting the right type of intelligence officer wasn't hard. The OCG recruited within family or within close old school friends. Allegiance amongst both groups was high and the likelihood of them being 'grasses' minimal.

"Right, what we got from the field, Kirk?" said Rob, a young skinny lad, who was sitting with two laptops tops in front of him. Kirk stood balancing on his skateboard, looking at the screen on his burner phone.

"He's got us a phone number, address, and the first name of Kate." Rob's fingers started dancing across his keyboard as he started trawling for information.

"Stick the kettle on, lad. This'll take me a few minutes." said Rob, his face looking intently at the screen. "You're also gonna need to contact Al with the phone number. He'll do his magic with that." Kirk propelled himself to the kitchenette area and stuck the kettle on. He'd been given Al's burner phone number by the hub and texted the telephone number for Kate to it. Al would be waiting for the message and would know what to do.

"Here we go, girl. Into her Facebook account, Kirk," he called out. "She's not got it locked, this is too easy." The account gave Rob nearly all the information he needed. He commenced copying and downloading everything he needed, whilst drinking his coffee. Just one open door was all he needed and today's door was Facebook. Other platforms made it just as easy. The problems only occurred for Rob when someone was switched on, with accounts locked and passworded. That's when Rob faced his real challenges. Today his luck was in as he copied images of friends, family, workplace and relations as further personal details were gleaned.

An hour later and he was done. All data was transferred onto the second laptop, ready for onward movement. Rob and Kirk packed up and went downstairs to the office, which was empty. A quick look through the door showed one customer browsing the phone cases. They entered the shop and walked through. Kirk stopped by the refurbished phone cabinet, whilst Rob walked out, turning left.

"See ya," said Kirk to the shop owner, exiting the front door, where he turned right, dropped his board to the ground, and skated away. His work was done for the day so he could dispose of his burner phone now.

Rob headed towards the railway station where he could jump on the Merseyrail. His last job was to pass the second laptop on, where it would be taken to an analyst, who would map out their target's known life, thereby identifying the best means by which they could find her.

* * *

Kate sat in the rear of the traffic car travelling away from the A1 motorway into the countryside of North Yorkshire. Alone on the back seat she kept silent, having been briefed by Rachel beforehand to keep quiet. Rachel had impressed upon her the need to disclose nothing about their next intended actions, reinforcing to her that the least people that knew the better. They'd been travelling for about an hour and were getting close to their meeting location.

"About a mile up here on the left there's a small farm cafe," said Rachel, "There's a lay by just prior to it. You can drop us there. We'll be fine."

"Yes, Ma'am," replied her driver. A sign for a farm shop and cafe came into view and seeing the layby, the driver indicated and pulled in.

"Grab your rucksack, Kate," said Rachel, opening her car door. "We'll walk up from here, it's not unusual for walkers to drop in here."

"Thanks," said Kate to the traffic officer and climbed out of his car, hitching her rucksack onto her shoulder.

"No problem. You take care." The car headed off, the traffic officer now transporting Kate's camera to the investigation team.

She'd packed everything she thought she'd need. Her phone, switched off, in her bag just so she could get numbers out of it if she needed to. Her purse, with one hundred pounds in it, which was given to her by her grandparents, and her laptop. The rest was just clothing.

"Come on, help an old woman," said Rachel, indicating to her stick as she started walking. Kate stepped alongside her, grabbing Rachel's bag too, trusting her, but worried.

"Where are you taking me?"

"One of my team is up at the cafe with a car. It's not a police car, we've hired it. We'll have a quick toilet stop and a brew, then we'll get you across to Barnston. The officer is called Tina and she will be looking after you. You'll get on great with her. She's not from Barnston, so the cops across there won't know her."

"I'm scared, Rachel." Rachel stopped and took Kate's hand.

"I know love, but you're safe now. Matt's looking after your grandparents, and Rosie, and I'm looking after you." Rachel held direct eye contact. "I will not let anything happen to you. I promise." Kate smiled nervously and they walked on.

Chapter 5

The car park had six or seven cars within. A couple of families sitting on some outside tables were enjoying a snack, and the fading warmth of the sun. Rested against the bonnet of a dark Nissan Juke was a middle aged lady wearing a white T-shirt and jeans.

"Tina," whispered Rachel quietly, to Kate. "Just go with it."

"There you are," said Tina walking up to Rachel and smiling. "I've not been here long." She embraced Kate with comforting arms, and held her back at arms length. "It's great to see you again. It seems to have been so long since last time." Tina smiled which was reciprocated by Kate. Tina linked arms with her and walked her towards the cafe. "Now you'll have to tell me everything that you have been up to," Tina continued. Kate went along with it and like the best of friends they entered the cafe, followed by Rachel. *They'll be fine together,* thought Rachel.

Two hours later, Tina was driving on the main road towards Barnston town centre. Traffic was light and as they approached the centre the tell tale signs of the ruddy faces of holiday makers, demonstrated that the weather had been good in Barnston today. Groups were sitting outside of the pubs, drinking wine and beer, with not a care in the world. Relishing the good weather and numbed to their reddened skins which would guarantee an uncomfortable night's sleep.

"We're going to drop Rachel at the train station, Kate, and then I'm going to take you to the hotel. We'll get you settled, then I'll take you out for a bite to eat."

"OK" replied Kate, now comfortable in Tina's company. Tina pulled up to the station car park and parked in the rear car park. Rachel climbed out.

"You sure that you're alright walking from here, Rach?" asked Tina.

"Yes, I'll be fine. I've been sitting in the car for ages. The walk will do me good. Look after her and I'll speak to you later."

"Will do." The car pulled away heading for the car park exit. Rachel picked up her bag and slowly walked to the pedestrian exit and headed towards Barnston Police Station.

A few minutes later she entered the station and headed to her office situated on the ground floor. Thankfully it was empty as everyone had finished for the day. She shared the office with her team and they desk hopped depending who was in and when. Two jobs to do for her tonight before she grabbed a lift home. She knew that Kate would be safe with Tina so she could just do a last phone check in with her, later on this evening, and leave Tina to it until the morning. The first job, she'd thought a lot about. She logged on to her account where a barrage of emails awaited her attention. However, she only wanted to read one, and searched for the one that she knew would be there sent from the Chief's Staff Officer. Sure enough, there it was, posted today about an hour ago. *Not even a phone call*, she thought, *I suppose they'll want the Fed rep to deliver the news gently tomorrow. To be fair, they know I've been away.* She opened the email and digested its contents. It was as she expected 'early retirement due to her disability REFUSED'. In essence, they still felt that she was a valuable asset to the organisation. *Well, North Yorkshire, I have other thoughts.* Kate took out her personal mobile phone, opening its email. She had spent time on the journey from Scotland drafting her resignation. Resolved in her purpose, she emailed it to her work account. *The job has been good to me, but it's time to look after myself.* Completing the address fields, she paused the cursor over 'send', and with a smile pressed the button, feeling a weight immediately lift from her shoulders.

***

Kate and Tina walked out of the hotel where they were staying. Luxurious for Kate, she had her own double room with a view of the sea. Tina had arranged the accommodation which had been booked covertly, explaining to Kate that they were just booked in for a couple of nights. The hotel believed them to be two friends, who were just having a couple of nights away.

"I've googled an Italian restaurant, and found one around here that looks cracking," she advised Kate. "I'm paying for everything, so don't worry. Tonight, we are just going to relax so that I can get to know you. The real work can start tomorrow."

"What do you mean?"

"Getting a statement from you, getting your account of what you've seen. Then I need to know about you in detail. If we are going to protect you, then we need to profile you. Then we can close any loopholes where someone could find you. I'll sort a new mobile phone for you tomorrow, so that you can contact me. However, tonight lets just chill. Here we are." Andrea held her arm out in the direction of Carlucci's Italian Restaurant.

Having enjoyed the meal at Carlucci's, Kate now lay back on her double bed within her room, finally feeling relaxed. Tina had kept things very light-hearted as they'd had pizzas and a glass of wine. She had steered the conversation, with small talk centring around Kate's personal life, and only gently touched on what tomorrow would bring. Tomorrow would comprise Tina learning as much about Kate as possible. Not just about Kate personally, but about her finances, friends, medical history, family, and social media activity. The list seemed endless. Before Tina even started on that, Kate would need to provide a statement about the event that she had witnessed. *Well, I'll worry about that tomorrow*, she thought, walking through to the en-suite and turning the taps on. The wine had made her tired, and a bath and comfortable bed was what she craved. Kate had been told not to use her laptop or contact anyone on her mobile phone. She dug them both out of her bag, placing the laptop on the bed and looking at her phone. *I'll just need to write down a couple of numbers, then I can use the hotel phone tomorrow*, she thought, switching on the mobile phone. *That should be safe, numbers are just logged in the phone's memory, not on the network.* Kate switched on her phone and watched the screen illuminate, checked her contacts and jotted down the numbers on the hotel pad and pen. *Done,* she thought, pleased that she had what she needed. Tina said that she'd get a replacement phone tomorrow, so she'd await her instructions until then.

In the few minutes that Kate's phone was switched on, the device had connected with the network. As soon as it was powered up, it sought the nearest phone tower and "shook hands" with the closest telephone mast. It mattered not that no text message, call or internet search had been made by the phone. It had been activated by Kate and, in her hotel room, may as well have sat up, waved its hands and shouted out 'Here I am'.

***

Rachel had arrived at home and had just put her phone down following a conversation with DS Kaur. He appeared fine on the phone and was willing to trust Rachel with his witness for the time being. He'd told her that he'd update the superintendent and that they'd need a phone conference in the morning. Kaur had also directed her traffic driver to headquarters, to deliver the camera to the digital department, so that they could evidence any of the imagery and provide it in a format for the SIO to view. A quick call to Tina reassured her that everything was alright with Kate, and it was now time for a bath. She was tired out. *What a day, and it'll only get busier tomorrow.* She slowly climbed the stairs to the bathroom, her leg aching, but happy in herself. Kate was safe, the investigation would get everything that Kate could give them, and Rachel had made her decision. She could now think about a new life, and couldn't wait to tell Matthew her plans.

* * *

In a quiet telecoms office in Merseyside, Al sat with two other operatives, fielding calls from members of the public in relation to their phones. The office also supplied an on-call facility for the police or agency enquiries. Tonight Al was on the late shift and on-call with the two others. He'd nipped out to the vending machine, returning with three chocolate bars and a diet coke. The bottom of his computer screen flashed, showing him that he had an alert, and he unlocked the screen to view it. Squeezing into his chair he smiled and checked over the top of his screen, ensuring that the other two were busy, before taking out his small burner phone. He typed in to the phone and sent his message to the hub phone, informing them that he had a cell site location for their phone of interest.

Chapter 6

Bill drove towards Sterndale with Matthew as his passenger. Things seemed to have gone smoothly with Rachel and Kate last night, and Matthew had been given the job of going to Kate's house to let her friends know that she was alright. They'd met Bill before so he'd come to help and between them they could grab some of Kate's things that she may need. He drove into the street and got out stretching his arms wide.

"Tired?" asked Bill.

"No, no, I'm good," replied Matthew. "Still ironing myself out from the long drive down yesterday. Fell asleep last night, as soon as my head hit the pillow."

"Anne and I couldn't settle, lad. Worrying about our Katie."

"Rach will take care of things, Bill. It's hard not to worry, but she'll be fine." Matthew looked across the street, where he saw an old lady watching them from her living room window.

"Neighbours are sharp around here," said Matthew, indicating with a tilt of his head towards the old lady's house.

"Not necessarily a bad thing," replied Bill. He raised a hand and waved to the lady. "Don't do any harm to be friendly. This way son." Bill walked towards number 10, knocked on the door, and waited. One minute later the door was opened by a young female with dark brown hair, wearing shorts and a T-shirt.

"Hi there," she said

"Hello love, I'm Kate's grandad, I don't know if you remember me?"

"Yes, of course. She's not in, I'm afraid. I haven't seen her. Ginnie's just gone out too, but I know that she hasn't seen her either. Is she OK?"

"Hi there," Matthew intereceded. "I'm Matt, Kate's godfather. Can we come in?" Emma held the door open, allowing them in and took them through to the lounge.

"Everything's fine," said Matt. "She's had to nip off for a few days. Said that she left a note outside her room for you and just asked us to nip round to grab some of her stuff." Matt wanted to make sure that this was a quick, casual visit. He was sure that they would get contacted by the police at some point today, so he'd leave the police to tell the housemates whatever they thought they should. He didn't want to interfere.

"I haven't seen a note," replied Emma, "her room's upstairs. I'll show you." The trio went to the landing where Bill and Matt were shown Kate's room. Emma looked around the hall.

"No notes lying around here!"

"I'll check with her," said Matt. "We'll only take a couple of minutes." He entered Kate's room with Bill. Matthew immediately noticed that the bedside drawer was open and walked over to look.

"Right," said Bill, grabbing an empty sports bag that was lying on the floor. "She said that she wanted some clothes, toiletries and her trainers." He started looking in a wardrobe and chest of drawers, grabbing items randomly. "Oh, and her address book and diary, which are in the bedside drawer," he said over his shoulder.

"This drawer?" asked Matthew. Bill turned around to look.

"Yes, that's the one," confirmed Bill.

"You sure she didn't grab them last night?"

"She said she hadn't, Matt. Now just grab them son, let's get this done quickly."

"The drawer is empty, Bill. No books in here."

"She must be mistaken then." Bill zipped up the sports bag and headed to the door. "Come on, we've taken enough of...," he paused, looking at Emma, trying to recall her name.

"Emma," she stated.

"Enough of Emma's time." continued Bill. Matt exited the bedroom and they all descended the stairs towards the front door. Matthew's mind was ticking over. *We won't get back here again. At least not before the police call.* He turned to Emma, as she held the door open for them.

"Emma, we were just looking for a couple of Kate's books in her room that aren't there. You haven't borrowed them have you?" He had not named the type of books on purpose, so as not to lead her.

"No. We all have strict rules. No going into each other's rooms unless you are asked to. The door was slightly open last night, so I peeked in, but it was empty."

"Can you remember whether her bedside drawer was open?"

"Sorry, not a clue."

"OK, no problem. We'll speak to her later. Has she had anyone call for her?"

"We only have mobiles. Only other person was some Scouse weirdo who called here yesterday, looking for number 29. I pointed to our house number," Emma reenacted her movement "and sent him off in the right direction. The idiot walked the wrong way!"

"Probably some delivery driver," replied Matt, smiling. "Right, we'll be off. Thanks for letting us in. I'll get Kate to text you."

"Thanks, love," said Bill, carrying the sports bag over his shoulder as he walked away.

"Bye," said Emma, with a cheery smile, closing the door. Bill and Matt walked back towards Bill's car.

"Hello there." said the old lady, who had been looking out of her window, now in her front garden. Bill wandered over.

"Hello there, love. Grand day in't it. Just been calling round at my granddaughter's."

"It's lovely," she replied. "Callers there yesterday too," she said, conspiratorially. "Is something going on?" *This one's clearly up for a bit of gossip*, thought Bill.

"Callers yesterday? What for?"

"I don't know, but he came out the side of a white van and marched over there," she pointed to Kate's house. "Knocked like a madman on the door. When it was answered, he just walked away and got back in the side of the van. A few minutes later, a different man wearing work clothes came to the van and drove it away. It all looked very strange, I can tell you."

"Well, there's no accounting for folk," replied Bill moving back to his car. Matthew approached the passenger side of the vehicle.

"I'm part of the neighbourhood watch, you see," said the lady to Matthew. "Looking out for anything strange. You know, in case it's important. I wrote down the van registration number. Wrote it here in my notes." The lady produced a small red notebook, from a pocket in the front of her house apron.

"Very efficient of you," replied Matt. Looking at the page in her book as she showed it to him.

"See, there," she pointed to an entry, timed and dated with the registration and description of the men. One of many entries. The lady clearly took her role seriously.

"I'd ring the police with that," said Matt, noting the registration.

"No, no." she replied. "I'll follow the correct procedures and ring Mr Moss. He's the neighbourhood watch coordinator, he'll know what to do with it."

"Make sure you do," replied Matt, climbing into the car. He got his mobile phone out and quickly entered the registration number into it, before he forgot it. He raised his hand in farewell to the lady. Bill had started the car.

"Let's go, Bill." Bill pulled away slowly and they headed out of the close.

* * *

Detective Constable Dave Brindle walked into the living room of his small flat, squinting at the state of the room, head throbbing from the booze he'd consumed last night. He'd mixed red wine and spirits knowing that he'd suffer. Looking at the coffee table which was strewn with old newspapers, the *Racing Post* prominent, he spotted a half full glass of water. Popping two paracetamol in his mouth, he reached out with a shaking hand and lifted the glass to his mouth, swallowing the tablets and contents. The burn of neat vodka seared his throat and burst against his stomach lining, almost causing him to vomit. Mouth closed, he controlled the reflex. *Oh, well,* he thought, *my mistake.* He walked to the kitchen and switched the kettle on.

Brindle's life was a mess. He'd never recovered from his wife leaving him ten years ago. She'd kept the family home, leaving him with nothing, as he attempted to claw his way back to normality. They'd grown apart as he had dedicated himself to his work, to the detriment of their relationship and their two kids. Long shifts, combined with an hour or two in the local pub afterwards, drove a wedge between them. He had thought her happy with the money he was bringing in, but had since realised life wasn't all about the money. The divorce had favoured his wife and financially he'd had to support the kids too. It had left him staying with friends and then eventually renting the little flat he had now. Brindle had struggled to see a way out of his crappy little life and trying to make ends meet had dabbled with gambling. First on the horses, which he still did, and then he joined a couple of casinos and started online too. He was always chasing the elusive big win. He was close a couple of times though but he knew that it would come in and that his worries would fade. On his days off Brindle would go on the occasional 'bender' and twelve months ago, whilst in Manchester, had got to know a couple of good lads, whom he now met up with once a month. They regularly drank together, had some fun, and met some ladies, not hurting anybody. He'd ended up telling them about his financial worries, when drunk with them one night, and the following day they'd taken him to an accountant who would help him. Since then life had gotten easier. The accountant consolidated his debts, ensuring that anything he owed to casino's, betting shops, and online were cleared and arranged for Brindle to pay cash, on a monthly basis, to the accountant to slowly pay off his arrears. It worked great for Brindle, he now only dabbled on the horses and went on the occasional drinking spree. They'd given him a solid base to work from and though he still couldn't see where his life was going, at least it was now stable. Obviously, he'd kept his problems hidden from his work colleagues and like them, worked hard for his money. He was respected by his peers and known to do a good job.

Life was 'on the up', until two days ago. He'd nipped across to Manchester to pay some cash and was given an ultimatum by his 'friends'. Luck had brought Brindle within their sights. They weren't looking for him but when a gift horse landed they took the opportunity. The accountant explained that interest had accrued on his debts, which was substantial, showed Brindle some photos of the policeman in the company of prostitutes, and prominent in the picture were lines of coke placed across a coffee table. They had him and he knew it.

"What do you want?" asked Brindle.

"Well, Detective Brindle, it's not what I want. It's what the boss wants. The boss wants you to work for her," explained the accountant.

Brindle walked away from the meeting desperate, confused and defeated. He'd been told that they would be in contact and he'd been given a burner phone. That was it, he was on his own. He headed out of Manchester, straight home, where he opened a bottle and sat staring at the phone. He had nowhere to turn, nobody to turn to. It was either help them or lose his job.

Now, dressed for work with coffee in hand he stared at the phone resting on the work surface. He'd had no call or messages on it since he'd been given it. *Maybe they've forgotten,* he thought, hopefully. He went to the bathroom, brushed his teeth and straightened his tie. Putting his suit jacket on he looked at himself in the mirror. He looked tired. He looked beaten. He heard the ping of a text. His face crumbled.

"No, no, no." Brindle walked to the kitchen where the burner phone screen was illuminated. He picked it up with his fingers and looked.

Find her, was the text displayed on the screen. That was it. Nothing else. He turned the phone to silent, deleted the message, placing the phone in his jacket pocket as he walked out of the flat. Brindle's bad luck had just hit new depths.

***

Andrea and Jamal sat looking at an image on his computer screen depicting two men on the walkway above Sterndale Falls. The image was dated and timed and corroborated the time of the call that had come in from their witness. Duffield could be clearly identified from the image but the second male, unknown to them, was a different matter. Andrea had taken a call from Rachel Barnes this morning and had been given a full verbal update about what the witness had seen. The current location of the witness had also been disclosed to Andrea, as the SIO had full responsibility for all aspects of the investigation. The full witness statement would be obtained this morning and forwarded to the investigation hub. Andrea had worked with Rachel before and trusted her judgement and expertise in relation to the victim.

"Andy Burrows will be with us soon," said Andrea. "He's going to ensure that the intelligence cell are getting tasked correctly and he'll keep us on track."

"Great," said Jamal. "I've sent some detectives down to the witness's house to complete enquiries there. They'll speak to her housemates and do some door to door. If neighbours have seen anything suspicious it will help us to verify whether this guy is looking for her." He indicated to the image of the unknown male on the screen. "NABIS have been provided details of the seized weapon so that they can try and develop any other intelligence about it."

"The pathologist report confirms the cause of death as blunt trauma to the head causing a cerebral bleed. We've done everything we can at the scene so that's clear now. We need to identify this man," said Andrea pointing to the image.

"Yes," said Jamal, standing up, "I'll go and speak to our Field Intelligence Officers. They can start putting some force bulletins together with this image, and I'll see what any analysis of Duffield's phone is telling us. He walked out of the office, leaving Andrea to her paperwork, crossing the corridor where they had set up the intelligence cell. The intelligence office was only small with two FIOs and an analyst who were now dedicated to working on the enquiry.

"Morning guys," said Jamal as he entered, "and morning Dave, you back from days off?" he continued, seeing David Brindle standing in a corner, coffee mug in hand.

"Yes, J. Here for whatever you need."

"You OK, mate? You're looking tired."

"Just a couple of busy days. Yeah, I'm fine."

"Good, we could do with all the help we can get." Jamal's mobile phone rang, he answered it.

"Jamal Kaur."

"Hi J, it's Col. I'm down at The Close, doing the house to house. Thought I'd better ring you with this straight away."

"OK." Col then recounted the neighbourhood watch lady's tale of the van in the street and provided J with the registration. There was a light tap at the office door. Jamal moved and turned to see the head of Andy Burrows peer around the door. Jamal smiled, and waved him in.

"Right, repeat that registration," said Jamal, who grabbed a pad and pen lying on a desk and scribbled it down.

"Great work, Col. We'll get on with it. Keep me updated with anything else." Jamal terminated the call.

"Hi, Andy. Good to have you here." He reached out and shook Andy's hand.

"Nice to be invited," replied Andy, with a smile on his face. "Don't let me interfere. You crack on, I'll listen in."

Jamal recounted the telephone call that he had just received to the officers in the room.

"Let's start getting some checks done on that registration plate number," said Jamal. Dave put his coffee cup down.

"I'll get out of your way J. I'll nip and have a cig then I'll be in CID when you need me."

"OK, mate." Dave left the room to go outside.

Now outside, Brindle walked out of the grounds to a small park opposite the station where he sat on a bench. It was warm, he was sweating and he was nervous. Brindle had to make a choice but felt he had no choice. He was pinned. Exactly where they wanted him. He took the burner phone out of his jacket pocket as he lit a cigarette. Switching it on, he selected the only number on the phone and wrote his text.

If it's your van in The Close, they know about it. They have the registration.

He hesitated, drew deeply on his cigarette, *Stuff it*, he thought, and pressed send. *Time to look after number one. That's it now, I'm committed.* The phone buzzed in quick reply.

OK. *Find her*

***

Rachel walked slowly out of the superintendent's office, following a lengthy hour of discussion and pressing the button for the internal lift, waited for it to arrive. She felt lighter, a great weight lifted from her shoulders. Her resignation had been accepted – not that they had much choice – and she knew that it was the right decision for her. The lift doors opened with a 'ping' and she stepped in, pressing the button to go down two floors to her office. With accrued leave, she could actually have walked out of the police station today, but she would take a couple of days to hand over her work and clear her desk and computer. Her replacement had already been identified as being her current Sergeant. She had run the office in Rachel's absence as Rachel had recuperated, and she would be given the rank of Temporary Inspector when she took over. *Good luck with that*, thought Rachel. *Don't step out of the office, you can never guess what may happen!*. She had newly been given the rank on the fateful day that she stepped out to help on the murder enquiry. Her knuckles whitened on her stick as she tensed with the memory of her accident. The lift stopped, she took a deep breath, and unclenched her hand. The doors opened and she slowly walked out, hobbled down the corridor and entered her office. Beth, Rachel's sergeant, walked in. She had already confided in Beth.

"There's a coffee, Rach," she said, placing it on Rachel's desk for her. "How did that go?"

"Surprisingly easy, Beth. Thanks." She smiled, picking up the coffee mug. "They're going to give you my role, as a Temporary Inspector."

"Well, there's no one much left at the bottom of the barrel to scrape around for," replied Beth laughing.

"You'll do a good job. Don't put yourself down. You've been carrying me for the past eight months as it is."

"Nonsense, we've supported each other."

"It's funny though, Beth. The Super didn't even ask me to stay. It's like she's given up on me."

"Rubbish."

"No, not at all. I don't blame her, it's just business and I'm just a person filling in a role. It doesn't matter that it's me, Rachel Barnes, as long as it's someone doing that role. Obviously, it helps if whoever is in the role can do it well, but you know, I'm not really sure that they even care about that really." She sipped her coffee. "Ignore me, Beth. It's been a hard few months." Beth smiled in response. "The next couple of days will just be me sorting out my desk, computer and files. You know everything that's going on. Tina's looking after Kate, so we'll get her to drive out somewhere and we can meet her. Then it's over to you."

"Sure enough, Rachel. Just give me a yell when we are going."

***

Tina finished taking her notes and looked up at Kate who looked tired.

"That's enough for now, Kate. Let's get out of here and get some fresh air." Kate smiled.

"It's horrible remembering it all again," she said, "and now knowing that the poor man died, I feel terrible." Tina took Kate's hand, reassuringly.

"You did all that you could, Kate, and a damn sight more than other people may have done. You couldn't have stopped the fight, but you reported it to us, and you took a photograph of the killer. I've got everything I need to draft your statement. Let's get some sea air and grab a coffee. We're meeting Rachel later on today. So come on," she nudged Kate's shoulder as she stood up. "I'll meet you at reception in five minutes." Tina left the room whilst Kate grabbed her trainers and the new phone that she had been given. Her old phone and laptop lay in her bedside drawer.

Five minutes later the women walked out of the front of the hotel into beaming sunshine, with the sound of seagulls reverberating from the building walls. The air was tempered by an onshore breeze, the waters cooling the air prior to it climbing up the south cliff to the building. The front of the hotel had a small seating area where customers were enjoying a lunch time snack, beer or glass of wine, enjoying their holiday breaks with no worries in the world.

"Come on," said Tina. "Let's walk along the cliff and into town. We'll grab a coffee and check what Barnston has to offer. You'll probably be here for a few days so you may as well get to know the place." Kate smiled in return, and just went along with it. She felt lost really.

A few people strolled along the upper cliff paths, whilst others rested on benches which were interspersed along the cliff top, enjoying the view out to sea. The sound of seagulls permeated the air as they glided on the thermals, and wheeled through the air. In the distance Kate could see the harbour, its lighthouse prominent, and various fishing boats tied within the quay. An old fashioned style tall ship exited the jaws of the harbour, with masts but no sails, heading out to sea, powered by an engine. An expected tourist sight on the East Coast, allowing customers to experience a small part of bygone days. The town itself crawled from the harbour ascending the bay, the small historic fishing port now morphing into the large town of Barnston.

Tina and Kate descended a steep concrete staircase towards the valley floor before climbing a road to the town.

"There's a Costa on the main street," said Tina, slightly out of breath, with Kate beside her breathing easily. "You're younger and fitter than me. I don't know about you but caffeine is calling me."

"Hot chocolate for me, please."

"Hot chocolate it is," said Tina, checking google mapping, on her phone. "This way." They headed into the town centre, and having ordered, took a seat within Costa.

* * *

Joe walked out of Forsetti's and headed into town for some lunch, leaving the shop in the hands of Rich, Matt's university mate. The town was busy with tourists and the season was at its busiest. He wheeled his way through crowds, and seeing an opportunity at the counter of Thomas the Baker's, dived in and ordered.

"Two cheese and bacon rolls please, love," he said to the elderly assistant who was sporting an attractive hairnet. Carefully selected with tongs and placed in a paper bag, the assistant handed the goods over to him with a smile and took Joe's money. He exited happily and flinched as "Next" was bellowed out by the elderly assistant. *Who would have thought she had it in her*, he thought, as he squeezed past a family of five entering the shop. Joe bit into the first roll, enjoying its warmth, crumbling flakes of pastry decorating his chin and shirt, and approached Costa, wiping his chin before entering.

There were only two or three people in front of him, and looking around he knew that he'd be able to grab a table. Joe's eyes were immediately drawn to an attractive woman who looked like she was sitting with her daughter, or younger friend. He flashed a friendly smile in her direction, receiving nothing in reply. *She can't have seen me*, thought Joe. He ordered his coffee and when ready, carried it over to a table adjacent to the female couple, where he sat down.

The ladies appeared to be talking to each other about the town and it sounded like they were visitors. *Nothing ventured*, thought Joe, comfortable in himself.

"Hi ladies," he said to them both, "visiting the town?"

The older lady smiled, "Yes, just for a couple of days."

"You've come at a great time," continued Joe, "lovely weather. You should see it in winter," he leant towards them "it's bloody awful." He laughed, at his own joke, winking at the older woman. She smiled in response. *Positive*, thought Joe, *keep going son*. "I'm Joe," he said.

"Tina. Nice to meet you," replied the older woman, turning back to face the younger woman. Not to be deterred Joe continued.

"I work in the town meself," he continued. "Own a bookshop, just in one of the side streets over there," he indicated with an arm in the general direction of Forsetti's. The young woman's eyes brightened. "Bring your daughter in for a look, I'll see if I can give you some discount."

The women finished their drinks and stood up to leave.

"That's very kind of you," replied Tina. "We'll think about it. Bye."

"Bye, girls," said Joe, happy with himself. *Well, that was OK*, he thought, watching them leave. *Tina looks about my age and is a good looking woman. Well, she knows how to find me.*

Tina and Kate left Costa onto the main street. Kate laughed out loud.

"What?" said Tina.

"He was hitting on you," said Kate, smiling. "I own a bookshop," she mimicked Joe's voice, "My name's Joe." Tina laughed.

"Cheeky little sod wasn't he," said Tina. "That sparkle in his eyes. I bet he's trouble."

They walked away, heading back to the hotel. Kate smiled, and despite herself Tina felt flattered.

* * *

Chris and George sat at a motorway service station on the A1 awaiting further instruction from their boss. The cab of the vehicle was warm and the boredom was wearing them both down. Their working relationship had deteriorated over the past couple of days and it was taking all of George's patience not to walk away from it all. Chris had put them both in this situation by being overzealous with Duffield, and then again by his subsequent actions at the house, putting them both in jeopardy.

"I'll go and grab us a burger and coffee," said Chris.

"OK," replied George. Chris left the car as George opened his window, lit a cigarette, and inhaled deeply.

The services were busy with a combination of business commuters and tourists stopping off for a quick break. George had noted that the car parking was monitored by an ANPR system and that there were various CCTV cameras positioned around the site. He had ensured that he had remained in the vehicle whilst here. Chris could flaunt his face all over the place if he wished, but George was careful. *The man's a fool*, thought George, not for the first time, *the quicker this whole job is over with the better. I'm not working with him again.* George's mobile phone buzzed in his pocket, taking it out, he noted that the calling number was blocked. He pressed a button to receive the call and held the phone to his ear, saying nothing.

"George, it's me," sounded a Scouse accent in his ear.

"Boss," replied George, slight surprise in his voice. *The boss, calling me directly. Something's up.*

"Listen George, and listen carefully."

Chris walked out of the public toilets, within the services, pulling his trouser zip up, ignorant of common decency or of cleanliness. Trouser belt adjusted and hands wiped across the back of jeans, he walked to Burger King, pushed in front of two young lads, and ordered food for George and himself. A few minutes later, he walked back towards the car carrying food and two cokes and saw George ending a phone call as he approached. George reached over to the passenger side, opening the door for Chris and reached across for the drinks to help him.

"Cheers, lar," said George. Chris climbed in and passed George his burger and chips.

"Who was on the phone?" he asked.

"New instructions from the top," replied George, as he crammed a mouthful of burger into his mouth.

"What we got?" Chris mumbled, through a mouthful of burger, ketchup running down his chin. *You really are a tool,* thought George, looking at Chris.

"We've to move from here. Somewhere a bit more secluded. Off the track a bit, but they want us in North Yorkshire. They're going to give us more to do in a couple of hours."

Chris nodded in reply, slurping on his coke. *Enjoy it whilst you can,* thought George.

George placed his coke in the cup holder, and started the engine. Balancing his chip carton on the seat between his legs, he set off, heading East. George now knew that this vehicle was 'hot', the police were aware of it and he'd been instructed to dispose of it. He'd also been instructed to keep the information to himself and en route to his destination he planned his next moves. Chris lay asleep in the seat next to him as George drove steadily, calm but adrenaline infused excitement building in his body. He drove past fields to either side with a small trail of traffic preceding him. Signs indicated that this route was not suitable for caravans and ahead he could see that the road wound up a steep hill. He was due to stop in a car park at the top of the hill where he would collect his next vehicle.

"We'll stop at the top of this hill," he said out loud. George stirred next to him.

"What was that?"

"There's a car park at the top of this hill. We'll stop and change drivers."

"Sound lar, I'm busting for a piss."

Their van slowly climbed the hill, in low gear, progress slowed by the cars ahead and a lorry, which was tentatively crawling up the steep road.

"Here we are," said George, pulling into a visitors' car park. The area was busy with vehicles, and walkers who were enjoying the temperate weather. George drove to the far end of the park, having already spotted the dark BMW which had been parked up for him to collect.

"It's busy here," he said, driving through the car park and stopping at a junction where another road crossed. "I'll just nip to the right here. There'll be somewhere we can park up and stretch our legs." He turned right and found an opening to a forest track which he pulled the van into. Chris jumped out.

"Back in a minute, Georgey." He climbed out of the seat and walked into the forest.

George moved quickly out of the driver's side, to the rear of the van. Within, he had his rucksack stored. He lifted it out. Checking the road. It was empty. He placed his bag against a tree stump to the right of the vehicle. Leather gloves now on he took a pack of antibacterial wipes from his bag and wiped down the wheel, door handles and gearstick. He'd been careful to place seat covers on both seats and gently removed the driver's one, and placed the sterile wipes within, folding it up and placing it next to his bag.

"It's lovely here, like." said Chris, approaching George from the trees. He stood looking at George. With a whip-like strike, George's open hand hit the side of Chris' neck. Chris' legs buckled as he collapsed to the ground, unconscious. George dived on him, flipped him on his back, and placed a choke hold on his neck.

"You're done," he grated through his teeth, into Chris' ear, "a liability, surplus to requirement."

He felt Chris's body turn deadweight. Now wired with adrenaline, George stood, picked up the body and placed it in the driver's seat.

Reaching under the seat he pulled out a spectacles case, within a full syringe of dirty coloured liquid; high dose heroin and cocaine mixed ready. Chris sat unconscious and as George tilted his head, Chris' reddened neck was exposed. He pushed the needle to the carotid and injected it. No remorse, and hardly out of breath, Chris applied a tourniquet to George's left arm, introduced the used needle to the inside elbow and then removed it, placing it in Chris' right hand. The keys remained in the ignition. *Job done, instructions carried out in full,* thought George. *Time to clean up.* George removed Chris' burner phone from his pocket, placing it in his own. Closing the door to the van he then methodically swept the area of marks and footprints using a pine needled spruce branch. *Luck is still with me, nobody around.* He hefted his rucksack and walked to the road, checking for vehicles and people before he strolled away from the van. *That's one problem dealt with.* Taking out his own burner phone he texted to the hub that the job was done as he walked to the BMW, whistling to himself. Reaching the car and placing his bag by the exhaust, he knelt down as if checking his bag, and retrieved the set of keys that had been left for him within the exhaust. His phone vibrated with a message received.

Head for the East coast. Barnston.

Chapter 7

Matthew sat on the patio, having enjoyed a light tea, prepared lovingly by Anne. Bill joined him, bringing him a cup of coffee.

"Village show on Saturday, lad," he said. "It'll be a busy day."

"Are you entering it?"

"Oh yes. Course we are. Most folk in the village will be. Competition will be hot."

"Anything I can do to help?"

"There'll be loads to do and your help will be greatly appreciated, but tonight…," Bill took a sip of coffee, his eyes holding Matt's, Bill looking over the lip of his cup, "Tonight we are off to the pub, lad. Our competition starts here and now." The seriousness of Bill's tone confused Matt.

"But it's just a small village show, Bill." Bill nearly choked on his coffee.

"Just! Just! You're joking, lad. It's the event of the year here in High Harton," said Bill excitedly.

"Oh! Sorry, I didn't realise that it was so serious."

"That's fine, Matt. You're not to know. Being a towny, and all that. You'll see in the pub."

"Can't wait," replied Matthew, now intrigued.

"We'll go about eight," continued Bill, taking a leather pouch out of his pocket, from which he removed a pipe, tamper and Zippo, placing them gently on the patio table. "They'll be a few in by then and the chatter will have started." Bill picked up his pipe and gently filled it with pinches of tobacco, taken reverentially from the pouch. He placed the pipe in his mouth and lifted the lighter. Matthew sat mesmerised at the ritual, performed in the warmth of the evening sun. Bill stared down the garden. "Aye, we'll see what they have to say." He brought the Zippo flame to the pipe and placed the stem in his mouth, took a couple of shallow draws and the smoke drifted from the bowl enveloping his head. Now lit, Bill picked up the tamper and gently pressed the tobacco within the pipe bowl and placing the tamper back down puffed again, blowing a circular smoke ring into the air.

"Right," said Matthew. "I'll go and give Rach a ring and see how young Katie's doing."

"OK, lad." replied Bill, with a smile. Matthew left him enjoying his pipe.

* * *

Matthew sat on his bed and dialled Rachel, pleased to hear her voice when she answered.

"Hi darling, how are you doing?" she asked.

"I'm fine, love. I'm off to the pub with Gandalf tonight and it's the village show tomorrow."

"Gandalf?" Matt explained the scene he had just witnessed on the patio to Rachel.

"Well, it's clearly serious business at the show, Matt. You can use your detective skills to determine who the front runners are and who is going to win."

"Can't wait," he laughed. "How's Kate doing?"

"She's doing well. We've got her statement, and the photograph, of course. We are just mapping out her current life so we can work out what we need to do to protect her and teach her what she needs to do to protect herself."

"How long is it all going to take though?"

"How long's a piece of string? She'll have to stay with us until we at least get the guy arrested. Then we can reassess. She sends her love to Bill and Anne, by the way."

"I'll let them know. And are you still happy with your decision? Ready to leave?"

"Yes," said Rachel. Matt could hear the relief in her voice. "Obviously, I'll keep in contact with Kate, as I'm here. I've also made a call to a couple of retired cops, but I'll talk to you about that when you get here. When are you coming?"

"I'll help Bill and Anne with the show preparation and I'll be with you for the weekend, if that's OK? Bill and Anne are doing fine. Let me know if Kate needs anything brought over."

"I will do love. I'm off to see her now. Better go. Enjoy the pub."

"I'll try to. Love you loads."

"Love you." The call was terminated. *Right, time to get ready for a pint,* thought Matthew. *Let's see what this show is all about.*

* * *

"Right, Bill, Ready when you are," said Matthew, walking into the kitchen.

"Right you are lad."

Anne stood by the cooker studiously observing a jam thermometer, which was resting within a cooking pan. The air smelled sweet with the aroma of strawberries which bubbled gently on the stove top.

"That smells wonderful, Anne," said Matthew looking over her shoulder at the rich red berries simmering merrily.

"Oh, it'll be a good one," said Bill looking over her other shoulder.

"Oooh, get back. You're crowding me. It won't be any good if you don't get out of the way." Anne turned and gently pushed the men back. "Now, give me room, I need to get the jars out of the oven." The men stepped back. Opening the stove door, Anne placed on some oven gloves and gently removed three jam jars from the oven placing them on a wooden chopping board.

"Delicate operation," said Bill, jokingly to Matt. "Sterilises the jars you see," explained Bill. "Look what I've got for her here," he continued. Bill proudly produced an oblong piece of wood with three circles rebated in a line, along its centre. The wood was polished to a shine and branded in neat letters along its edge the word 'Jam'. "It's for holding the jars you see," Bill clarified, as if Matthew hadn't realised.

"I get you, Bill," said Matt smiling. *This could be a long night.*

"Right, love, we'll be off." Bill gave Anne a peck on the cheek.

"Don't be too late."

"We won't. Come on lad. The first pint's on me." With that they headed off to the pub, leaving Anne to complete her show entry jam.

* * *

A low murmur escaped the room as Bill and Matt entered the bar of The Crown, skipping a beat as people within checked the new entrants, before recommencing.

"All right, Bill. How's things going?" asked the landlord.

"Fine thanks, Jack. Just in for a couple. Lots to do."

"Usual?"

"Yes, please. What would you like, Matt?"

"Pint of lager, please. Fosters will do," replied Matt, having spotted it on tap. Bill stepped back and looked him up and down.

"You sure? There's real beer here, you know. No need to settle for second best."

"Lager's fine. Beer doesn't settle well in my stomach." Matthew would have preferred a nice glass of red, but felt that that may have been one step too much for Bill.

"OK, your choice." Bill turned his back to the bar checking out the people within the small room.

"You ready for the show then, Bill?" asked a white haired gent, who looked as if he was enjoying a whisky.

"Nearly there, Alf, nearly there. How about you? How've you done with yer onions this year? They were pretty miserable last year."

"This an' that," replied Alf, guardedly.

And so it begins, thought Matt, picking up his lager and taking a large mouthful. *A couple of hours of wordplay, wits sharpened ready.* Bill had come to hold court, and with a glint in his eyes and the attention of the crowd, Matt could tell Bill was about to have some fun.

* * *

Paula had met Rob in the city centre earlier and, after stashing a laptop and burner phone in the bottom basket of her kids buggy, had done a bit of shopping before catching an Uber home. She'd returned to her little two-bedroomed flat, and having sorted out her child's dinner, bath and bedtime, now had some time to herself. She looked at the laptop on the table reluctantly, knowing that she had to get started. *How the heck did I ever get mixed up in all of this?* she thought, reaching into her handbag for her cigarettes.

Paula had been brought up well. She had enjoyed school and was a bright girl. Strong in mathematics and computer science she excelled in her classes with the school expecting her to be a high achiever. Things hadn't worked out as they had anticipated though.

Influenced by pressure from her parents and school, Paula had started staying out late at night, regularly partying with some of the local guys and girls. Underage drinking, cigarettes and late nights started affecting her schooling and although still sharp of mind, Paula wasn't producing the results on paper. Like many teenagers, discipline imposed by her parents had the reverse effect, and then she met Jimmy. Jimmy was a bad lad, but boy she loved him. Although mixed up with gangs and drugs, he protected her and always looked after her. At seventeen Paula became pregnant, which was the last straw for her parents. She refused to split with him and seeing no alternative she left home, moving in with Jimmy. She knew it wouldn't be easy, but Jimmy always seemed to have money and he genuinely cared for her. Their lives were fine until two years ago, when the bizzies came knocking on their door and took Jimmy away with them. He was now residing at Her Majesty's pleasure.

One year ago, following a visit to Jimmy in prison, Paula was given a lift home. This had been her first contact with Jimmy's 'friends' and the rules by which she now lived were made blatantly clear. As she was now part of their 'family', they wanted to use her skills with computers and her organisational mind. They would ensure Jimmy's safety in prison, and ensure the safety of Paula and her child. If she helped them then they could guarantee it, if she didn't then ....! The meaning was clear.

Now, a year further on, and with Jimmy due out in six months, she sat looking at the computer. Opening the laptop and logging on, she started. Paula never asked why, she didn't want to know. Her role was to profile whomever was given to her. To look at their accounts and any intelligence gained and gather it together in a format which could be easily understood. She'd selected specific software to use and to help her. Paula was good at this, and she knew it. Her reward for doing the work? Her family's safety and a good wedge of cash for completing the task. *OK, Kate, who do you know?* Paula started an association chart which placed Kate in the centre and her associates circled around the outside, with lines drawn from the centre outwards, like a spider's web. Interlinking lines would identify relationships between the associates. Following this Paula would complete the same work with locations and overlay this onto the associate chart. The work made it easy to visualise Kate's network and primary locations. A brief summary would identify key factors. Working late into the night Paula sat and looked at her work. She was satisfied that her 'boss' had what was needed in the report. Core family, grandparents Bill and Anne at High Harton; Matthew Forster (godfather) and his partner Rachel Barnes (POLICE) at Barnston. She downloaded the information on a memory stick and closed the laptop. She was tired. Paula opened her front door and placed the stick within her electric metre cupboard, leaving it open, and sent a text. It would be collected before morning when she would fetch the phone data that she was bound to receive. All Paula could think was *Kate, what have you got yourself in to?* as she switched off the lights, and checked on her safely sleeping child, before going to bed.

* * *

Andy and Jamal walked out of the lengthy morning briefing which had lasted two hours.

"She's thorough, J," said Andy, putting the kettle on.

"Yes, she knows what she's doing, doesn't suffer fools, and gets results," replied Jamal. "We're only just behind this guy, Andy. Everything's falling into place and it's only a matter of time. He's made mistakes and that's what we need to capitalise on."

"Have you heard anything else from Rachel?"

"No, but she's supplied everything that I need at the moment. I'm sure that she'll look after our witness."

"Well, she would, if she wasn't leaving. I'm sure that her team will though."

"Leaving?"

"Yep. Leaves at the end of the week. Handed her notice in. Shouldn't affect us though, her deputy has more or less been doing her job on and off for the last year."

"Why's she going? What about her pension?"

"It's to do with the Wellbury murder. She's had enough, mate. Job won't pension her off, so she's decided to resign. Cash in a smaller pension early."

"Bloody hell, she must be hacked off. As long as my witness is looked after though."

"She will be. Anyway, more important things to crack on with. As I said in the briefing, we've taken a still image from the witness photograph and put it out on an All Forces Bulletin. That's been circulated throughout the UK. We've also done some ANPR work around that white van that the neighbour reported in her street and Gemma here hopefully has some results for us." Gemma sat behind one of the desks in the office looking intently at two computer screens.

"What have you got, Gemma?" asked Jamal.

"In summary, Jamal, the van appears to be on cloned registration plates. The plates' PNC data is linked to a van that was recently purchased in Cornwall. Checks have been done down there and the owner purchased it via Autotrader. The VIN plate has been checked and he has the real vehicle and the documents to prove it."

"OK, that's a good start." Gemma smiled, obviously happy with herself.

"It gets better." Gemma continued. "I've done ANPR checks on the registration plate and filtered the results, removing all movement in the south of the country. The data that I am left with indicates that the same registration plate has been sighted in Merseyside and on the natural route from Merseyside to North Yorkshire, where it terminates. The last known movement on the vehicle was yesterday."

"The vehicle is still in North Yorkshire?"

"Looks like it," she beamed.

"Brilliant, Gemma," said Jamal enthusiastically. "Any intelligence on it?"

"I've just started looking, but an initial report indicates that it's linked to a Merseyside OCG."

"That would link in with the accent of the delivery bloke that called at the witness' house. We need to make sure that the plates are circulated to all the cops and get out there looking for it." said Jamal. "Where was the last hit?"

"Travelling east from the A1." replied Gemma.

"Right,"

"Can I suggest that we get the east side armed response vehicles to patrol that corridor, from the A1 to the east coast?" asked Andy.

"Yes. Let's ensure that all the shift briefings are up to date. I'll need to speak with Silver command and update them about the van. I'd also better inform the boss."

"I'll deal with Silver, the ARVs and briefings, Jamal," said Andy, "You update the boss. She'll want to update Gold. We don't want a bobby coming across it and going head to head with our murderer without the proper back up."

"We don't," agreed Jamal, standing up. "Great work, Gemma." Jamal left the intelligence unit heading for Andrea's office.

***

PC Simon Jones was busting for the toilet. He'd called at a couple of coffee spots this morning, to reassure them with a police presence, and his bladder was full. He took a steady drive up the steep hill. There was a car park at the top with a public loo where he could have his pack up and enjoy the view. The morning shift had been a quiet one for him. He hadn't picked up a job and was just enjoying having a drive around the villages, reassuring the public that the police still had a visible presence. Simon pulled into the car park, secured his vehicle and took a brisk walk to the gents. Walking out of the gents he was confronted by a young boy.

"Are you a real policeman?"

Simon patted his chest and looked down at himself then at the boy. "Well, I believe that I am, young man," he replied, smiling.

"Have you ever shot anyone?" Simon squatted down to the boy's height.

"No, I haven't. I don't need guns, you see. These hands are lethal." He held his hands out in a karate style, in a parody of Bruce Lee. "No one can get past me." A hip gently nudged Simon's shoulder, knocking him off balance.

"Now, Jonny. Stop annoying this nice policeman," said a middle aged lady, taking hold of Jonny's hands. "Oh, sorry dear, I didn't mean to knock you." said the woman, who had turned to see Simon balanced on his hand.

"That's fine, madam. No problem." Simon stood up and brushed his palms together, clearing dried soil from them.

"Problem, constable, problem. I think you've got a problem," said an old gentleman walking up, wearing a khaki shirt, shorts, and cap, and looking up at him with a reddened nose on which was balanced reflective red sunglasses. "There's a white van, just down the road there," the male pointed, "with a bloke in it who doesn't look well. He's not moving. I'll be honest. He looks…" The old man looked down at the young boy, pulled Simon to one side and said quietly "dead!" Simon looked at the man, as the words sank in. "Yes," said the man, directing Simon again, "just down there." Simon ran to his car, climbed in and started the engine. As he drove gently out of the car park, he turned the vehicle in the direction that the old man had indicated and increased speed.

Ahead, Simon saw a white van, parked nose in towards the forest. Blocking the rear of the van with his own vehicle, he quickly climbed out, and ran to the driver's side. He swiftly opened the door to the van and was confronted with a male, tourniquet on his arm, empty syringe in his right hand. He checked for a pulse and found nothing. The male was dead, and had been for a while, his left arm already discoloured from the impeded blood flow. Simon contacted the control room and reported the discovery and was advised to protect the scene pending a further update.

***

"Andy."

"Yes, Gemma," replied Andy Burrows.

"A PC Jones has just found our vehicle. There's a dead bloke in it!"

"What?"

"The control room has just telephoned me. Silver is asking what we want to do with it. They're ringing Jamal."

"I'll go and find him. Ring them back and tell them to protect the scene, until we know what the boss wants."

"Will do." Andy left the office, heading towards the superintendent's office, meeting Jamal on the stairs.

"You heard?" asked Andy.

"Yes, I'm heading out there. You coming?" replied Jamal.

"No, I'll find whichever officer is Silver Command today and keep them right. If you need any enquiries, put them through us and we'll sort them."

"Cheers, a marked unit is going to run me across to the scene. I'll ring you with anything whilst I travel."

Forty minutes later Jamal arrived at the scene. SOCO were already in attendance and an ambulance was waiting to take the body away. A cordon had been set up and everything looked to be under control. Jamal approached the constable, who was recording all officers who visited the location, and provided his details.

"Do we know who he is?" Jamal asked the officer.

"I think SOCO has his details, Sarge, the ambulance crew are just removing the body now." Placing on blue overshoes Jamal entered the area which had been screened off using a temporary barrier. The ambulance crew were just covering the body on the stretcher.

"Just a minute," said Jamal, raising his hand, and approaching them. "DS Kaur. I need to take a look." The crew waited and pulled back the face covering. Though discoloured in appearance, the resemblance was clear. Jamal was looking at the face of the male in the photograph his witness had taken at the falls. He had found his murderer.

"Any identification on the body?" asked Jamal.

"The SOCO officer over there has his wallet." replied one of the crew, indicating to a male wearing a white forensic suit. Jamal saw bruising to the cadaver's neck.

"Anything else obvious?" The same male pulled back the covering showing the ligature encircling the left arm.

"Empty syringe was found in his other hand. Looks like he'd been shooting up. Overdosed himself."

"Thanks." Jamal walked over to the SOCO officer, as the trolley was wheeled to the ambulance and the body placed inside.

"DS Kaur." Jamal introduced himself. "Have we got a name?" The SOCO officer produced an exhibit bag containing the male's driving licence and showed it to Jamal.

"Christopher Sydnam, born 10/02/73, from Liverpool." said the male in the suit. Jamal wrote the details down in his pocket book and checked the photograph, confirming that it was the male on the stretcher.

"Cheers, mate," said Jamal. "I'll leave you to it." He walked carefully away from the scene and exited the cordon. "One of my detectives will be here shortly," he stated to the officer on the cordon. "It's Dave Brindle who will be coming. He'll sort out the search team and staffing when he gets here. Thanks for your help."

"No problem, Sarge." Jamal went to his car, removing his overshoes before he climbed in. He picked up his phone and rang Andy Burrows, advising him of the deceased's details and providing him with a brief description of the scene. He knew Andy would commence the intelligence collection plan on this male and would have some information for him when he returned to the police station. He then searched his contacts for Andrea's number and dialled, listening to the ringing tone as he waited for her to answer. *There were two of them there though*, he thought to himself, *the witness saw two men looking for her.*

***

Jamal arrived back at the police station and headed straight to Andrea's office, where she had called a meeting. He knocked on the door and entered. Andrea sat behind her desk talking to Andy, both of them looking relaxed.

"Sit down, Jamal," said Andrea, pointing to an empty chair. "Coffee?"

"That would be great." Andy poured him a cup from the warm carafe, sitting in the percolator machine, and handed it over.

"Thanks."

"Good work, Jamal. For once we've had luck going our way." said Andrea.

"Yes, I'm confident that it's our man," he replied.

"We waited for you to arrive, Jamal, before going over things. What's the intelligence update, Andy?"

"So, Christopher Sydnam, from Liverpool. Not recorded on our systems, that we can see. However, extensive reports about him on Merseyside's intelligence records and on the Police National Computer. To summarise, he served time as a youth for offences of theft and burglary, and seems to have been in and around the drugs world for most of his life. Nothing recorded to say that he is a user himself, but definitely has links to the county lines network, so it's possible. He is recorded as being a violent man, though nothing that links him to firearms. During the past two or three years there isn't a lot recorded about him, apart from Merseyside have him linked to an OCG which runs some county lines into Fenchurch, Grimsby, and Barnston. There's one piece of intel that says he does a bit of enforcement for the group. We're continuing to develop our intelligence as we speak."

"Thanks, Andy. Jamal?"

"The scene is secure and our images match. So, he's the male that the witness photographed and the male whom she says committed the offence. We still have no idea why. On the face of it, he looks like he's driven to a quiet location and taken an overdose. Whether deliberately or not, we may never know. We now have the full witness statement and pathology report, but nothing has come back on the firearm that we found at the river. There's still CCTV to trawl, a second pathology report and a lot of work to do to tie everything together."

"There is," interrupted Andrea. "However, we appear to have our man, and therefore, have negated the threat to our witness. It's time to slow things down now. Gather what we have and concentrate on getting everything done thoroughly. Gold is over the moon and is going to the press this evening. We all know that the hard work starts now but Gold is informing the press that we've caught our man." She smiled at Jamal, noting the concerned look on his face. "What's up, Jamal?"

"What about the second bloke? The one that the witness saw in the field and that the old lady in The Close saw getting into the van?"

"He's not our murderer, Jamal, Sydnam is; whether on purpose or by accident, it's him that the witness describes as committing the act. The other male may have been driving him around, trying to help him locate our witness, who knows. Currently, we have no evidence that he's done anything more. The investigation continues, Jamal, but the pace can slow. If we ever identify him, then we decide then what to do. It's the long hard slog of investigation now. Gold is happy, and our witness is safe. That's what matters. Now, I'm contacting

Gold, if you can both go and discuss what resources we need and Jamal, let Rachel know that we have our man. Well done, gents."

Obviously, a clear dismissal, both left the room with coffees in hand. Andy placed a comforting hand on Jamal's shoulder.

"It always goes the same way, mate. They throw everything at it to begin with, but as soon as the threat has gone, it all gets thrown back to us to deal with. Not their fault, and not ours. There will be another big job in the force tomorrow and the same will happen." They both walked into the intelligence office to discuss the way forward.

* * *

Rachel had cleared her desk in preparation for Beth taking over. Surprisingly, to herself, she felt no regrets at leaving the police. She also held no antagonism to them for not pensioning her off early with her disability. They had a business to run and although the Chief Constable held the final decision, he was advised by many specialists when making that decision. Rachel knew that the choice to leave was right for her though. It was amazing how quickly the organisation could move when they wanted to. She had been provided with the financial details of the early closure of her pension and had been made aware that the criminal injuries compensation board were due to make the decision on a financial settlement soon. Financially, she would be fine, as long as she spent her money sensibly and usefully. She had the plan, had made her contacts, and today she had a meeting planned to formalise and recruit. Later in the day she had a meeting with Tina and Kate and was just awaiting a further call from Jamal Kaur, this afternoon, advising her of his proposed plans. She could then consult with Beth and make a decision regarding Kate's protection and update both Tina and Kate.

Looking at her watch Rachel realised that her meeting was at eleven o'clock. *Subconsciously, have I done that on purpose?* she thought. She had planned to take a taxi, from the railway station to the meeting location, and realised that she would be walking the same fateful route, to a meeting, just as she had done last year. Only last year, she never made the meeting, in an event which altered the course of her life. Rachel stood up and took her suit jacket from the back of her chair, she placed it on. She reached for her stick, rested against the desk, and was unnerved to notice that her hand was shaking. She was nervous. Not scared, but now aware of the ceremonious nature of her actions and the finality of her decision. There would be no Geoff Brown out there today, ready to push her into the oncoming traffic, but she had avoided walking that street since it happened. Had avoided facing it, and now she felt she had to. *Come on girl, you can do this.* She bolstered herself. *First steps to my new life, and that bastard isn't going to hold me back.* Rachel squared her shoulders, straightened her back and walked resolutely from her office. The next two hours would determine her future, and she was looking forward to it.

* * *

Dave Brindle looked at the recovery truck approaching the scene and watched as a uniformed officer moved forward and, with a raised hand, halted it. The cordon remained, closing off the entrance to the forest where the van had been parked from members of the public. He stood confused as to what had occurred, and though an accidental suicide didn't ring true, there was nothing else here to indicate otherwise. He had arranged recovery of the vehicle, via the control room, and had requested a full lift to preserve its integrity for Scenes of Crime. The full lift onto the back of a recovery truck would ensure that the vehicle wasn't driven, but instead lifted mechanically onto the vehicle, and subsequently transported to the SOCO garage for examination. He saw no need to have the area searched. After all, they had their man, and he was in the van. He fiddled with the burner phone in his pocket. *I need to update them,* he thought, as he walked up to the officer on the cordon.

"Hi mate, any toilets around here? I'm busting," he asked.

"Up in the visitor's car park," the officer replied, indicating the direction with a pointed finger.

"Cheers. Don't let them recover the van until I get back. I'll only be gone for two minutes."

"OK."

Brindle walked to his unmarked car, climbed in and drove to the car park where he stopped, and switched on the mobile phone. There were no waiting messages for him. He composed a quick text.

Cops found the van. Dead bloke inside. Looks like suicide. He pressed send and sat staring at the phone. The phone vibrated with a message received.

Good.

"That's it! Good," he said to himself. *What's bloody good about that?* He sat confused. *They're on to you, you bloody fools.* He tossed the phone onto the passenger seat where it bounced into the car footwell. *Boy, I need a drink.* He checked his watch. He had a runner in a race at Catterick, called Lucky Jim, and he had a good feeling about it. He'd studied his form, liked the rider and was feeling lucky himself. A bit of a risk with one hundred on the nose but 'you had to be in it to win it.' He grabbed his own mobile and tapped his app, the race was on the final straight.

"Come on, come on." Dave checked the screen for his horse. *Bloody hell, he's leading.* "Come on." Second place was catching him. "You can do it." The finish line was close. The horses closed a neck, now a nose in it, now together. "No," said Brindle, annoyed. "No," his voice raised, hands clenching the phone tighter. The commentator continued.

"And approaching the line, by a nose, it's … Red Admiral. Red Admiral wins the race. Lucky Jim, second…"

Brindle smashed his phone onto the steering wheel, once, twice, then punched the door with the back of his fist in an explosive rage. He now gripped the wheel, taking deep breaths, his sudden anger spent by his actions. He steadily calmed.

"Another day, Dave, another day." He looked at his phone, the homepage now ruined by spider webbed cracks. *Just my luck*. He reached into the footwell to recover the burner phone. A further message.

Find her

"I'm bloody trying to," he spoke angrily at the inanimate phone. *This lot are not gonna stop*, he thought, as he deleted the messages before returning to the cordon.

Chapter 8

Rachel climbed out of the taxi after the twenty minute drive up the coast. The journey had given her time to compose her thoughts, in final preparation for today. She had spent the last two nights at home going over her plans, ensuring that her proposition was realistic. She believed in her own heart that it was, and also felt that the people whom she had chosen were right for what she needed. Rachel tipped the taxi driver and walked to an empty table, situated outside in the sun but offering a parasol for those seeking shade. There were a number of tables and a large car park, though at this time they remained empty. It was still early and the lunch time trade hadn't started yet. She sat down with a view of the small private road leading to the pub and when asked, ordered a coffee and waited.

After a short while Rachel watched a black BMW 1 series drive towards the car park. She raised her hand in greeting to its occupant and smiled as it pulled into a parking place. *Here we go*, thought Rachel, standing up. The vehicle halted and a middle-aged man dressed in blue shirt, beige trousers and brown Oxford wingbacks, climbed out and walked towards Rachel, a smile on his face. He looked well and it was clear that retirement suited him. At five foot ten with thinning brown hair and a slim physique, he could blend in anywhere. Nothing stood out about him, he was unremarkable. He reached Rachel, opening his arms.

"Hi, Rach. You're looking well." They greeted each other with a friendly hug.

"You too, Tom. Do you want a drink?"

"I'll wait for the others, if that's OK?"

"They won't be long." Rachel nearly made it to sitting, then changed her mind, standing straight back up. "In fact, here's another one." A grey Skoda Fabia slowly drove down the road towards the pub, both occupants raising a hand in greeting as it manoeuvred into the car park and came to a stop next to the BMW. A bald-headed male, dressed like a school teacher, climbed out of the driver side, and out of the passenger side a short, dumpy and dishevelled man appeared, his bearded face with a large grin on it. Rachel smiled across at them both. "Gents, welcome." Both shook her hand. Rachel turned to Tom.

"Tom, meet Jim and Ronnie." The men all shook hands.

"Who's in the chair?" asked Ronnie. "The bar will be open and I fancy a drink."

"I'll be buying," replied Rachel.

"That's what I like to hear. Mine's a pint of Landlord," replied Ronnie.

"Just one more to come," said Rachel, cocking her head to one side, "and if I'm not mistaken she's about here." The growl of a motorbike engine increased, and travelling towards the pub a rider and bike appeared, the rider easing the throttle as they negotiated the road towards the car park. Pulling the bike next to the Skoda, ignition switched off, temporary silence dominated, before the natural sounds of the countryside reasserted themselves. The rider, clad in dark protective clothing climbed off, and removing her helmet, brushed back her shoulder-length red hair, using her fingers like a comb. Hanging her helmet from the handlebars, she unzipped her jacket and walked over to the group.

"Rach, good to see you," she reached her arms out to Rachel and cudded her.

"And you, Sarah," replied Rachel. Rachel stepped back, looking at the group. "Right, we're all here, let's grab a seat and sort out introductions." A member of staff approached the group when they sat down and their drinks were ordered.

Rachel looked at the group, satisfied that she had the right people here. She had spoken to them all on the phone separately but this was the first time that she had pulled them all together. *The first time, of many times to come*, she thought. *May as well get started*. Looking around, the surrounding tables still remained empty. A couple of elderly couples had entered the pub but had not reappeared, so she presumed that they were settled inside.

"So, guys," she started, "we all know why we are here and I'm hoping that this will be a fruitful meeting. You all know me, and you all know that I retire tomorrow."

"You won't regret it," piped up Ronnie. She smiled graciously.

"Let's get some intros done. Ronnie, will you start us off?"

"No problem," he replied, taking a sip from his pint. "Ronnie Cuthbertson, retired detective. Done my thirty years, currently sitting at home doing nowt. Bored out of my brains and up for it."

"You may wish to wipe that." Jim interrupted Ronnie as he pointed to the line of beer foam that had settled on Ronnie's moustache. Ronnie wiped it away.

"Jim Scott, twenty-five years and now retired due to some lucky pension choices. Trained detective, CHIS handler, and surveillance foot trained. I'm pretty nifty on a computer too." Rachel nodded to Tom.

"Tom Fairbank. Retired too. Surveillance trained and also a surveillance trainer. Worked in a few forces but finished off in Northumbria."

"And finally …." said Rachel looking at the female biker.

"Sarah Milford. Surveillance trained, worked in covert ops and, clearly, a bike rider."

"That's us." stated Rachel. They all looked around, quietly appraising each other. "I've spoken to each of you on the phone, so let's get down to it. We are all going to put a bit of cash into this venture. I'm going to put the largest amount in, and the rest of you are putting in an equal share. The bank account is set up and awaiting your transfers. It's a risk, but we all think that it could work or we wouldn't be here. How are we going to get this team up and running? What do we need?" Rachel took a pad and pen out of her bag to take notes. They all looked at each other, waiting for someone to lead. Then they all looked at Rachel.

"Right," she commenced, "we need a secure base, an office." The others pitched in as Rachel took notes.

"Equipment"

"Computers"

"Training"

"Another pint," said Ronnie, holding up his half empty glass. The rest of the team laughed. Jim cuffed Ronnie's shoulder.

"Always the joker!"

"What?" replied Ronnie with an innocent look on his face. "We've definitely got to have some bloody fun." Rachel sat back as the team made good-natured jibes at each other. *This is going to work*, she thought, *we're going to make it work*. Two trained surveillance operatives (one of them a trainer), a computer whizz (steady and thorough), and a comedian (who behind it all was one of the safest pair of hands that she knew). They spent the next two hours discussing plans. She had her team. A small team to be sure, but it was a start.

* * *

George looked out of the window onto the North Bay beach where wetsuit-clad surfers could be seen bobbing on the water, waiting for the next set of waves to assault the beach. The top floor room in the guest house gave him a panoramic view of the bay, and he had spent the morning enjoying the view and waiting for a call or text. Outside, tourists held their positions on the sands, or tracked up and down the steep grass bank leading from the top road to a lower road and the sea wall defence. An open-topped double-decker bus regularly drove along the seafront ferrying tourists from one end to the other.

Early this morning he had checked that the sash window opened fully and had climbed out onto the flat roof, then to the side of it. Keeping low, he had ensured that he had an escape route if required, and sure enough the adjoining terraced guest houses could be traversed over their rooftops to fire escapes at either end of the block. Experience and instinct had taught him to always have an escape plan. Nobody would know him in Barnston but self preservation never went amiss. He'd received a call late last night advising him of his task for today but he was just awaiting the finalisation and authority to move forward. His phone buzzed on the table next to him.

Complete recce. Moira is en route

He had no need to reply. The sender would know that he had received the message and would trust that he would get on with the task. *So, they're sending Moira!* George was happy with that. Moira was a consummate professional. He'd worked with her before. She knew her stuff and was reliable. He opened his photo app, checked the image of Marsden he'd received, grabbed his cigarettes and a baseball cap. A quick visual sweep of the room, all was tidy. He stepped out, closing the door gently behind him, and placed the DO NOT DISTURB sign on the handle. Room cleaning service had already been this morning. Taking a box of matches from his pocket, he removed one, and pushed it between the door and the doorframe. Old habits die hard, but they were habits that he lived, and survived by. He took the stairs to the ground floor where he exited the building and headed for the town centre.

He'd checked the route on his phone and the walk was barely ten minutes. The streets were busy, as everyone enjoyed the sunny weather. George halted short of the main road and watched a police van cruise past completing its patrol. He was happy in the crowds. Just another tourist enjoying his day. Now on the main precinct he headed towards a side street and spotted the shop sign for Forsetti's. George took a seat on a bench in the precinct which gave him a view of the shop front. He took out a cigarette. *No need to move in close yet. I'll see how busy it is first.* George lit the cigarette, inhaling deeply, and relaxed. He was patient and his patience was rewarded. As he finished his cigarette a light-haired man exited the shop and turned to look at the window display. He pointed as if indicating to someone inside and then reentered. George stood up and an elderly lady, pushing a wheeled shopping trolley, shuffled towards the now unoccupied space.

"I thought you were never going to move," she joked, as she squeezed past him, claiming the seat.

"Why don't you help yourself, love," he said, walking away and tossing the dead cig butt at her feet. She gave him a disgusted look but held her position. George approached the shop and looked in the window at the books on display. He moved to obtain a clear view of the serving counter and smiled as he moved away. Turning right at the end of the side street, he sent a text.

Positive sighting of Marsden at bookshop.

Wait for Moira, came in reply.

That gave him time to familiarise himself with Barnston. Moira would arrive in town by train and he would greet her on her arrival. He hadn't been told how Marsden fitted into the equation but he knew that Moira would have been given more information and would let him know when she got here. He was aware that the OCG had a drugs line to the town, and was not surprised as he spotted various smackheads wandering around. *Must be grafting to get funds together for their afternoon fixes.* He'd seen the pattern in many places. Heroin abusers scurrying around in the morning trying to get their pennies together for a fix, and then again in early afternoon up to tea time doing the same. Rats in a trap living their relentless groundhog day.

The train station was easy to find with its large clock tower at the top of town. The main area, pedestrian precinct, with a road circling the centre. He'd seen the police station and courthouse on his way in yesterday and intended to stay well away from there whilst here. He'd noted that the town CCTV coverage was pretty good and would take a drive out later around the outskirts of the town to identify any more cameras. Fixed ANPR in Barnston looked non-existent but obviously the cop cars may have mobile ANPR fitted. He was aware that his current vehicle would probably have been recorded as he travelled in but if he kept its use to a bare minimum then he should be able to slip in and out of town unnoticed. His phone buzzed in his pocket.

With you in five, he read as he checked it. He doubled back and headed towards the vicinity of the station. He didn't want to meet Moira within the station but she knew that he would be around and would facilitate them meeting. Walking towards the station he saw a bus stop opposite. *That'll do.* A bus had just pulled away but there were two or three people milling about waiting for the next one. He checked his watch, though expecting that the train would be late, he knew that Moira's timings would be correct. *Two minutes.* He moved forward, taking his place in the small queue waiting for the bus. George watched as a few people started walking out of the station. It was clear that a train had arrived and sure enough there was Moira. Dressed in shorts and T-shirt with a small backpack, tanned skin, curly-haired, with a slim and toned body, Moira walked out of the station and halted, orientating herself. She checked her watch then headed towards the town centre. George removed himself from the queue and walked parallel to her route, his eyes sweeping behind her to see if she had been followed. With practised ease Moira halted and checked her backpack, allowing anyone behind her to walk past, then resumed her route. Crossing a road to the precinct, Moira moved from the right to the left of the path as George took the right side of the footway. Now held looking in Waterstones' window, Moira waited. George checked around and was happy she hadn't been followed. She continued walking as he moved closer behind her right shoulder, and closed the gap.

"Hi G," said Moira "Thought you were never going to join me."

"All's clear."

"Cheers. Saw you at the bus stop." He smiled, happy to be in the company of a professional. "Where to?"

"Let's head to the sea front," replied George. "It's busy there, we can grab a coffee and you can let me know why we are here." They walked through the town heading for the beach.

Twenty minutes later George and Moira sat on a low wall with a view of the beach and the sea. The sands were busy with screaming children and people in various states of undress, braving their bodily exposure to the elements. All hues and areas of skin were on view; from skinny pale legs, formidable oiled beer bellies to sunburnt scalps and noses challenging for supremacy in tanning capability.

"What's the job then?" asked George, sipping on a tasteless coffee from a white polystyrene cup.

"They think that she's here, or that she's been here."

"I guessed that much. Are they not happy that Chris' suicide will offer them enough protection?"

"They're not convinced. The bizzies know that there were two people there. Her statement describes two men and they have a description of you. Depends how far they look into it, and if they look hard enough they'll start asking questions. The boss just wants it to go away and wants loose ends tidying up."

"What's Marsden got to do with it?"

"I'm not sure, but our instructions are to get behind him, establish his routine, and report back. Eyes open for her as well."

* * *

Rachel had just got off the phone from Jamal, on her last day in the office. Beth had nipped out for a sandwich and would be back shortly. Although dissatisfied with the outcome, Jamal had been given clear instructions from his boss. They'd found their suspect and were now collating all their evidence to prove that he was the offender. Long term enquiries would continue as to the capability of the OCG and how it was impacting North Yorkshire, but for the meantime the threat to the witness had gone with the discovery of the body. The pathologist had found nothing untoward with the suspect's body, albeit deep bruising to the neck, but no defensive injuries to indicate that he had been in a struggle. The heroin/cocaine cocktail was unusual, but was possibly a lack of judgement by the suspect, who may not have been of sound mind after murdering Duffield. The police still didn't know whether Duffield's murder was an accidental result of a fight gone wrong, but the death of Christopher Sydnam appeared to be a death by misadventure. Jamal had left Rachel and Beth to inform and deal with the witness.

Beth walked back into the office and Rachel updated her regarding her conversation with Jamal.

"Great, Rach. Last case closed. Do you want me to tell her?"

"No, if it's OK with you then I'll meet her this afternoon and that's me done. Tina can update all the paperwork."

"That's fine. You having a drink on your last day?"

"No, I'll pass, thanks. Maybe in a couple of weeks I'll arrange something."

"Let me know and I'll let everyone else know." Rachel smiled. She had no intention of having any sort of leaving do. She didn't want to hear the sympathy, or the well dones for being brave. She just wanted to move on. She picked up her mobile and arranged a meeting with Tina.

* * *

Rachel entered the front doorway of the garden centre. Situated ten minutes' drive from the town centre it was a safe location for her to meet Kate and Tina. She had never actually visited before, and on entering felt immediately relaxed by its ambient atmosphere. Towards the back of the building a large tea room looked out onto the outside area, beautifully designed to display plants, pagodas, and pots for sale. Rachel had never had time for her garden, trusting a local gardener to cut the grass and keep the borders tidy. She doubted that her current plans would afford her any free time either.

Sitting at a table at the rear of the café were Kate and Tina. Both appeared to be chatting away like the best of friends. On seeing Rachel, Tina excused herself and walked over.

"I'll get you a coffee, Rach. I haven't told her anything."

"Thanks, Tina." Rachel walked over to Kate's table, using her stick for support and slowly sat down. Tina watched in sympathy, a feeling she hid from Rachel for fear of offending her. Tina walked back to the table having ordered the coffee.

"So, Tina says it's your last day," said Kate, "you're leaving her to look after me."

"Well, yes and no," replied Rachel.

"What do you mean?" Kate had a confused look on her face.

"There's good news, Kate. They've caught him."

"What!" exclaimed Kate, sitting back astonished.

"They've got the man you described. You're safe." Rachel explained the outcome of the police enquiry, watching the relief on Kate's face as she did so.

"What about the second man?" asked Kate.

"They have no idea who he is. They'll keep going with enquiries but the chances of finding him are slim. Also, he didn't kill Duffield. He may have been there, and he may have been driving Sydnam around, but at best if they identify and find him, he'll get questioned, will tell the cops nothing, and probably get released."

"Can I go home?"

"Not yet. We've got a B&B booked for you this weekend. Tina's got some bits and pieces to finish off with you. Hopefully, next week."

"I'm missing Gran and Grandpa."

"I know, love. Matt's picking me up tonight and I'm going over to see them. I just need to check everything's clear with them and explain to them what has happened. Are you OK with that?"

"If that's your advice, then yes. Tell them that I love them though."

"I will do, but you'll be telling them yourself soon." Kate smiled.

"And you're not going back there without a treat for Rosie," continued Kate. "I'll get one from here." Kate stood up and walked in the direction of the pets section.

"Nice one, Rach. You're going to miss it."

"You know, Tina, I'm not. I've done my bit for the force and it's time for me to move on."

"That's your final job done for North Yorkshire Police."

"Yes, it appears so."

* * *

Matthew approached the outskirts of town as he headed into Barnston. He was due to pick Kate up in an hour but he wanted to go and check up on the shop first. Though not concerned at all he could say a quick hello to Joe and Rich and check that they were happy with everything. He'd travelled across country, thereby avoiding the main road from Fenchurch to Barnston, which would be heaving with tourists towing caravans, driving motorhomes, or with cars packed to the gunnels, as they flocked to the coast for the anticipated good weather. The Brits loved the beach in the summer, and Matthew wasn't complaining as footfall would increase in the shop too. He drove down the hill, past the hospital and headed towards the police station where he could park the car on the roadside, and walk to Forsetti's.

Strolling down the precinct, he noted that nothing had changed. Matthew hadn't expected it to but he hadn't been in the town for a few weeks. The cuddle of familiarity encompassed him as he walked beyond Costa and Briggs' old law firm, the same *Big Issue* seller selling the magazine. Matthew approached him,

"I'll take one," he said, holding out a fiver.

"Cheers mate, I'll just get your change." said the male, gratefully accepting the note and handing over a copy.

"Don't bother. Grab yourself a coffee."

"Oh! OK, thanks."

Matthew walked on, rolling the magazine into a tube and approaching a nearby bin, stopped, and checked the front cover of the issue. He hesitated, then rolled up the copy, and tucking it under his arm, continued walking, hands in pockets. *Is this town still right for me?* He'd not put too much thought into it recently but now seeing it again it made him think. The people were great, and business for the shop was good, but the reality was that Rachel and him didn't have to stay here if they didn't want to. That was part of the reason for travelling to Scotland. To see what else was out there. The town held a lot of good memories for them both but the memory of last years 'accident' weighed heavily on Rachel, and Matthew knew that. *Something to discuss later.*

The shop window was looking good with a section dedicated to holiday reading and travel. The lads were obviously looking after things and peering through the window he could see that there were a few customers browsing the shelves. Rich stood behind the counter serving a couple but no sign of Joe. *He's probably in the storeroom.* Matthew entered the shop and walked to the counter.

"Afternoon Rich, how's things?"

"Matt, good to see you. I didn't expect you until next week."

"Just thought I'd nip in. I'm picking up Rachel and going away again for the weekend."

"I'll get Joe to get us a coffee. Joe?" he called to the back of the shop. Joe appeared holding a stack of books. "Look who's called in." Joe smiled.

"Well I never. The wanderer returns." He placed the books down and walked up to Matthew. "Well, how the hell are you?" he asked.

"Good, mate. Good. How are you? You're looking well."

"Couldn't be better. You want a coffee?"

"Yes, I do." He looked at Rich. "I'll just make sure that he makes it properly." Rich laughed.

"Help yourself, it's your kitchen." Matt and Joe went to the small kitchen behind the till. Ten minutes later, they reappeared, having caught up, with coffee in hand.

"I'll leave you two to bitch about me," said Joe, handing Rich a coffee and walking back to the books he had placed down.

"Anything to report?"

"Nope. All seems good. Takings are reasonable and picking up. The sun's bringing out the shoppers and trade is good."

"You're doing a great job here, Rich."

"Well, you're paying me a good wage, and I enjoy the work. Joe is a good worker and doesn't cause me any issues. We work well together. When are you coming back to it, full time?"

"I'm not sure, mate. Does that cause you any problems?"

"Not in the short to mid term, but in the long term I dunno. I've learnt a lot here. Maybe, I'll eventually open up my own shop somewhere in the country," he joked, laughing.

"You could do worse than do that, but hold that thought. I need you here at the moment. Can we discuss it next week?"

"Of course, you get yourself away and enjoy your weekend."

"I fully intend to." Matt checked his watch. "Right, I need to go and find Rach. See you next week." He stood up to leave, and looking for Joe, saw him speaking to an older lady within the poetry section of the shop. *Well, wonders never cease, he's settled in fine. Good for you, Joe.* Matthew walked to the exit and stepped onto the street. *Time to call Rach.* Taking his mobile phone out he selected her number, dialled and, holding it to his ear, turned around inadvertently nudging a male to his right-hand side.

"Sorry, mate," he said, continuing walking and turning, raising his hand in apology. The dark haired male stared at him with cold eyes. Matt shrugged his shoulders. *No pleasing some people.*

"Hi Rach, it's me."

"Hi love, where are you?"

"Just at the shop. Where are you?"

"Out at the Wyke. Can you collect me?"

"On my way." He terminated the call and looked back at the shop. *Have I seen him before?* However, the man whom he had bumped into was no longer there.

* * *

Matt arrived at the pub to see Rachel sitting alone outside, a small half-full glass of red wine in front of her. He watched as a waiter brought her a glass of coke and placed it on the table. Matthew parked the car. *She looks content*, thought Matthew, climbing out. He walked over to her, kissed her cheek and sat down

"This for me?"

"Yes. Lovely to see you."

"And you. You're looking happy with yourself."

"Last day, Matt. I'm out. Couldn't be happier."

"Cheers to that." He picked up the coke, tapping his glass to hers, and took a sip. Rachel raised her glass and downed her wine.

"Steady, girl." He laughed.

"Let's get going. We've got some stuff to collect from the house then let's get over to High Harton. We can talk on the way."

"Right, you are, Miss Barnes." Matt took a swig of coke and, leaving the rest, walked slowly back to the car with Rachel.

An hour later they were back on the road leaving Barnston and heading for the A1 motorway. Matt had told Rachel that all was good at the shop. They both were happy to be leaving as they saw the queue of traffic entering the town.

"It's going to be a busy one, Rach."

"I'm glad we're heading in the opposite direction."

"So, what have you been up to?"

"I've been making plans for the future."

"Go on." he enquired. Rachel updated Matt on the meeting she had just held with her prospective team. He listened attentively.

"So, let me get this right. You are putting a team together of ex-cops."

"Specialists," she corrected him, "some of them were cops."

"You're going to stump up the majority of the cash to get it up and running, for equipment and whatever you need."

"Yes, but they are all putting some of their cash in too."

"Like shareholders?"

"Yes."

"And you are going to investigate… what?"

"We are going to find work. Tom's got a contact in an insurance company. A private surveillance/investigative team can save them a fortune in payouts. People claiming they can't work, false claims being made by them. There's loads of opportunities in the private sector. People who may want private surveillance, on wives or husbands cheating, business partners not pulling their weight. It's an untapped market."

"OK, but you haven't got the work, yet."

"No, we have to go out and find it. The team that I've picked have got the skills though. The police get great training in the job, and when they retire, that's it! The training isn't used. I'm going to use it. We'll start small and see where it takes us."

"And they're all up for this? They're prepared to take the financial risk?"

"Yes. They all believe that it could work."

"And where do I fit into all this? You're going to be busy setting this up."

"I want you with me, Matt. I want you in the team."

"Me! I've got no training."

"You don't, but you know me. You know how I think. We can train you. I'm not the same since the accident, I'm getting stronger but I can't get out there as easily, like the others. You can do that for me. You can do the bits that I can't and I think we will be great together." Rachel's shoulders slumped, following her impassioned speech. "Just think about it." Having slowed the car, as he listened, Matthew slowly accelerated. *A change of direction. A new life.*

"I will. Just let me process it all and I'll let you know."

* * *

George was having a good day and felt that he was making progress. Moira had booked into a bed and breakfast not far from him and they had met up on the north bay, at a small independent cafe frequented by bikers and tourists. The spot had no CCTV and was busy enough that they could just blend in. They had sat outside and in shorts and T-shirts looking like a couple who were out for the day. It had given them time to plan and to check in with the boss. Their instructions remained the same: to keep an eye on Marsden and track his movements. Moira had visited the street where Forsetti's was located and had seen Marsden opening up the shop, so now they both knew what he looked like. They'd had a couple of coffees at the cafe and then parted ways so they could continue familiarising themselves with the town. He'd moved the car again, giving the appearance that it was in use and therefore not attracting undue attention.

George had arrived in the town centre a good hour or two before the shop was due to close so he could check on Marsden's appearance today. He was glad that he had, as luck was with him when Forster accidentally bumped into him outside of Forsetti's. Forster was busy on the phone, barely noticing George as he mumbled an apology. George walked away, into an adjoining shop with a smile on his face. *So Forster is in town.*

Now, close to four-thirty he sat outside of Costa with a view of the side street where Marsden would appear on the precinct. He'd passed the information into control regarding Forster and they were happy. With Forster in town, and the intelligence about the girl, there was a fair chance that she was here. He checked his image of the girl on his phone, hoping that he would spot her. George sat patiently and was rewarded as Marsden walked around the corner, eating a McDonalds, and heading towards the station. He called Moira.

"On his way."

"Ahead and waiting."

Moira had positioned herself at the bus stop outside the station. George watched Marsden as he continued walking in the centre of the precinct and allowed him enough distance before he stood up. Moira knew the score and would know that George was loosely following Marsden until he arrived with her. Hugging the building line as he casually strolled, George watched as Marsden continued on his expected route towards the bus stop. A quick text to Moira, *Over to you,* and George peeled away heading for his car.

***

Moira stood ahead waiting. *There you are.* She moved into the queue ahead of Marsden as the bus pulled up. She'd travelled on the bus earlier in the day so she knew the route. Checking the driver as she alighted she noted that it was a different male than earlier. *That's good.* The bus was busy but there were spare seats. Moira managed to get one near the front next to a lady who was busy texting on her phone. She didn't want Marsden near her, not yet. She sat and watched as Marsden presented his ticket to the driver, and as he walked past her down the centre aisle, she smiled at him and received a smile in return. Moira then kept her eyes forward, knowing he had probably grabbed a seat to the rear. The bus commenced its journey and Moira texted George confirming to him that she had Marsden on the bus with her.

Twenty minutes later a ping sounded as Marsden's bus stop, situated near the estate where he lived, came into view. Moira stayed sitting as Marsden walked past her to the front of the bus. The only person waiting, the bus pulled to a halt, and turning before leaving, Marsden smiled at her. She returned the favour, saying, "See ya," to him. He stepped off, hesitated and now looking back through the window, raised his hand in farewell. She responded with a small wave as the bus pulled away, enjoying the slightly confused look on his face.

George, now wearing a different shirt, walked towards the stop as Marsden exited the bus. He saw him wave and also saw the smile on his face as he walked away. *Job done.* He took a small side path which would take him back to his car in order to collect Moira, who would get off the bus at their pre-arranged bus stop.

Moira sat on the bus happy with herself. *Men are so predictable. Marsden had no idea what was coming.*

Chapter 9

"Come on then, Anne. Let's check over the entry form and then we can start getting our stuff together. Matt and Rachel will be up soon and they can help."

"It's pinned up there on the board, love." Bill walked over to the cork notice board as the kitchen door opened.

"Speak of the devil," said Bill as Matthew walked into the kitchen.

"What have I done now?" Matthew joked.

"We were just saying that you could help us with the show entries, love. Ignore him." Anne indicated to Bill. "Do you want a coffee?"

"I'll take one up to Rach, if that's OK? She takes a bit longer to get going in the morning."

"Of course, dear. I'll stick the kettle on." Anne moved over to the kettle, switched it on, and reached into the cupboard for a cafetière and cups. "I know that you like the proper stuff, help yourself." Matthew took a bag of ground coffee from the fridge and measured it out.

"You ready for today, lad?" asked Bill.

"Can't wait, Bill. When's it all start?"

"It already has! We're just checking the categories then we'll pick some veg and flowers, and Anne will sort the baking and jams."

"Entries have to be in by midday, dear." Anne clarified for Matthew. "Judging during the afternoon, and doors reopen at four-thirty."

"A full day then," stated Matthew.

"Yes, lad, and all the hard day's graft in the garden and kitchen getting our entries ready. It's almost a full time job!" explained Bill. "If we want to win, then we have to put the effort in. Highlight of the village calendar, it is."

"No burning of local witches and warlocks this evening then?" joked Matthew. Bill glared at him.

"I'm sure that I could arrange for a set of stocks for you to spend some time in if you like, young man." Matthew laughed.

"Only joking, Bill. Let me take this up to Rach and I'll be down to help." Matthew made a hasty retreat out of the kitchen carrying the coffee.

"Right, Anne. Where were we?" Bill placed the entry form on the kitchen table and they both started discussing their plan of action.

* * *

"Here's your coffee, darling." said Matthew entering the bedroom. "It's getting serious out there and Bill's wanting a hand. How are you doing?"

"I'm OK. In a bit of pain though. Can you pass me my pills, please." Matthew reached for them and gently threw the box to Rach. "Thanks love."

"Looks like it'll be a busy morning but I think that we'll get the chance to relax this afternoon."

"At least the weather looks good for them," said Rachel. "I'm not sure how much use I'll be though."

"You just sit and relax, love. It's your first official day of retirement. Plus, you've got lots of planning to do." Rachel smiled, pulling her legs to the side of the bed, gently standing, and clutching the headboard for support. The skin of her leg patterned by a large keloid scar, tracking from her hip to knee. She gently raised her heel from the floor as she started her exercises to loosen the stiffness of her limb.

"No time to rest here, love. You had any other thoughts?"

"Still mulling it over, Rach, but some, yes. Let me help Bill and Anne with their entries and I'll take you into Sterndale this afternoon and we can discuss it." Rachel lowered herself down and, taking her pills, used her coffee to help her swallow them.

* * *

"He's out in the garden, dear. He'll have set up in the greenhouse," said Anne as Matthew entered the kitchen.

"OK, I'll head down there." A tray of warm fruit scones sat upon a cooling rack, their sweet aroma tickling Matthew's nose. Anne was facing the oven as he reached out for one of the smaller ones casually walking towards the back door.

"I saw that," said Anne, still facing the cooker, "No more now. I need to choose the best four."

"They taste wonderful." Matthew mumbled, crumbs of scone escaping from his mouth. He headed out the door where he could see Bill at the greenhouse scratching his head.

"What's up, Bill?"

"Nothing lad, just viewing the crop." An array of vegetables sat within two trugs balanced at one end of the garden table. A cauliflower and lettuce dominated each basket with a selection of carrots, onions, beetroot and peas separated between each. At the other a selection of potatoes had been placed upon some white garden fleece.

"That's quite a collection you've got there, Bill."

"Yes, lad, but it's the task of choosing the best that is now the challenge. I'm looking for uniformity in most things. Three or four of the same veg that are the same in size and colour. You can start out by sorting the potatoes."

"What about the tomatoes?" asked Matthew, indicating to the greenhouse. The glass room was burgeoning with ripe tomatoes that had climbed their string lines and now bowed heavy heads majestically to each other. Reds were predominant with globe and cherry tomatoes hanging from different vines, interspersed with a small amount of yellow and green.

"They're fruits. We'll move on to the fruits once we've got the veg done. You sort the potatoes into size and shape, whilst I get on." Matthew stood by the bench and looked at the selection. *Where to start?* thought Matthew. Bill noticed Matthew's hesitation. "Shape up, lad, we've not got all day. They're the same variety. You're looking for clean skins, no marks and about the same size and shape. Put them in groups of four." Bill moved over to an area of soil which had three drain pipes stuck horizontally into the earth with bright green fronds adorning their tops. Matthew started his sizing project whilst keeping an eye on Bill.

"What you got there?" he asked.

"Carrots! Longest carrot competition, you see. Grow them in drain pipes with a mixture of sand and soil. The tube helps them grow long. I split my tube down one side and then tape it up. Then…" Bill laid a pipe flat, tape uppermost. "I undo the tape and start loosening the soil and sand. If I'm careful I can remove some of it. Then I gently tease the carrot out. Sometimes it works, sometimes it doesn't."

"I didn't realise that it was so complicated."

"I'm just an amateur, experimenting. There are some real pros out there." Matthew shook his head, amazed at the amount of time that people put into their produce, but sure enough Bill extracted a healthy looking carrot with the longest root that Matt had ever seen. Bill stopped and rubbed his hand on his chest.

"You OK, Bill?"

"Yes, just a bit of indigestion, that's all. It'll go off." Bill finished off and then walked over to check on Matthew's efforts.

"Not bad, not bad." He checked the separate piles, discarding some potatoes and realigned the groups. "These three groups, lad. We'll take them up to the kitchen, with the onions and we can check on the runner beans on the way." Matthew gathered the potatoes and with onions in hand Bill marched up towards the kitchen.

"Time check, Anne," he bellowed as he entered the kitchen.

"We're on schedule, don't panic."

"Me, panic? Couldn't if I tried. A couple of Rennies though, love. I've a little bit of indigestion."

"In the top cupboard." Bill found them and chewed on them.

"Right, Matt. That'll settle it. Now to the runner beans." Bill removed six newspaper tubes from the cold larder cupboard and started unwrapping one. Within lay a straight green runner bean. "You wrap them in wet newspaper the night before, you see," he explained to Matthew. "Straightens them out. I'll choose the best three." Matthew stood in the kitchen watching as beans were unwrapped, cakes iced, onions topped and tied neatly. The whole process was an education in itself.

"Anything else I can do?" Bill looked at him thoughtfully.

"You know what, son. You take a rest and sit and have a coffee with Rachel, when she comes down. Being a towny you're probably best leaving the rest to us. You can help me carry the stuff to the hall later. How about that?"

"Whatever you wish, Bill." The kitchen door opened and Rachel stepped in.

"More coffee, love?" asked Matthew, quickly.

"That would be great."

"I'll bring it out." Rachel walked slowly towards the patio where Matthew joined her with coffee. He whispered quietly. "I think I'm getting in the way."

"Why's that?" Rachel replied quietly.

"I've been asked to sit and have coffee with you and leave them to it. It's clearly to get me out of the way."

"How rude," replied Rachel in a queenly voice.

"Absolutely." They both giggled like children, and enjoyed the relaxation of doing nothing.

***

Sarah and Tom pulled onto a small industrial estate about five miles away from the A1 motorway. Both dressed smartly in suits, they were there to view some office premises which were available for rent. Cover story already in place, they were here to meet the agent who was managing the rental. They had been reviewing places for the past week and this was looking like a good one. Situated near a main motorway, which gave them access to the road network, yet tucked within a small estate which was still big enough to move in and out of without drawing attention to themselves. Tom had made contact with the estate agent during the week, advising him of his interest, and she was due to meet them shortly. When the team had all met last week they had allocated the task of finding premises to Tom and Sarah.

"It's that small unit there, Sare," said Tom. A light grey security fenced building sat within a small compound next to a large industrial hanger. A small entrance door stood at the side of the building with a roller shutter door, currently closed, to the front.

"There's a small garage where we can keep your motorbike or to use for any cars if we need to. Two small offices upstairs. Kitchen and a small wetroom, with toilet and shower. Only one loo, I'm afraid."

"What about CCTV?"

"Each building has its own. Nothing public and nothing at the entrance. We can install our own, no one needs to know. The entrance gate to the compound is electric, which is handy. Good mobile phone signal, with internet and landline already installed. What do you think?"

"It's looking good from the outside. They just think that we are a private business, running a health and safety consultancy?"

"That's what I've told them. Jim's been putting together the website, business cards, paperwork and anything else that we may need. I can't see them asking much about the business, unless they want to be bored to death."

"Here she is now," said Sarah, indicating to a lady pulling up in a Porsche Cayenne. "Business must be booming." She raised an eyebrow and the estate agent stepped out of their vehicle with a large smile on her face.

* * *

"The site is looking good," said Ronnie, who had been watching over Jim's shoulder as he had been completing the initial stages of the build.

"It'll take a while to get it looking really slick but it's a new business, so we can build it over time."

"Well beyond my capabilities, mate. Pen and paper man myself."

"That's why I'm doing it, Ron. Computers are my thing."

"What's next?" asked Ronnie.

"Well, we start with a bit of training next week. Priority now is to price up and check the spec on some encrypted radios. Body sets for us all and a couple of spares, car sets for our vehicles and one for the bike, also a base station for the office. We have a long list. Earpieces, microphones, transmitters and body harnesses. We need to research and price up a couple of vehicle trackers, and a couple of listening devices too."

"It'll cost a small fortune."

"It's just the initial layout. Once we do get some business, which I'm sure we will, we'll earn it all back. Oh! iPads too."

"For?"

"Research when we're on the ground working. Also to give us access to maps, should we need them."

"Loads of gadgets to play with," said Ronnie, rubbing his hands together greedily. "Can I have some spy specs, like James Bond? You know, that lets everyone see what I'm seeing?"

"I'm not sure that we all want to see what you're seeing Ron," joked Jim. They both laughed. "Come on, I'll show you the type of things we need on the web, then we may take a run to West Yorks. There's a shop over there that sells this sort of stuff."

* * *

George and Moira sat having a coffee in a small cafe situated within the gardens on the South side of Barnston. The cafe was a little suntrap and with clear skies the day was stunning.

"Plans for today?" asked Moira.

"Day off for us. I've got a small job to do tomorrow over the other side of the county. How about we take a ride over to Fenchurch. Book a Travelodge room for the night. Get some food and have some beers."

"Sounds good to me. I'm ready to go whenever you are."

"What about your kit and toiletries?"

"Always prepared, George. Clean knickers, toothpaste and brush in my bag. That'll do me. If I need anything else I'll buy it."

"Cool. We'll take my car. I'll need it tomorrow. I can either pick you up on the way back, or you can grab a train back tomorrow."

"What's the job?"

"The boss wants me in Sterndale, just to complete a little visit."

"Intriguing. You can update me en route."

* * *

Jamal sat at home reading the paper, his kids sat watching a film on Netflix in the living room with him. This was his first proper day off for a while and he intended to do very little. He was going with his family to visit his wife's parents this afternoon, her sister and brother would be there too, for a family party. The kids would be kept entertained by their cousins and he could just chill and enjoy the atmosphere whilst having a beer.

The investigation was winding up nicely. The intelligence hub was still beavering away, trying to identify the organised crime group behind the killing and Andrea was satisfied that they had caught their offender. Any identification of the group would be used for intelligence development. Jamal doubted that they would ever identify why Duffield was killed. It was often hard to identify a reason when you had captured a live suspect, nevermind a dead suspect. The motive was often reliant on the suspect's admission, and the reliability of that was questionable. In this case, Duffield had been very unlucky in a chance encounter, or he was involved in some form of criminality of which the police had no knowledge. The gun in his possession, an offence in itself, had yielded no results with NABIS. His wife appeared totally ignorant to any illicit dealings that he may have had. To be fair to Andrea, all the enquiries were leading to dead ends. In the back of his mind the second male still niggled at him, but with nothing to go on he couldn't progress things. *Oh well, we've done our best*. He closed the paper, folded it and placed it on a side table.

"Come on kids, TV off, let's get ready to go."

* * *

The doorbell rang.

"I'll get it," said Matthew heading to the front door.

"It will be Deborah, dear. She wanted to call round to give me a hand if I needed it." Matthew opened the front door to be greeted by a wide-brimmed sun hat, worn by a lady looking towards the front gate. She turned around and looked up at Matthew.

"Deborah?" Matthew enquired.

"Yes, and who may you be?" she asked, in a brusque manner.

"Matthew, a friend of the family. Please, come in, Anne is expecting you." He held the door open. Deborah entered, after looking him up and down.

"I know the way." *I bet you do*, thought Matthew, recognising her as a lady not to be trifled with. He followed her through to the kitchen, where she had already entered and flicked the kettle on.

"Right, Anne. What can I do to help?"

"A cup of tea, Debs. Then we can get the entries together." Matthew walked through to the patio where Rachel was sitting, as the ladies continued to talk.

"Who is that lovely young man?" asked Deborah.

"Our Matthew, Debs. I've told you about him before."

"The one whose partner is a police woman?"

"That's the one."

"How lovely, and how's things with young Katie?" continued Deborah, conspiratorially.

"Oh, she's still away on her trip. I do miss her, but hopefully she'll be back soon." Matthew closed the patio door behind him, leaving the ladies to their conversation. Rachel was standing by the greenhouse talking with Bill. Matthew wandered down.

"Just in time, lad. The doors close in an hour. Can you grab that wheelbarrow and we'll get loaded up. Has Debs arrived yet?"

"Just now."

"Good. She'll help Anne gather her bits." Matthew fetched the barrow and Bill loaded it with his produce.

"Do you mind wheeling that to the hall with me?" asked Bill.

"Not at all. I'll be back shortly, Rach, then we can head into town for a couple of hours."

"Lovely," she replied. Matthew wheeled the barrow across the garden, to a side gate, accompanied by Bill, who chatted with him. *Gives me time to check in with the team,* thought Rachel.

* * *

The men approached the hall where a table sat at the entrance, manned by two people. There was no queue, and what looked to be a couple of helpers stood waiting to take entries and exhibits.

"We've timed it well, Matt. I hate it when there's a queue. Gives other competitors an early heads up as to what you've brought. Best to keep them guessing."

"I see," replied Matthew, not seeing at all. *Surely by this stage it doesn't matter, you've brought what you've brought!*

"Here he comes," spoke aloud a ladies voice.

"Morning, Joan. Morning, Malc." The couple at the table smiled. Malc squinting through a paint speckled pair of spectacles.

"Now then, Bill." replied Malc. Matthew brought the barrow to a halt. "You got some extra help this year?" he asked, eyeing Matthew up and down.

"Only to push 'barrow, Malc. The produce is all my own."

"You sure?" joked Malc.

"Course I am, ye' daft fool."

"Long as it is. Right, down to business. How many categories are you entering?"

"You can go now, Matt. I'll park up the empty barrow here for later. Go an' tell Anne to get a shift on whilst it's quiet." Matthew took his leave and headed back to the house.

Arriving back at the house, Deborah and Anne were busy in the kitchen. Matthew passed on Bill's message and went to find Rachel, who was still in the garden.

"Right, love. Let's head out."

"Great," she replied. Taking a steady walk to the car, they climbed in, Rachel placing her stick between her knees as she fastened her belt.

Matthew took a gentle drive into Sterndale, enjoying the scenery as he did so. The outskirts of the town were dominated by new build houses, but on approaching the centre older townhouses stood prevalent, their stately architecture demonstrating the age of the town. Entering the market place the car's tyres rumbled as it negotiated a cobbled road surface.

"I'll take us down to the riverside car park that Kate described, if that's OK?" his voice trembling in empathy with the car.

"Yes, it'll be interesting to see it now that it's all over with," replied Rachel. Matthew drove across the bottom of the marketplace and headed down a steep hill to the river and the falls. The falls' car park was busy but Matthew managed to take the place from a car that was just leaving.

"I'll just nip and get a ticket, Rach. I think you'll squeeze out of your side." He walked off to pay for the parking, leaving Rachel, her grateful that once again he'd left her to fend for herself. She didn't know whether he did it consciously but Matthew treated her normally, leaving her to cope for herself, unless he thought that she really needed his assistance. *He probably doesn't realise how strongly his behaviour supports me. I should tell him.* Enthusiastically running back to the car with the ticket, Matthew stuck it to the inside of the windscreen. "I've just paid for an hour. That should do us."

"Let's take a gentle walk and take a look." The air thrummed with the sound of the waterfall, the atmosphere feeling heavy as they approached a viewing platform. They both understood the significance of the location whilst blissfully ignorant families and visitors enjoyed the atmosphere of the area. A stone wall at chest height protected the platform from the falls and both approached it, Rachel leaning on its boundary wall for support. Both immediately identify the small concrete pier leading out above the falls, with the pebbled area to its right. Families played on the pebbles, skimming stones across the water to the far bank as others walked along the small pier, teenagers jumping off its end into the chilly waters. Matthew put an arm around Rachel, pulling her close, and spoke into her ear.

"If only they knew." She nodded in reply. He pointed to the top of the rocks at the falls. Children in swim shorts now played there, some jumping into the plunge pools created by the falls.

"That must be where it happened," said Matthew. "Let's wander downstream and see if we can see where Kate was standing." They walked on the footpath in the direction of a large grassed area. Matthew stopped and pointed across the river to the far bank.

"It must have been about there, Rach. She said that she could see the falls. If she was back much further then she couldn't have seen."

"Such a beautiful place to be stained with such a violent act," said Rachel.

"Yes, love, but look at all the families here now. People soon forget, or don't even know what happened down here. I'm sure if they knew they'd feel sorry for the dead man's wife but it's easier to forget it and move on."

"I don't suppose Mrs Duffield will forget though."

"I don't suppose she will, but her heartache will lesson and she'll move forward."

After a short walk, they returned to the car, Rachel tired but relaxed.

"I'll find us a spot to park in the centre and we can grab a drink," said Matt, heading to an exit road which would take them away from the falls, the slope to the castle on their right. Another hill took them to the town where they parked on a cobbled road. Signs designated up to two hours parking which was ample for their needs.

"Right, let's find a pub," said Matt, "I fancy trying a beer. Glass of wine?"

"Lovely. Lend me your arm." Matthew put out his arm, allowing Rachel to link in. "The cobbles are a bit of a challenge to walk on," she explained, "but it's good for me. Makes me concentrate on my balance a bit more." Matthew squeezed her hand, making no comment, as they entered a small street leading to the centre.

The small street looked aged, its shops crowded down either side displaying local crafts and artwork. A small charity shop featured a window display of summer clothes and quality used products. It was clear that the town was blossoming and the busy streets indicated that too. A local butcher shop displayed its fine cuts of meats, boasting homemade pies, a red and white chained flynet allowing air to circulate into the shop. Approaching the end of the street the town opened up into a cobbled market place.

"It's lovely, isn't it?"

"A real nice town. A picture postcard. There's a seating area there." He pointed to a small cordoned area outside of a pub. They sat down and ordered. Rachel felt tense but she needed to know.

"So, Matt," she took a sip of wine. He looked at her, waiting for her to finish. "Have you had any thoughts about my business proposal?" He took a mouthful of beer and swallowed it.

"Well, actually, I have." She leaned forward in anticipation.

"I think it's a runner. It's got a chance of working. You're confident that it will." She nodded. "Well, if you're confident then I'd like to come along for the ride." Rachel's face beamed.

"Really! What about Forsetti's?"

"I've had a couple of chats with Rich about it. He really enjoys the work there and he mentioned, when I called in the other day, that setting up a bookshop may be the way forward for him."

"What's that mean for you?"

"We are going to go into partnership on the business. He's going to buy a major share in it. I'll keep a small percentage of equity in but he's going to take on the full running of it. That leaves me free to jump in with you." Rachel reached for Matthew's hands and raising them to her lips kissed the back of them. "I love you," she said, holding his gaze.

"You too. It will take a little bit of time to sort it all out but Rich is keen. He has Joe there as an employee but basically he can do what he wants with it, except for to sell it on without my say so."

"It's going to be such an adventure, Matt. The team's found an office premises. They're looking at getting equipment and sorting out training. I know that we can make it work."

"And I trust that you will," he laughed. "Where's the office?"

"It's just off the A1 motorway on an industrial estate."

"That's a bit of a hike from Barnston?"

"I know." Rachel scrunched her face up. "We may need to move house," she continued, squinting at him.

"Oh, we may have to may we, madam?" he joked. "Bloody hell you have been planning. New business venture, new house, new life. Are we mad?"

"No, just ambitious," she replied.

* * *

Deborah and Anne walked back towards the house having taken Anne's entries to the hall and handing them over.

"You're bound to win, you know, Anne. Your baking looks wonderful."

"Oh Debs, don't. You'll make me blush."

"Shall we have a cup of tea? Then I'd better get off home, my nephew's coming to visit and I'll need to make sure that the house is tidy." They both walked into the kitchen, where Anne started making the tea. Bill was in the garden pottering in the greenhouse. Deborah watched Anne's movements and noticed her pause, staring into space.

"What's wrong, love?"

"Oh, nothing. It's Katie, I'm just worried about her."

"Well, didn't you say that she was safe and that Rachel and Matthew had been looking after her?"

"Well yes, but still, I've not heard from her. I'm not even sure where she is."

"Well, that's ridiculous, what's this all about? Tell them to tell you?" Anne sat down at the table.

"It's not that simple. I'm not supposed to say anything, to anyone, you see." Deborah looked confused.

"Well surely you can tell me, who am I going to tell?" The kettle boiled. Anne stood up, poured water in a teapot and returned to the table, letting it brew.

"Yorkshire tea," she smiled, indicating to the pot.

"I know," Deborah smiled. "I've gotten quite partial to it since I've moved here. That's your influence." She took hold of Anne's hand reassuringly.

"You're a good friend, Debs."

"You know that you can talk to me about anything. I'll keep stum. Promise." Deborah mimicked zipping her mouth closed. Anne leant forward and whispered quietly.

"She saw something. She's a police witness." Deborah sat back and checked that Bill was in the garden still. She leant back in, whispering herself.

"What did she see?"

"You know that man at the river? The one who was found dead? She saw it all happen." Deborah now sat back, a look of shock on her face.

"You are bloody joking," she covered her mouth, having spoken out loud.

"I don't know much else. Rachel has been dealing with her. Kate thinks some bad men are looking for her so she's been moved somewhere safe."

"And you don't know where?"

"No."

"Does Bill know?"

"I don't think so, but he's been spending time with Matthew today so who knows." Anne poured the tea. "I suppose he may have told him. They've got a round of golf tomorrow, so they can chat then too. You know how men like to gossip." Deborah nodded. "I'm sure he'll tell me later, if he knows. I know that they are more relaxed about it all now. Matthew and Rachel, that is. I think they are going to let us know what's going on tomorrow."

"That's good news. Honestly though, I'm shocked. It all sounds a bit cloak and dagger, like something from a film. You'll have to tell me how it all goes." The ladies sat chatting for half an hour before Deborah left heading back to the nearby village where she lived.

Chapter 10

Matthew took his borrowed set of golf clubs from the rear of his car as Bill climbed out of the passenger side of the vehicle. The sun's warmth had already burned away the morning clouds and it was clear that it was going to be a warm day. Anne and Bill had done well at yesterday's show and Bill felt that he deserved this round of golf. They had left Anne and Rachel at home, enjoying a late breakfast from where they intended to travel to town, so that Anne could show Rachel around some more. Then they'd meet the men at the club later for a drink and a bite to eat.

"It's been quite a while since I played. I hope that I don't embarrass you."

"I'm sure that you won't, Matt. There's three groups off before us so why don't we use the practice green to warm up. There's the driving bays too if you'd like to loosen your shoulders up."

"I think I'll just get some putting in, if that's OK? What are we doing about our golf handicaps? What are you playing off at the moment?"

"Oh, don't worry about that. I'll give you two shots on a par five, one on a four, and none on a three. That ok with you?"

"Sounds good to me. What about you?"

"We'll work that out at the beginning of each hole, so that we're in agreement. How about a small bet of a pound a hole?" Bill rubbed his hands together, as if in anticipation.

"Yes, that's good." Matthew changed into a pair of borrowed golf shoes as Bill unpacked a golf trolley, assembled it and placed his clubs thereon. Matthew carried a near full set, put together from old clubs of Bill's that he'd never got rid of. Bill looked at the set, now carried over Matthew's shoulder.

"Always hoped that Anne would take it up, but she never did. She can't see the point of walking round a course, getting frustrated with a little white ball and a stick."

"She has a point, Bill. Keeps you fit though."

"That it does."

Sterndale Golf Club stood in a beautiful mature setting. Having been established for a number of years, the course looked resplendent, its fairways and greens looked to be in pristine condition, the clubhouse giving views of the number one and ten tees. *No pressure there then*, thought Matt, knowing that he could be watched on his first tee off by anyone in the clubhouse.

"Lovely," said Matt, as they walked to the practice putting green.

"Wait until you see the eighteenth green," said Bill, smiling. The men rounded the side of the clubhouse and, looking left, Matthew saw a green surrounded by trees.

"Where's the tee?"

"Yon side of those trees, lad." Bill pointed to the ring of trees.

"Well you can't see the green," said Matthew. "How do you know where to aim?"

"You don't," laughed Bill. "It's a hit and hope. Sorts the men from the boys."

"I hope you've brought enough golf balls."

"You'll be fine, lad. It'll be fun." They walked to the practice green to warm up.

* * *

George stood on a small grass bank leading from the public footpath to a dry stone wall which stood at his chest height. He wore trainers, dark trousers, and a plain dark collared shirt. Tucked in his waistband was a peaked cap and, hanging from his back pocket, a single black leather glove. He placed a solitary golf club on top of the wall. He'd checked the area out earlier this morning, when the roads were quiet, and knew that he would gain a good view of the first and tenth tees of the golf course. Dressed differently when he recced he'd been careful not to get noticed. He only required a quick look to ensure that he could obtain the view that he needed. Having checked, George walked back to his car, which he'd left on a housing estate, and went to check out the driving route to the course. All it had taken then was a little bit of patience. Liverpool had provided him with the details of two cars to look out for, and sure enough he'd watched Forster's car drive past, towards the entrance road to the course. Forster had been busy talking to an elderly gent as they headed for their morning round. First task of the day complete, knowing that nine holes would take about two hours, he headed off for an hour's sleep before prepping for phase two.

Now back at the stone wall he was ready. He had timed it right, and secreted at the wall with a tree behind him, using a pocket set of binoculars, he watched Forster and the girl's grandfather, Bill, walk up to the empty tenth tee. Forster placed his clubs down and spoke to Bill, resulting in both men walking quickly to the clubhouse, presumably to use the gents. Having seen enough, George quickly clambered over the wall, picked up his club and casually walked towards a small copse which ran down the right-hand side of the eleventh fairway. Entering the wood he melted into the trees. Previously, he'd researched the course on the internet and had decided that this was the best spot for him to wait. He moved forward through the woods. No golfers had preceded Forster, which was in George's favour. Now he had to trust in luck. The eleventh hole was a par four with a right-handed dogleg. A sliced shot would take you into the woods, and a hook take you back across the tenth fairway which gently sloped downhill. If lady luck didn't shine on George here, he had identified two other locations on the course which he would be happy to use. George crouched down, now with a clear view of the tenth tee, and checked the small of his back for his sheathed knife. *Always handy if required,* he thought.

***

"By, I needed that," said Bill, returning to the tenth where Matthew stood taking a couple of practice swings on the grass behind the tee. "Bladder's not what it used to be. Right, I believe that it's my honour," continued Bill, checking the score card. "You're two shots behind."

"That I am. I'm allowed an extra shot on this one. What about you on this hole. It's a pretty straightforward one?" Bill looked at him, one eyebrow raised.

"Not as easy as you think, lad." He looked at the scorecard thoughtfully, pencil to his mouth. "Think I'll allow an extra shot here for myself too." Matthew smiled. Bill's flexible approach to his own handicap had put him in the lead, and it was clear that he wanted to keep there. Bill placed his ball on a tee, lined his shot, and took his position. One look at the hole, a wiggle of his bum, head held down, he whipped the club back with a quick awkward stroke and drove through the ball, with a swift swing and solid strike. The ball flew straight. Bill turned to Matthew and smiled, flexing his left hand.

"Must have caught it wrong. That shot travelled through the club." He moved from the tee allowing Matthew to approach. After nine holes, Matthew still couldn't work out how Bill's awkward swing brought him a consistency in hitting it straight but it did. Matthew had consistently driven the ball further than Bill but Bill's accuracy, and handicap scoring, kept him in the game. Matthew took his shot and they headed to the tenth green.

***

George had watched it all. Still crouched in the wooded area, the trees offered a slight reprieve from the sun for himself, and the various flying insects that occupied the copse. He felt calm and composed. He was ready. Checking his watch he moved slowly forward as he heard the first strike from the tee. Watching the fairway the ball hooked left, hit the tenth fairway and rolled away down the gently sloping hill. He listened intently. The thwack of a second strike, the ball hit the grass at the end of the tree line, bouncing right towards the direction of the green. *Good shot. Now whose ball is whose?* He heard two male voices approaching,

"See you later, lad. I'll meet you on the green." Looking left, George watched Forster walking towards the tenth fairway away from the wood. George moved forwards and right, entering the rough to the right of the short cut grass. Spotting the ball that had landed he picked it up and threw it towards the tree line. He stood and waited, taking a few practice golf swings as if aiming to the green. The old man came round the corner. George raised his hand and pointed towards the tree line behind him, indicating where the player's ball had landed. Bill raised his hand in reply, a confused look on his face, but moved towards the trees to find it. George moved in the same direction, approaching Bill.

"I didn't realise that you were in front of us," said Bill. George moved quickly, closing the gap on the old man.

"I wasn't." He grabbed Bill's arm. "This way."

"Oi, what the …" Bill tried to pull away. A blow to the back of his head forced him to his knees. His antagonist crouched in front of him.

"Where's Kate, Bill? Where the hell is she?" Bill tried to speak, when an open hand crashed to the side of his face knocking him to the grass. Bill clutched the side of his face as a weight drove onto his chest. A man's face leaned in close. "Where, Bill? You don't want me to visit Anne." Bill pushed with all his strength, forcing the man back. An arm raised to strike him again. He raised his arm to block but then a vice squeezed his chest. He couldn't get his breath. Acute pain shot towards his jaw. He groaned.

George knelt back. The old man was grasping his chest, his face going blue. He looked around but could see nobody. However, he spotted a yellow golf ball on the fairway behind him. Forster was probably coming. Bill lay there gasping, holding his left arm.

"Watch yourself, old man." George moved and walked away calmy, following the line of the rough to a drystone wall separating the course from a wheat field. Looking back he saw Forster's head appear on the horizon as he looked for Bill and his ball. Forster stopped, dropped his clubs, and ran towards Bill. George moved further to a stile in the wall, climbed it and halted looking back. Forster had reached Bill and leant in as if speaking. He looked around. George raised his hand, stepped down into the field and walked away. *Not the outcome I wanted*, he thought as he moved along the field, out of view.

***

"Don't worry, Bill. I'm here." Bill lay on his back breathing but clearly in pain. "Is it your heart?" A faint nod. "I'll ring for help." Matthew looked around for help, to see a tall man standing on top of a style by a drystone wall. The man raised his hand and dropped to the other side of the wall. *What the hell!* He rang emergency services, grabbing Bill's golf trolley as he did so. *If it's his heart then raise his legs*, was all he could remember. The services answered and looking around he saw two men running to help him from the direction of the clubhouse. "Help is on its way, Bill." Bill lay breathing but grey faced. His lips blue, with a trail of saliva running down his cheek. He didn't look in a good way. He mumbled something to Matthew. Matthew leaned in closer as he heard running footsteps towards him.

"What was that, Bill?" The running stopped as a man walked up to Matthew.

"I'm a doctor. Can I help?" The doctor leaned in and Matthew saw that the other man with him was the member of staff from the club shop.

"I think he's had a heart attack." The doctor moved forward as Bill looked at Matthew with a pained expression on his face. He tried to speak.

"What's his name?" asked the doctor.

"Bill."

The doctor leaned closer to Bill. "Bill, I'm a doctor." He took hold of Bill's wrist checking his pulse. Bill mumbled again.

"What's he saying?" asked Matthew.

"It sounds like a name. Katie, I think." Matthew stepped back, confused, and looked towards the drystone wall. *Katie?* The sound of an approaching siren dominated the air as blue lights could be seen at the course entrance descending towards the car park. The ambulance negotiated the car park and gently drove across the grass towards the small group of people. Matt advised the operator on his phone that an ambulance had arrived, and terminated the call. At the clubhouse a small collection of golfers looked towards them, their natural interest piqued by the unusual activity. Bill appeared to be passing in and out of consciousness. Matt stood back feeling helpless but appreciated that Bill was in the best hands, being cared for by the doctor and the crew. An oxygen mask was swiftly placed over Bill's nose and mouth as a second crew member placed the pads and leads in place for the portable heart monitor.

"Ventricular fibrillation," stated the crew member, reading the heart monitor.

"Let's get him into the ambulance." replied the other. The doctor had supplied the crew with the medical information that they required.

"Next of kin?" Matthew stepped forward.

"It's his wife, Anne. I'll get hold of her but here, take my business card, you can contact me if there's anything urgent. She's just in town. I'll fetch her and bring her to the hospital."

"OK, sir. Thank you." Bill, now lying on a trolley, was lifted into the rear of the ambulance. The doors were closed and the vehicle drove steadily away, blue lights flashing. The doctor turned to Matthew.

"Where's your car? I'll help you get the clubs in and you can get hold of his wife."

"Thanks," replied Matthew, in a slight daze. The doctor collected Bill's trolley and walked with Matthew to pick up his own set and both were placed in the boot of the car.

"Are you ok driving?"

"Oh, yes. Thanks for your help. I'll be fine."

"I'll leave you to make your call. Let the club know how he goes." The doctor walked towards the pro shop giving Matt his privacy. Matt took out his phone and called Rachel so she could prepare Anne for the bad news.

***

Anne sat in the back of the car quietly, hands anxiously clasped together. She had taken the news as well as could have been expected but was understandably concerned.

"We'll be there in about five minutes, Anne," said Matthew.

"I told him that he needed to rest more," said Anne, "he's been complaining of a lot of indigestion recently. I should have realised that something more serious was up."

"You can't blame yourself, Anne," replied Matt, thinking that maybe he should have noticed the signs on the day of the show. "We're not experts," he continued, "and don't always recognise what is right in front of our noses." Rachel, also sitting in the rear, took hold of Anne's hand and squeezed it reassuringly.

"He's in safe hands, Anne. A doctor on the scene and an ambulance crew arriving so quickly. He couldn't have received better care."

"I know, dear." Anne squeezed Rachel's hand back. "Thank you." She looked at Rachel and smiled, clearly appreciative of Rachel's support. They arrived at the entrance of the hospital and Matthew went to check with the accident and emergency reception desk as to the whereabouts of Bill. He returned within a couple of minutes.

"They've taken him straight to the cardiac ward," he advised them. "Anne will be allowed to see him but they have a strict one visitor only policy."

"That's fine," said Rachel. "I think I've had my fill of hospitals."

"I'll take you up there, Anne. Then we'll head back to the house, let Rosie out, and grab some of Bill's things."

"Oh, I forgot all about Rosie," Anne's hands went to her mouth, her eyes tearful.

"We'll sort her. She's not your worry." Anne climbed out of the car. "Now, let's go and find Bill. The staff have told me that he is stable. He'll be wanting to see you and you can tell me what I need to fetch for him." They both entered the hospital as Rachel waited by the car, grateful to be avoiding the corridors of the infirmary.

* * *

George drove his car heading from Fenchurch towards Barnston, and was disappointed with himself. He'd checked in with the boss, giving the update of the incident on the golf course. The boss was fine with him, but George liked getting results, which he had failed to do on this occasion. Even though the old man collapsing was out of George's control, he was still frustrated that he had gained no further information to locate the elusive Kate. The boss had hoped that pressure on her grandparents, with a veiled threat to Anne, would glean something, but fate had intervened. Still, something had come of it. He'd had a good chance to have a look at Forster, and he'd decided that he didn't like him. With his designer hair, neat beard and smart clothes, not to mention the time and money to swan around a golf course; George found him instantly detestable. *I wouldn't mind smashing my fist into his handsome face,* he thought, his hands clutching tightly to the steering wheel. He could feel his anger building. *He looks a right smart arse. Maybe I'll get my chance.* George took some deep breaths, his hands relaxing, unsure why the man irritated him but putting it down to tiredness in the exasperating hunt for the girl.

Anyway, he was now heading back to Barnston to meet up with Moira. She had texted and informed him that she had made her own way back there. They could have a couple of beers tonight and relax, before they commenced the week's plan. At least that would be a bit of fun for him. He held his speed steady as he passed a marked police car parked in a lay-by with a butty van in it. *Lazy tosser,* he thought driving past and increasing speed slowly as the road opened up in front of him.

* * *

Matt and Rachel pulled their vehicle onto the driveway of Bill and Anne's house. Both were tired following a stressful morning but the day wasn't over yet as Matthew had a few errands to run. He walked up to the front door of the house and, on opening the door, heard Rosie's bark coming from the kitchen of the house.

"Quiet, Rosie!" he yelled, to hear the bark turn to whimpering, and the frantic sound of claws pawing at the wooden door. "I'm coming," she had clearly recognised his voice. He walked to the door and opened it to be greeted by an excited dog, front end crouched, with backside in the air, tail wagging, and front paws almost tap dancing on the floor. She was beside herself. He moved to the patio door, where she now stood on hind legs, front paws clawing on the glass, scampering and whimpering to get out. He opened the door at last and she ran out, completed a circuit of the grass and froze. Nose and eyes looked upwards, to a pigeon that had resettled on the boundary fence. A solitary front paw raised, tail straight out she stood bonded in her 'pointing' pose and waited. Matthew closed the door, leaving her to her quarry, as he was confident she would never catch.

"Are you ok, hon?" Matthew turned to see that Rachel had entered the kitchen.

"Yes, fine. What a day."

"Well, they're both safely at the hospital now. What do we need to do?"

"I just need to grab a bag of Bill's. Can you believe it, they both always have a bag packed with essentials for themselves, for just this sort of emergency."

"Wow, that's organised."

"I know. Very considerate of them, but then it takes a lot of stress away for each other, or in this case for me. At least I know I'll be taking in the right stuff."

"Have you time for a coffee?"

"Yes, there's no rush. I'll just nip upstairs and grab the bag. Give me two minutes."

Matthew returned carrying a small sports holdall with a luggage label attached, which had Bill written clearly on it. He glanced out into the back garden where Rosie continued to stalk the elusive pigeon.

"What did you get up to in town?" he asked Rachel.

"Oh, nothing much. Grabbed a coffee and a cake. Looked in some shops, estate agents and looked around the market."

"Estate agents!"

"Just seeing what the house market is looking like. Don't panic. Anyway, what about your golf round?"

"I was playing OK. It's been a long time since I last played. Trust Bill to spoil the round," he half joked.

"Not in the best taste, Matthew."

"I know. Sorry. Just a bit shaken up."

"I'll let you off."

"That golfer is still bugging me. The one on the wall when Bill collapsed," he clarified. "Why didn't he come and help?"

"Maybe he didn't realise what was happening?"

"Rubbish. He had a clear view. He bloody waved to me!"

"Where did he go?"

"No idea. Into the field and then I was too busy with Bill. I didn't see him again."

"Some people just don't want to get involved."

"I suppose."

"Was it Kate that Bill was asking after?"

"That's the only name he said according to the doctor. I'm surprised it wasn't Anne, but who knows what he was thinking. He probably thought he was dying." Matthew finished his coffee. "Right, I'll head back. Are you happy to stay here with Rosie and mind the house?"

"Of course, I need the rest." Matthew stood to leave when his phone pinged. He took it out of his pocket.

"It's Anne. She says that he is settled and sleeping. No visitors allowed and she's arranged for Debs to come and get Bill's bag. She'll let us know when she's ready to come home and I'll pick her up then." As if on cue the doorbell rang. Matthew went to answer it holding Bill's bag. He opened the door.

"Hello dear. Now not to worry I've got everything in hand. Are you ok? It must have been a terrible shock to you? And poor Bill.

What about him? Village show one day and heart attack at the golf club the next!"

"Hi Deborah. I'm fine. How did you get to find out?"

"Oh, Mary from the club rang me. She told me the news." She reached for the bag. "I'll take that love." Matthew let the bag go. "Bolt out of the blue, Matthew. Did he say anything while you were playing or when he collapsed? Nothing that gave him a feeling that something wasn't right?"

"No, Deborah. It just happened." She turned to walk back to her black Range Rover.

"Well don't you worry. I'm here. I'll look after Anne and you look after that lovely police lady of yours." She climbed into the vehicle, gave him a wave and drove out of the driveway. Matthew stood looking at the driveway and took a deep breath. *Now, she is a force of nature. Good luck, Anne!*

* * *

Jim and Ronnie stood looking at a small cluster of equipment sitting upon Jim's kitchen table. The kitchen itself was immaculate, with clear and clean sideboards and a kettle that looked to have been polished to within an inch of its life. Ronnie moved over to the rotund kettle, looked at his close-up reflection within its mirrored sheen, and decided that he could do with trimming his nostril hairs. He stepped back briskly, wiping his nose with the back of his hand. *A job for later,* he thought. The aroma of coffee permeated the air, produced by the meticulous efforts of Jim, whom Ronnie had watched pick and grind the beans, which were now brewing.

"Absolutely parched," he said, "I feel like my throat's been cut."

"Patience, patience. It'll be worth it."

"It'd better be. I don't want to have to resort to drinking tap water unless I really have to."

"There's a jug of filtered water on the side there. Room temperature, just as it should be."

"I'll pass. Are you always so meticulous? I bet you bloody floss too."

"Attention to detail, Ron. Look after the small things and the rest will take care of itself."

"I wish you'd hurry up and take care of my dehydration." Jim smiled and started separating the items on the table into four separate piles. Ronnie reached forward to examine an item.

"Ah ah. Just wait. I need to record some details and label the items." Ronnie placed his hand in his pocket, as Jim checked his watch. "Coffee is ready. Let me get you a cup and you can sit and relax whilst I record all the details. It won't take long." He poured a coffee for them both, and reaching into a cupboard pulled out two tins labelled 'Biscuits' and 'Chocolate Biscuits'. With a quick glance towards Ronnie he placed one tin back and placed the tin marked 'Biscuits' onto the table. "Help yourself."

"Don't mind if I do." He'd watched Jim's actions but food was food, so he took three.

Jim separated the equipment. They had managed to purchase a radio base station, four radio body sets, and the requisite equipment to make them function. The equipment would allow the team to talk to each other when following a target, and also allow whomever was directing the team from the office, in likelihood Rachel, to listen to their transmissions when doing so. It was enough equipment for them to use for training. In a separate pile sat two digital cameras and one listening device. Initially Sarah and Tom would carry these as they were already fully trained in operating them.

"Right, Ronnie. If you are sufficiently replenished let me show you how this works and we can get a bit of practice in today."

"Ready when you are, Q." replied Ronnie, slurping the last mouthful from his cup.

* * *

"Turn left into the estate and then follow it round." Matthew steered the car into the industrial estate so that they could have a look at the building from the outside. "It's a good location for quick access to the motorway," continued Rachel. She pointed to a building and Matthew stopped outside the gates of the small compound.

"It just looks like a standard warehouse," said Matt.

"That's what we need. Nothing flash." They both had a look at the internet pictures of the inside on Matt's phone. "I'm not sure how much we'll use it but it's a year's rental so if it's not working out at least we're not stuck with it."

"How do you see the team practically functioning then?" asked Matt.

"Firstly, we're all committing our own money to it all. That will cover equipment, set up, fuel, and things like that. I've opened a business bank account, two signatories, and I can sort out how the team accesses that. Each team member provides their own car. We use technical equipment whenever we can, to do all the legwork and pull the team together when they are needed."

"Leg work?"

"Ok, so Matt Forster works for a large company as a travel rep, but is on the sick with an alleged bad back, having fallen whilst at work. He's looking to sue the company because they sent him to an unsafe environment to sell their goods. He has a company car. We get employed to see if he is really that bad and unable to work. We make an assessment of the client's needs, and decide to put a vehicle tracker on the company car for three weeks, with the company's consent. We analyse the data and it shows that every Wednesday the car goes to Barnston Golf Club. So the following Wednesday we put our team behind Forster. They follow him, find out where he goes, if he arrives at the club then film him lifting his clubs, and doing his practice swings before teeing off on the first. Put it all in a neat package for the client and it's up to them to decide what they will do with it. We charge for our three weeks' work."

"Sounds doable."

"Best thing is, because the tracking device is doing all the work for us, the team can be doing other work. It will be slow to start, but once we start building a reputation with a good client then word will spread, and I'm hoping that we'll be run off our feet." Rachel's face was glowing with excitement causing Matt to smile.

"What?" she asked.

"Nothing. It's great, Rach. It's been a long time since I've seen you this excited about something."

"I am and I know that it's going to work. I'm going to make it work."

"And I'm going to help you." Matthew checked his watch. "Visiting time at the hospital. We'd better head off."

"OK, love. I'll speak with Tom and Sarah about this spot and ask them to get onto the estate agent to tell them we'll have it."

***

Forty minutes later Matthew walked towards the hospital front entrance. He was met by the obligatory scene of a patient in a hospital gown holding a drip stand, inhaling deeply on a cigarette. Various patient transport ambulances stood at the drop off bay with hospital staff assisting people to and fro. He entered the main entrance of the hospital and, bypassing reception, checked a notice board on the hospital corridor, looking for the cardiology department. Turning left in the direction of the ward Matt negotiated past staff in various coloured uniforms, hospital trolleys and doctors in white coats who looked too young to be thrown into the traumas of medicine. *Thank goodness they do it though*, he thought. He turned into a right-hand corridor, then took a lift to the third floor where the ward was situated. The lift doors opened and Matt was confronted with Anne who was heading towards the lift.

"Oh, Matt. Thank goodness you're here." Her voice was trembling, and he noted her hands shaking as she took hold of his.

"What's up, Anne?" asked Matt, leading her to a chair on the landing, sitting her down, and taking the seat next to her.

"He wants to speak with you. He's adamant that it's just you and he won't tell me why, but I think it's to do with Kate."

"He mentioned her at the club. I think he's probably just worried about her and doesn't want to worry you. I'll go and see him now."

"Thank you, dear. I'm just going for a small walk to the hospital shop to get him some Werther's. He likes those." Anne walked to the lift as Matt walked towards the ward and pressed the intercom buzzer before being allowed entry.

Bill lay on a hospital bed surrounded by machinery. Leads attached to his chest led to a machine which displayed his heart rhythm. A pulse oximeter was attached to his finger showing his current oxygen saturation levels. Matthew understood none of it but, as Bill was sitting up in the bed, assumed that everything was relatively ok. An oxygen mask and bedside buzzer lay on the covers next to Bill's free hand and although nurses were around, none were attending to him. Matthew approached the bed.

"Hi, Bill. You gave me a shock on the course. How are you doing?"

"I'm doing fine, lad. Tired but getting better and being well looked after."

"I've just seen Anne …" Bill interrupted

"I need to speak with you. You don't know what's happened." Matthew sat on the chair next to Bill's bed. "Kate's still in trouble. That Scouser is still after her." Bill recounted the events at the golf club. Matthew could feel his own pulse quickening as a sense of unease invaded his senses.

"I saw that man on the course. The arrogant sod waved at me. He must have been waiting for us." Bill nodded as he observed Matthew absorbing the information. "We, I mean I, have to do something."

"You do. He doesn't know where she is, but he's trying hard to find out. You need to make sure that she's safe."

"I will, I will, Bill. Don't worry. We need to look after Anne too."

"Don't worry about Anne, son. I'll sort that out with her. I'm sure that Debs will help keep an eye on her until I get out." Matthew's mind was whirring.

"The police will probably need to speak with you."

"That's fine." Matthew checked his watch. "Bill, I'm going to have to go. Rach and I now have a lot to sort, but trust me, Katie will be safe."

"I know, lad. I know she will be, with you looking after her. Now get going. Don't worry about Anne. I'll explain things when she gets back." Matt squeezed Bill's arm, stood and walked calmly from the ward.

Now back on the landing area he pressed the lift call button impatiently. Unable to wait he saw the sign for the stairs, where he headed, moving swiftly down to the ground floor, through the hospital to the main entrance, and to the welcome fresh air of the outside car park.

The lift doors opened onto the cardiology ward landing area and Anne stepped out, oblivious of Matt's departure, balancing a bag of Werther's Original and two takeout coffees in her hands. She walked carefully towards the ward.

* * *

Matt ran to the car and climbed into the driver's seat as Rachel lowered her phone, having just finished a call.

"That was quick."

"Kate's still in trouble!"

"What do you mean?" Matthew recounted his quick meeting with Bill, as he started the car engine and negotiated his way through the hospital grounds and out onto the main road.

"Right, let's think this through," said Rachel.

"I saw the bloody man, Rach. The cocky bastard waved at me." He hit the steering wheel with his hand in exasperation. Rachel placed a hand on his knee.

"You couldn't have stopped what happened to Bill, Matt. We need to concentrate on Kate again now. Focus our efforts on keeping her safe. Now, drive safely, and keep to the speed limits. Firstly, I'm going to ring Tina and see where Katie is. The chances are that she's left her in Barnston to look after herself now that the police have caught their man." Matthew tried to interrupt her but she raised a hand to stop him. "Secondly, I'll ring Jamal and give him our update. I don't know if the police will do anything, as they are winding up their case now."

"Surely, they have to do something," said Matt desperately.

"I'm sure that they'll go and speak with Bill, love, and they'll probably want to speak with you at some point but look at it from their point of view. They're going to speak with an old man who has just been through a massive personal trauma. Everything he says that happened was whilst he was having a heart attack. Was he confused? How reliable is his recollection of the bloke's words? Can he describe him?"

"I can give a description of him?" Matthew interrupted.

"I know, love, but in reality what have you seen? A tall, thin man, wearing golfer's clothing, and even that was seen at some distance." Matthew's shoulders slumped.

"It doesn't sound good. What are we going to do?"

"I'm going to make the calls so at least we know where we stand. You keep driving. We're going to Barnston to get hold of Kate. She's a sensible girl and she'll be keeping her head down. She knew that we were coming back today."

"What about me laddo from the golf course?"

"Hopefully, he still doesn't know where she is. However, we have to make the assumption that he's headed for Barnston too."

"Barnston! But he can't know she's there."

"And he probably doesn't but somehow he's found Bill. So this lot has worked out the family relationship between Kate and Bill. What else have they worked out?"

"The book, Rach, the book," stated Matthew. "Katie's address book was missing from the house. Have they got hold of that somehow?"

"Will you be in that book?"

"I don't know. I doubt it, I've never given her my address. She knows about Forsetti's though."

"So, we have to assume that this man knows about the shop too. If he's checked your site then he knows about you. If he digs deep enough then he'll find that we are partners, and let's face it I was all over the local news last year. Hence, we assume that he knows about Barnston. Now, you concentrate on the road and let me make these calls." Rachel could feel the buzz of adrenaline as she was forced to apply herself to the problem of protecting Kate. She knew it was likely that the police would do nothing, as they had little evidence to go on. *I'm going to sort this out,* she thought. *I'm not entirely sure how, yet, but I am going to sort it out.* Rachel rang Tina. Matthew drove, his mind whirring as he listened to one side of the conversation. Rachel finished her call.

"So, Tina has left Kate in Barnston in a bed and breakfast on the north side of town. Tina's had to go off on another job but will be back later today. The police have made the decision that she doesn't need their protection now, so after today it's down to us."

"Bloody idiots. Kate's on her own?" said Matthew, concernedly.

Chapter 10

"Yes, but we'll be with her within the hour, so don't worry. We can give her a ring and tell her to wait at the bed and breakfast for us, and explain everything when we get there. I think that we'll move her out of the guest house and have her at ours tonight. Then we can plan our next moves." She smiled at Matthew who, with a worried look on his face, was concentrating on the road. Traffic was busy as people journeyed towards the coast to enjoy the summer warmth, and with bikers in their element it took his full concentration to keep them safe. *How things quickly change*, thought Rachel. *Last week I needed all the support that he could supply and now he needs my support. Right, next call to Kate.*

"Hi Kate, it's Rach."

"Oh, hello. Your telephone number was blocked."

"Yes, old habits. How are you doing?"

"I'm good, thanks. Tina has told me that everything is sorted and that I can maybe go home today." She sounded cheerful and Rachel regretted that she'd have to ruin her day.

"Well, Matt and I will be with you in ..." she checked her watch, "about three quarters of an hour. Are you at the B&B?"

"Yes, I was just about to go out for a walk though."

"I tell you what, can you just hang fire with the walk and wait for us there? We're not going to be that long."

"Yes, of course. Is everything OK?" Rachel detected a note of worry in Kate's voice.

"Yes, everything is fine. We'll be with you soon." *A white lie but better for her if I break all the news in person.*

"OK, I'll wait. See you soon." Rachel finished the call.

"She sounds fine," said Rachel to Matt. "Better to tell her in person." She finished explaining the conversation.

"Agreed," said Matt, checking his mirrors, as he heard the roar of a motorbike engine approaching. Rachel rang Jamal Kaur, and receiving no reply, left a message for him to call her back.

* * *

Kate sat in her room at the bed and breakfast in Barnston, wondering what to do. The weather outside was terrific. She'd already showered and made her bed. She now had nothing to do. *Surely going out for a little bit won't do any harm. I've got half an hour and I can be back before they get here. There's that little coffee shack about two minutes away.* She made her mind up, grabbed her laptop and left the room. *A coffee and check of today's news in the sunshine.* She felt safe for the first time since the incident at the falls at Sterndale.

Chapter 11

Rachel and Matthew arrived in Barnston and headed straight for the bed and breakfast where Kate was staying.

"I'll ring her," said Matthew, getting out of the car. He dialled the number and waited for her to answer, impatiently pacing up and down the footpath as he did so. Taking the phone from his ear he leaned in towards the passenger window. "She's not answering."

"Give it another go." Matthew re-dialled and waited, unconsciously tapping the roof of the car.

"Hi, Matt."

"Kate we're here. Just outside. Can you let me in and I'll carry your bags to the car for you."

"Oh! I just nipped out for a coffee. I'll be back in two minutes."

"You mean you're out of the building? Where? I'm coming to you." He covered the phone with his hand, "She's gone out! I'm off to get her." Rachel watched as Matthew strode off, talking on the phone, towards the north cliff. *He'll need to chill out a bit. She's obviously safe as he's on the phone with her.* Two minutes later Matthew walked around a corner, almost marching Kate towards the guesthouse.

"I've got her," he said aloud, stating the obvious. Rachel gave Kate a wave and a smile, receiving a timid wave and silently mouthed "What's going on?", before she was whisked away to the front door of the house. Rachel checked around the area, for anyone watching or for occupied cars. There was nothing obvious, but then if this guy was a professional they'd probably never see him coming. She sent out a group message to the team. *Availability to work for the next three days?* They weren't ready and weren't set up properly, but this was an opportunity to see how it could all work. Matthew and Kate walked out of the guesthouse towards the car with Kate's things. She'd wait for the responses to come in.

"Hi, Kate. You're looking great."

"What's going on, Rach? Matt won't say anything."

"Let's go to our house and we'll explain everything. There's nothing for you to worry about but there's a lot for you to take in. How have things been going with Tina?"

"Oh, she's been great." Kate replied, feeling a sense of reassurance in the tone of Rachel's voice. Matthew drove them away from the guesthouse heading north towards their own home, descending a hill to a large roundabout.

"Let's just take a run along the seafront, Matt. See what the tourists are up to." Matt negotiated the roundabout and took the exit towards the sea. Rachel kept a view in her door mirror whilst he did so, noting the two cars behind them as Matt slowly drove towards a further roundabout.

"The traffic is horrendous. Are you sure we should bother?"

"Maybe not the best of ideas," she admitted. Matthew approached the roundabout and indicated right, manoeuvred all the way around and headed back towards the first roundabout, taking the original exit towards their home. Rachel was confident that none of the cars behind them had followed their route. They climbed a hill away from town and as they headed out Rachel's phone rang.

"It's a blocked number," she advised Matt. "Pull into that car park at the top of this hill will you. I'll take the call there." Unquestioning, Matt followed her instructions and pulled into the car park, choosing a temporary pick up point facing the road to park the car. Rachel climbed out mid call and studiously watched the road as she talked. Matt and Kate sat in companionable silence as she took the call, each contemplative in mood. After five minutes Rachel climbed back in the car.

"That was Jamal. Let's get home, and I can tell you both everything that is going on."

* * *

Kate sat at the kitchen table, her eyes puffy from crying and darkened with smudges of eyeliner.

"It's all such a mess," she said forlornly, "and I've got us all into it by witnessing what that stupid man did."

"It's not your fault, Kate," said Matthew. "You did the right thing. There's nothing else that you could do. This is all just a set of circumstances beyond your control."

"But what about Grandad? Is he going to be OK? What about that man at the golf course? Are you saying that I'm not safe again? Are Grandad and Grandma not safe now?" Rachel moved from the sideboard, where she had been standing, sat down next to Kate and cuddled her around the shoulders. She looked at Matt, who nodded and she took over the conversation, holding Kate's hand and looking at her directly as she did so.

"That's a lot of questions," she smiled. "Let's deal with them one at a time because if we don't, this whole situation is going to overwhelm you."

"I think that it has already."

"You know something Kate? It hasn't. You are a strong young woman and you can deal with this. You are not going to let this man control your life."

"Why is it always a man?"

"Because they can be weak, Kate. They are inherently vulnerable and need strong women to support them. Those without go off the rails a bit." They both looked at Matthew who stood with arms crossed with one eyebrow raised, glaring at them. They both laughed.

"Don't worry, love. I'm your strong woman." Matthew opened his mouth to speak and was forestalled by Rachel's raised hand. "A nice cold drink each would be lovely, darling. Don't panic. I need you too." He closed his mouth and walked to the fridge. Rachel winked at Kate.

"OK. Number one, Grandad Bill. He's doing well. He managed to have a full conversation with Matt and told him that he would tell Anne himself. They have Deborah to support them. The police are sending Detective Brindle to go and speak with him and they'll take it from there. I'm sure DC Brindle will do the best that he can."

"Can I call Grandad or Grandma?"

"Of course you can. We can call them at tonight's visiting times at the hospital from Matt's phone. Then you'll probably get to speak with both of them. How does that sound?" Two glasses of orange juice were placed on the table. Matt stood drinking a glass of water.

"That sounds good." Kate took a sip.

"So secondly, are they both safe?" Rachel counted off on her fingers. "They're both together. They have Deborah to support them. The police are going to see them. Rosie's at home to look after Anne." Kate nearly choked on her juice.

"Rosie. She'd run a mile," she laughed. Matthew could see that Kate's tension was diffusing, as he stood admiring Rachel's manner of controlling the situation.

"Well, at least she'll bark if she's concerned," she joked. "So, they are as safe as they can be. Which brings me on to you." A concerned look passed over Kate's face. Rachel continued. "I'll be honest with you, I don't know how much more the police are prepared to do to protect you."

"Why?"

"They've got their man. They're winding that case up and they're probably going to deal with this threat separately, if at all. They haven't got a lot to go on, but the good thing is that you are with us." She took Kate's hand again. "We think that there is a threat to you and so we are going to do something about it."

"What though?"

"Firstly, we are all going to get away from Barnston. Well away from Barnston. We have to assume that he knows that you are in town. So we need to get away from here. The rest of today and this evening is for making plans. Tomorrow, we move."

* * *

Brindle walked out of the hospital having been to visit Bill where he had listened to his tale about being confronted at the golf club. He had concluded that this wasn't really a job for CID but it suited his purposes, so he would string it out for a bit. He had Bill's wife that he could speak to, see if he knew anything about the whereabouts of young Kate. Unusually, her location had been kept quiet in the enquiry. There were always some gobby cops who spoke of things that they shouldn't but in this case there had been no leaks. Bill had also told him to speak with Matthew Forster about it all. He'd check in with Kaur, spin him a line and see what he could get out of it. Reaching into his pocket he pulled out his phone and, fumbling it, watched it drop to the ground. "Bollocks," he said aloud, unconcerned about anyone around him. He reached down to pick it up, noting that his hand was shaking, and picked it up. The screen had cracked again. "Bloody typical." It was a job phone, so he didn't care much, but the damage was just another symptom of his current run of bad luck. Wiping a bead of sweat from his forehead, he dialled Kaur and awaited his reply. *Must be nearly time for the pub*, he thought as he waited.

"Jamal Kaur"

"Sarge, it's Dave."

"Alright, Dave. How'd you get on?"

"Well it's something and nowt really. I need to do a bit more digging. He seems a little confused but claims he was approached at the club, pushed over, and asked for Kate's location. He gives a vague description of the fella but it could be anybody. I need to speak with his wife and he says that Matthew Forster can describe him. Says Forster's probably not in town though."

"No, he's gone back over to Barnston with Rachel."

"When all this has just happened? That's a bit strange."

"They'll need to let Kate know."

"Surely they could just ring her?"

"I'm sure that they probably are." Dave clenched his fist jubilantly. Kaur had slipped up. *They've gone to see her*, Brindle surmised.

"Tell you what, Sarge. I've got a mate over there that I can stay with. It'll take me an hour and a half to drive there. I could finish my shift in Barnston, doss over at my mate's, and interview Forster tomorrow. I think it would be better done in person and get this one nipped in the bud. I've got nowt else on at the moment, that can't wait, and it'll only cost the organisation a bit of petrol money." There was a pregnant pause at Kaur's end as he thought.

"Go on then, mate. The car will need to be parked at the nick though, and give me a bell tomorrow when you sort your meeting with him."

"Will do. Cheers."

"Bye." Brindle barely heard as he punched the air in front of him. *Get in, Brindler the Swindler does it again.* He was confident that Kate was in Barnston. He didn't have any mates over there but could book into a Travelodge, and he knew of a nice little casino in Barnston that he could spend the evening in. He felt his luck turning, and tonight he'd prove it.

Brindle took out his burner phone. *No wonder I'm dropping these bloody things. I'm carrying too many.* He sent a text.

She's in Barnston, and awaited a reply. He didn't have to wait long.

Excellent. You need to get over there.

Already sorted. On my way.

Brindle deleted the messages and tucked the phone away. *Right, time for a quick pint and I'll be off.*

* * *

Kate had finished her phone call with her grandparents and appeared to Rachel to look more settled in herself.

"How's he doing?" asked Rachel.

"He's sounding OK. His voice is a bit shaky and he says a policeman called Brindle's been to see him. He told me that I've got to stick with you two," she laughed.

"Well, you've no choice there," said Matthew. Kate stood and helped herself to a glass of water from the tap.

"Is it OK if I go for a shower?" asked Kate.

"Of course," said Matthew and Rachel together. "I'll grab you a towel and show you the way," continued Matthew. He led Kate upstairs. Rachel checked her phone seeing that the team had all replied, and that everyone was available. She sent out a further message with a time for a meeting and its location. She had already booked a meeting room at a Holiday Inn on the outskirts of town during the drive over from Sterndale. One more text to Ronnie, asking him to collect her in half an hour, received a thumbs up in response. Matthew walked back into the kitchen.

"She seems to be coping well."

"She's doing brilliantly, Matt."

"What's the plan?"

"We're all going to move first thing tomorrow. We'll get somewhere booked well away from here so we can work out how to resolve all of this."

"Have you heard from Kaur?"

"No, nothing. Bill has obviously spoken to Brindle so that will just run its course. I'll have a word with Tina later to see if she's heard anything but I'm not expecting them to tell me much."

"But you've only just left the service. Surely they'll tell you something."

"I doubt it, Matt. It's a closed shop. I'm not one of their gang now, so they'll do me no favours. It's more than their jobs are worth." Matt checked his phone reading a text that he'd received from Anne.

"Anne and Bill have put some money in my account to help pay for looking after Kate. I'll tell them to keep it and give it back."

"No you won't. They obviously want to feel like they are helping. People don't give away money that they can't afford to so accept it graciously and we'll use it for Kate." Matt texted back his thanks and acceptance.

"Where are we going to go?" he asked.

"I'm not sure. Do you have any ideas?"

"How about seeing if the North Berwick house is free? Or is that too far?"

"That would be ideal. Can you get on to them and see if it is? If not, can they recommend any other places up there? I know it's short notice but let's see what we can get. Also, whilst Kate's out of the room," Rachel had walked to the hall doorway and closed it. Matt looked up from his phone. "I'm bringing the new team with us. It'll be a training exercise for them."

"Do they know?"

"They know that I need them for a few days. They don't know the job yet."

"And they're up for it?" said Matt excitedly.

"Yes, love, but calm down. Kate can't know that they're with us."

"OK," he replied, with a confused look on his face.

"You'll have to get used to this," she laughed. "Seriously though. Remember that they've had no practice together and that only two of them are fully trained. I'm going to ask them to follow us, covertly, to do counter surveillance. You know, watch our backs. Check that we are safe. It won't be watertight but it'll be a damn sight safer than doing nothing. Kate can't know that they are there. It will worry her."

"I understand. What do I have to do?"

"Just be you. Act naturally. We three stick together and let the team do their own thing. I'll talk to you properly about it tonight when I get back."

"Get back?" Rachel checked her watch.

"Ronnie's picking me up in ten minutes. I'm going to brief the team. You are going to find us a place to stay and pick me up later. If that's OK? If you could order a takeaway we can collect it on the way back too."

"Sounds good. What can I tell Kate?"

"Involve her in the booking. It will keep her occupied but make sure she understands the importance of telling no one where we are going."

"Loud and clear." Matthew felt proud. Rachel was in her element and she was thriving on it.

***

Rachel and Ronnie entered the car park of the Holiday Inn, where Ronnie let Rachel out at the entrance and then manoeuvred his car into a free parking space. Rachel waited for him at the doors and they entered the reception together. She approached the desk.

"Hello, Madam. Can I help you?" asked the receptionist politely.

"Yes, I'm from Hastings Associates. We've got a meeting room booked."

"Oh yes. Some of your colleagues have arrived. Down the corridor there," she indicated with her arm, "second door on the right."

"Thank you." They walked in the direction shown and entered the room.

The other three had already arrived, their chatter halting as the door opened, and recommencing once they realised that it was Rachel and Ronnie.

"Complimentary coffee on the side there," said Tom, pointing to a silver Thermos pump flask and some mugs.

"Complimentary?" asked Rachel.

"Yes, I know. I think that the staff just wanted something to do. Looks like they are having a quiet night."

"That's good for us," said Rachel, watching as Ronnie examined all the small packets of biscuits, before choosing three packs for himself. "We'd better get started. The room is only booked for an hour." Rachel grabbed a coffee and then took her place at the table.

"What's the job then?" asked Sarah. Rachel looked around the room. Everyone was casually dressed in shirt and trousers. Not scruffy or over smart, just normal. A group of people that could blend in anywhere. *A great start.*

"Thanks all for coming at such short notice. This is unlikely to be the normal way that we do things. In the future we should have more time to prepare, plan a job thoroughly and get a good chance to discuss it all as a team before deploying on it. However, circumstances have overtaken us and I thought this could be a job where we can assess our capability, get to know our skill set, and give us a taster of how our working future may look." She looked around the room noting that she still held her audience captive. Rachel then explained to the team the nature of the threat to Kate and her proposed plan. "In summary," she concluded, "I want you to keep behind Matt, Kate and I for the next few days and watch our backs.

It's a babysitting job but it will make me feel happier to know that you are with us. Questions?" The team all began to talk at once. "One at a time," interrupted Rachel loudly, pointing to Tom first.

"Who's paying for this?"

"Essentially, for our time controlling the subject 'Kate', then we are all paying individually. It's a training exercise and we have to invest some of ourselves into this venture to make it work." Tom nodded in agreement. "For expenses, fuel and accomodation, I'm paying. I have a small budget from the family but essentially I'm the client. So, all reasonable expenses I'll cover. Any unreasonable ones we will discuss. That OK for all of us?" Nodding assents came from the room. "Sarah. Any questions?"

"Just clarification. Should Kate leave you and Matt at any point, I'm guessing that you want us to stay with Kate."

"Yes, but either Matt or I should be with her at all times."

"And if we identify anyone whom we believe is following you?"

"Photographs, descriptions, as much intelligence as you can. If I have any concerns I'll be on to the local police as soon as possible." Tom interjected.

"I'll want to put a tracking device in your car."

"No problem. Prep it tonight and I'll take it tomorrow. Jim, what about you?"

"Does she know that we'll be following her?"

"No. I'll know and Matt will know. Nobody else."

"Have you got a photo of her?"

"Yes. On my phone. I'll send it out on the group Whatsapp. Ronnie?"

"What about breaks? We can't be with you twenty-four seven."

"When we get there you can stand down. Matt and I will have her with us. After that we'll speak to you regularly and co-ordinate when we go out."

"Where are you taking her?" Rachel checked her mobile phone.

"The Scottish Borders." She could feel an air of excitement in the room in anticipation of their first deployment. Tom looked at everyone.

"It won't be as easy as we think, guys. There'll be a lot of on the hoof learning and we've got a bit of planning to do."

"That's right," said Rachel, "but the opportunity is here so let's take it. Matt will be here in ten minutes to collect me, so take your chance to fire any last minute questions at me. Then I'm off and I'm going to leave you all to do the planning." The ten minutes passed quickly.

"I'll walk you to the car, Rach." said Tom, as she stood to leave. He opened the door for her and she exited, happy that the team was focussed.

"It's a big ask. We're only a small team and Ronnie has no training at all."

"I know, but we have to start somewhere. Anything that we can do is better than nothing."

"True," he replied, as they approached Matt's car waiting at the pick up point.

"Hi, Matt," said Tom, "give me a minute." He ran over to his car and retrieved a black peli case from the boot. Returning he opened the back door and placed it on the rear seat. "Radio base station, Rach. Put it in your room when you land and I'll set it up for you when Kate and Matt go out. Don't think for one minute that you're getting out of being trained too." Rachel laughed.

"Never thought that for one minute." Tom looked at Matt.

"We'll get you sorted once this little job's done." He winked at Matt and walked away. Matt looked at Rachel.

"Did you tell him that I was joining the team?"

"Nope, but he knows that we need you so it looks like it was never up for discussion."

"So it seems." Smiling, Matt climbed back into the driver's seat and waited for Rachel to climb in.

"All set?" he asked.

"All set. We leave at 10 o'clock tomorrow." They drove away, Rachel with a confident smile on her face.

* * *

George had found a small secluded layby on the coastal road where he had parked his car away from sight. Now walking with Moira they both climbed over a three barred fence and tracked along the side of a field of rapeseed. The scent of the canola dominated the air with its acrid, cabbagey aroma. A grass verge at the side of the field allowed easy walking alongside the impenetrable wiry stems of the crop, but George wasn't concerned about the crop, if anything it was likely to deter ramblers wandering around the area. He was interested in the small abandoned building that he had spotted from the road side. Both were dressed in T-shirts and shorts, George carrying a backpack.

"We'll have a look at it and see if it's in use. Doesn't look like it though."

"All right, mate." George walked, alert to his surroundings. A small gated track led from the roadside towards the building, with the hedges not having been cut. All the other hedges around had been so it looked like that this was just an area that the farmer wasn't concerned about. *It's looking ideal*, he thought. They approached the stone built structure with its corrugated iron roof and doorless entrance. The aperture stood at the side of the building with a stone wall facing the road. They proceeded cautiously, sweeping the ground for any recent footwear or tyre marks.

"There's only been a tractor up here," said George, "and not as far as this spot. I saw them spraying the fields a couple of days ago so no one should be back here for a while. You keep a look out and I'll nip inside and take a look." Moira positioned herself towards the hedgeline as George went in, his face brushing against a large spider web spanning the doorway. *Not used then.* Inside the sandy soiled floor was dry with a couple of rotted pieces of wood fallen to the floor. *Not placed, clearly fallen. No footprints. No one's been here for ages.* The air felt dry with the doorway failing to provide a draft inside. He flicked on the torch on his phone to illuminate the walls and, shining it around, saw that there was little else inside except from a couple of metal tether hoops protruding from the walls at either end of the room. He walked back out and returned to Moira.

"It's ideal. Nobody has been here for ages. Secluded and dry inside. We're not going to get disturbed here."

"The track's got a slight bend in it too, so once you're up here you can't be seen from the road. A good spot by you, G."

"Let's head back to the car and into town. I just need to source a couple of bits for this week."

"We checking up on Marsden again?"

"Yes, same routine. Let's confirm that he hasn't altered his pattern of behaviour. Don't push it too much on the bus though."

"I won't. Just enough for him to notice me again."

Twenty minutes later they had parked back at Barnston. George was getting bored with being here. He enjoyed Moira's company but he just wanted this job over and done with.

"We'll split here," said George. "I'll check that he's working and buy some stuff. I suppose we'll need some bottled water. If you can sort that out?"

"Sure." They parted company.

George headed to the town centre and, approaching a hardware shop, saw that a workman was changing the shop sign name. The 'W' of Wellbury's was just being removed. *Passed into new ownership.* He continued walking. *I'll buy from there though. A bit of poetic justice.*

Forsetti's was open as he approached and looked at the window display. The other guy stood behind the till serving a customer with no sign of Marsden. *Damn, I'm going to have to go in.* He checked his reflection and pulled his baseball cap lower over his face, and prepared to enter when Marsden appeared in the shop speaking to an elderly female. *Gotcha.* George walked beyond the door and kept going. A circular route would take him back towards the hardware store. Now, only displaying 'bury's' George smiled to himself. *Very apt.* He entered and paid for his goods in cash before returning to the car and emptying the bag onto the passenger seat. The bag with Wellbury's emblazoned on the side he placed under his purchased items which were a tow rope, cable ties, gaffa tape and a large dog collar. He whistled as he drove back towards his booked accommodation and would meet with Moira later, once she had made her penultimate bus journey.

Chapter 12

"That's the car packed," said Matt returning to the house.

"Kate's just in the living room speaking with her grandparents," said Rachel.

"How's she doing?"

"Really well, love. Really, really well. She must be scared but we'll work it all out. The first thing is to get safely away from here."

"Are the team ready?"

"They will be. I trust them to do their part." Matt heard the postman pushing a letter through the letterbox and walked off to get it.

"Something for you. Not the posty though. There's no stamp on it." He handed it over to her. She opened it, recognising the small black metallic box inside.

"It's the tracker. One of the team must have posted it so I guess that they're here." She placed it back within the envelope and put it in her handbag. Matthew rubbed his hands together in anticipation.

"It's a little bit exciting really, isn't it?" he stated.

"Do you think so?"

"Well, I know that it's worrying too but I can't help but feel a smidgeon," he held his fingers millimetres apart, "excited."

"Let's just get away safely. Though, I'll admit, the first deployment of the team is a big moment for me."

"What do we do when we get there?"

"I'll work that out on the way. This guy isn't going to go away, so somehow we need to stop him." Kate walked into the room.

"Everything OK?" asked Matt.

"All good. He's slowly improving but they're keeping a close eye on him."

"You didn't tell him anything?" asked Rachel.

"No, and he didn't ask. He knows not to."

"Great." Rachel checked her watch. "Let's go then. The sooner we leave the sooner we get there and then we can relax. Ready, everyone?"

"Ready." Matt and Kate replied in unison.

* * *

"Movement indicated at the vehicle," Tom transmitted to the team over his radio. He was sitting next to Ron within his BMW, an iPad showing a map of the area on his lap. Jim sat next to him looking at the same device. "See the green car on the screen?"

"Yes."

"That's our transmitter which Rach will have in the car. So we let that do the work today. We can keep our distance and track it as we go. You are going to keep an eye on the iPad and, to start with, Sarah and Jim will commentate on the vehicle's movement, to let us know where it is. After half an hour we'll switch the jobs round and it will be your turn."

"Talk about being thrown in at the deep end," mumbled Ron.

"Don't worry. I'll keep you right. This is the best practice you can get. You've got the crib sheet to help you also. Watch the green car on the map and listen to what they say on the radio to give you an idea."

"What if I mess it up?"

"The iPad will always show where the vehicle is so we won't lose it. This is your chance to get some good practice in. I'll start us off so you can see how it's done and then we'll give you a spell at it. We can pass control back to the other car at any point and then concentrate on something else."

"OK then."

"I'll take the first drive to show you how to follow at a distance and we'll talk tactics as we go."

"Bloody hell, there's a lot going on at once. A lot to take in." Tom laughed.

"That's surveillance for you. No one said that it was going to be easy."

"Control to you, Sarah," Tom transmitted on his radio, his voice sounding out aloud in the other car as well as in the team's personal earpieces.

"Sarah has control," replied Sarah's voice in their earpieces. Local tennis courts stood to the left of the T junction at the end of the road and were currently in use. Sarah sat in the car park of the club courts within Jim's Skoda and concentrated on the iPad. Club members occupied the courts with pairs matches ongoing. Jim watched an older couple steadily managing their side of the court with gentle and accurate returns making their younger opponents work hard for their points. He sat on a bench within the club grounds, which gave him a clear view of the road. Dressed in shorts, shirt and baseball cap with a racket bag on his lap, he blended into the scene.

"Vehicle moving towards you, Jim."

"Received," came his reply.

"Approaching the T-junction," said Sarah.

"Sighting of vehicle one. Three persons within." Jim conveyed on the radio. "Confirmation subjects one, two, and three within the vehicle. Subject one wears a white T-shirt. At the T-junction the vehicle turns right. Back to you, Sarah."

"Sarah has control. Confirmation, the vehicle has turned right and drives North away from town." Jim watched the road end for any further vehicles approaching the junction. He checked his watch.

Two to three minutes should do. During that period three cars had approached the junction, all turning left towards the town. Only one dark blue Corsa had turned from the main road into the junction. *Unmarked police car,* thought Jim. Five or six cars had driven the main road from the town in the same direction of the subject vehicle, the last being Tom's BMW. He picked up his bag and strolled down to the car park where he climbed into the driver's seat next to Sarah.

"Good job, Jim. Let's get going." He started the engine and they headed off.

"You've got them on the screen, Ron?" asked Tom.

"Yep. Heading north."

"Great. And what do we refer to as the vehicle on the radio?"

"Subject vehicle one, or SV1."

"And who have we got in it?"

"Subjects one, two, and three, or S1, S2, S3."

"And who is who?"

"S1 is Kate, S2 Matthew, and S3 Rach." Tom smiled.

"Great. You'll get the hang of this in no time." Ron relaxed in his seat, pleased with himself, and produced a pack of cigarettes from his shirt pocket.

"No smoking in the car." Tom hadn't even looked at him, his eyes focussed firmly on the road. "Back on the iPad, Ron." He placed the pack back in his pocket and picked up the device. *This is going to end up being harder work than I've done in years!*

"SV1 continues in a northerly direction passing a post office to the right side." The commentary continued from Jim's car.

* * *

Dave Brindle slowly turned into the road where Forster lived, passing the tennis courts to his right. His head was banging and although it was just after 10 am, he wasn't sure that he should be driving yet. *How the hell do they get up and play tennis at this ungodly hour?* Unless he was working, Jim usually got up late morning and although at work now, was only up and about as he'd had to check out of his hotel. He'd had a great night last night though. After checking into his room, he'd nipped to the local Tesco and bought a cheap little bottle of vodka, just for a 'pick me up', before heading into the town. A quick shower, change of clothes, and a splash of Lynx and he had headed out. He'd spotted a Wetherspoon's pub at the top of town and had headed there for their cheap drinks; later on heading to a local casino. Payday had landed and he'd been able to get some cash from the cashpoint. He'd worry about the bills later. Although the evening had been a haze he was confident that he'd had a good time. Checking his jeans pocket this morning he was chuffed to bits to find that he still had a tenner. That would get him a pint and a sandwich at 'Spoons' before heading home later today.

He concentrated on the houses on the road, counting down until he reached Forster's. With no car on the driveway the building looked empty. He parked across the drive and stumbled as he climbed out of the car, landing on his knees. Head throbbing, he still managed to giggle at his clumsiness and stood up, brushing down the knees of his suit trousers as he did so. He checked his reflection in the car window, flattened his ruffled hair and, using the same hand, checked his breath. *Not bad.* Just to be sure, he popped a piece of gum in his mouth. He walked to the front door and knocked, waiting patiently for an answer. Brindle peered into the front window and, finding the room empty, walked around the back, opened the rear gate and entered the garden. *They are doing bloody better than I am.* Brindle looked in the rear windows. *No one home. I'll check the shop first before I ring him.* Twenty minutes later, Brindle walked in the central precinct of Barnston, Lucozade in hand, heading to Forsetti's. His head was clearing and he was enjoying himself until a *Big Issue* seller tried to sell him a magazine.

"Bugger off, you scrounging smackhead," he said directly into the man's face.

"Oi, I'm just trying to make a living, and I'm not a smackhead."

"Bollocks to you," replied Brindle, walking away. He hated beggars, hated smackheads, hated anyone who tried to scrounge from others. *At least I have a home, a job and I don't scrounge from anyone.* Brindle's selective memory ignoring his reliance on alcohol and the criminal fraternity to which he owed money. He turned right on the precinct and, spotting the sign for Forsetti's, entered the shop.

A tall man stood behind the counter studiously working away at a computer. The shop was quiet and Brindle approached the counter and waited. The male was clearly engrossed in whatever he was looking at.

"Whenever you're ready," said Brindle sarcastically, as he reached into his back pocket for his wallet.

"Oh! Sorry sir, I didn't notice you there."

"Well, you have now." Brindle produced his warrant card. "DC Brindle. I'm looking for Matthew Forster. Do you know where he is?" Looking left, he saw a skinny male approaching him.

"He's not here," replied the tall male. Brindle looked at him, waiting for him to carry on.

"OK. Where is he?" *These bloody university types.*

"I don't know. Do you know, Joe?" he asked the skinny male.

"He's gone away for a few days. Dunno where." He stepped back from Brindle, as the smell of stale alcohol was overpowering. *Great,* thought Brindle.

"Come on, guys! Give me a hand here. Can you ring him?"

"I'll try," said Joe, picking up the office phone and moving towards the back store room.

"He'll know what it's about?" stated Brindle, his voice raised. Joe walked into the store room and returned a few minutes later. He didn't like the look of Brindle but then cops, apart from Rachel, weren't his favourite sort.

"Is it about the golf club?"

"Yes," replied Brindle, looking at Joe as if he was thick. He took the phone from Joe and held it to his ear. "There's no one there." He looked at Joe incredulously.

"No. He couldn't speak for long, mate. He's driving. Said for you to leave your business card and that he'd ring you later." Brindle put the phone on the counter. *This just gets better. A wasted trip.*

"I'm not your mate. You got a pen?" Joe pulled a pen from behind his ear. "Write this down."

"Dave Brindle."

"As in rhymes with swindle?" asked Joe. Brindle glared at him. *Smart arse.*

"Yes." Joe wrote the name down and the phone number as Brindle gave it to him. "Tell him to ring me." Brindle turned in disgust and walked from the shop. *I'll bloody ring him myself*, he thought. *Half a mind to do him for wasting police time.* He walked up the precinct, giving the *Big Issue* seller a wide berth, and rang Matthew's number. The phone rang out and diverted to its answer phone. Brindle left a message requesting a return call and decided to go to the local police station so he could check the intelligence held on the shop and Forster. He could ring Kaur from there and update him with the little he had. He was more worried about the criminals that he was apparently now working for than he was the police. Brindle was confident that he could blag his way through with Kaur, but the criminals played by different rules and he didn't want to get on their wrong side.

* * *

George watched a male wearing a suit walk from Forsetti's, clearly unhappy about something. On leaving, the male had immediately taken a mobile phone from his pocket and dialled a number. George noted his drawn looks, facial stubble and crumpled attire which didn't correspond to his arrogant stride as he buffeted his way through the busy town. George had learnt to trust his instincts. *Cop, and a man under pressure.* He followed him loosely and sure enough the man headed towards the police station. *Not ideal, but shouldn't change my plans.* He had a good description of the man but to be sure he'd text the hub and let them know. A couple of minutes later he received an image on his phone.

Is this the man?

Yes, he replied.

Police. He's one of ours

George's instincts had been right. *A bent cop too. I'll remember you, fella. Never know when you might come in handy.*

George gently weaved through the pedestrians towards the front of the shop. He just needed a quick look at Marsden to check what he was wearing, then he could meet Moira and confirm the go ahead for later today. Sure enough Marsden stood with the other male in front of the shop counter. He was wearing dark jeans and a dark polo shirt. *See you later, Marsden.* George walked away melting into the crowd.

* * *

"And it's right into the car park of Morrisons. SV1 moves towards a parking space and stops."

"That's great, Ronnie. They are stopping here for a quick break. It looks like there is a cafe and a loo in there. Tom to Sarah, can you take control on the iPad. We'll get out on foot and put them into the store."

"Yes." Sarah replied over the radio.

"I'll keep an eye on them, Ron. You just come and watch me for this one. How do you think it's going?"

"It's really hard. There's a lot to think of all at once, but I think my commentary on the vehicle movement is coming on."

"It is. You're picking it up great. Hang on ... here they come." Tom opened his door slightly ready to get out. "Just listen on the radio and watch how I position myself." They were parked in line with Matthew's car but at the far end of the car park a number of spaces away. Tom watched them exit and start walking to the shop. Reaching to the back seat into an Asda carrier bag he pulled out an orange Morrisons bag before getting out of the vehicle. Tom started transmitting on his radio which was secreted on his body, a button in his hand allowed him to press and talk, transmitting his voice to the other members of the team.

"Tom has control and it's an identification of S1, S2, and S3. S1 wears a white T-shirt, light blue jeans, and white trainers. They walk towards the store entrance."

"Jim supports you." Jim's voice transmitted on the radio. Ron climbed out of the car and sparked up a cigarette as he watched Tom and their subjects. Tom slowly traversed the car park in the general direction of the store doors, keeping at a distance and behind the subjects. Ron looked for Jim but couldn't see him anywhere.

"Received Jim," replied Tom. "Subjects towards the store doors, stop outside. S3 looks at her mobile. She looks like she's texting." Tom's phone vibrated in his pocket. "S1 moves towards the doors and all three walk into the store."

"Jim will enter."

"Loud and clear, Jim." Ronnie had noticed that Tom had now folded the orange bag up and tucked it into his pocket. He was removing his phone from his pocket. *Where the hell is Jim?* Ronnie checked the car park, but couldn't see him. Then a bald pate caught his eye as he spotted Jim wearing a dark green polo shirt and black trousers walking towards the doors. *The sly beggar. He looks like a member of staff.* Though not wearing the uniform, Jim's appearance was similar enough that at a glance he could be mistaken for a member of staff. *Luck or preplanned? I'll ask him later.* Jim entered the store.

"Jim is in." said Jim. Silence then reigned on the radio. After a pause came Jim's voice, now quieter. "S1 and S3 sit within the cafe. S2 is at the cafe counter." The radio went quiet. Ronnie looked across to Tom who was looking at his phone and slowly walking back towards the car.

"Tom to Jim."

"Go ahead."

"You can exit and return to your vehicle."

"Received."

"Tom to the team. Text from Rachel. They are grabbing some lunch. We can take a break and she'll text me when she is ready to set off." The team all acknowledged receipt of his instruction on the radio. Tom returned to his car as Ronnie was finishing his cigarette.

"I'll ring Sarah and arrange a place away from here that we can meet and discuss how we are doing."

"Right you are," replied Ronnie, flicking his cigarette butt to the ground and, seeing Tom's look, picked up the discarded end looking for a bin to place it in.

"It's just best practice," said Tom in explanation. "Don't leave a trace of yourself, wherever you have been, if you can help it. That butt has your DNA on it. Stick it in a cig bin and it'll never be found. Nevermind the fact that it's littering and contains microplastics, can you believe?"

"Got ya," replied Ron.

***

Matthew returned to their table carrying three coffees.

"I've ordered us all a poached egg with avocado on toast," he said sitting down in the small booth the ladies now occupied.

"Lovely," said Kate.

"All OK, Rach?" asked Matt, referring to the team's progress.

"All fine. Do you think we should give Dave Brindle a call? Get it out of the way."

"I will, but Joe didn't seem that enamoured with him."

"To be fair, I don't think that Joe's particularly keen on any cops."

"True. I'll give him a quick call whilst the food is being prepared." Matthew walked from the table towards the exit, his phone now to his ear.

"Are you happy that we are safe, Rachel?" asked Kate.

"Yes, love. Very happy. You're going to love the house when we get there. No one has any idea that we are going there so you can relax."

"What about you?"

"I've got some work to do. We need these people off your back and I need to work out how."

"I wish I could see my grandparents."

"I know, love, but Bill needs to recover. Maybe we can find a chance to see Anne. Leave it with me and I'll see what I can do."

***

Dave Brindle sat within the CID office at Barnston Police Station. With the office currently unoccupied he'd had free reign to interrogate the intelligence system in privacy. After helping himself to a cup of coffee, he reviewed his findings, happy with the results. A search of the system had confirmed Forster's home address, landline, and, with a little bit of digging, he had identified Forster's current vehicle and registration. A quick check of that vehicle on the ANPR system had shown him that the vehicle had travelled north this morning and was now beyond the Tyne Tunnel. He'd noted it down on a piece of paper when his mobile rang.

"Dave Brindle speaking."

"Hi Detective Brindle, it's Matt Forster, I believe that you've been trying to get hold of me."

"Ah, the illusive Mr Forster," replied Brindle sarcastically.

"Well hardly," replied Matt, a confused tone to his voice.

"Well, I'm in Barnston and it appears that you are not."

"No, I've gone away for a few days."

"Oh, anywhere nice?"

"No, just away for a break."

"I'd like to come and see you as a witness to the golf club incident. Is that OK?"

"Of course. As soon as I get back. I don't think there will be much more that I can tell you that Bill hasn't already told you."

"Well, you never know, Mr Forster. Have you time to talk now?"

"A few minutes." Matt advised Brindle about what he had seen at the club. Brindle realised that he wasn't going to get the end destination for Matt and presumed that Rachel Barnes had advised him not to tell.

"I'll still need to see you, Mr Forster. When will you be back?"

"Ehm, I don't know yet. How about I email you when I know?"

"That would be great. Can I have your email address in case I need it too?"

"Sure." Matthew provided the address which Brindle wrote down on his piece of paper.

"Right, Mr Forster. You and Rachel have a good time. I'll see you when you get back."

"OK. Thanks, we will." *So they're both there*, thought Brindle. "Goodbye. I'll let you know when we are heading back."

"Bye." Brindle terminated that call. *Right, I just need Rachel's number and that's me done.* Her personal mobile number was not recorded on the system, just her old number. He stood up and walked into a corridor leading from the office he was in. Doors were labelled with various job roles and the office he was looking for was there, door open, and labelled 'Witness Protection'. He knocked and entered, seeing a young officer sitting behind a computer.

"Hi there, I'm DC Dave Brindle from Sterndale."

"Beth," responded the lady introducing herself.

"You're the lady that has taken over from Rachel."

"That's me." she smiled. "How can I help?"

"I'm on the Sterndale enquiry. I just need to tie up a couple of loose ends with Rachel but I've only got her old work mobile. You haven't got her personal number have you?"

"I have indeed but it'll cost you." Beth said jokingly. She took out her own phone and flicked through her contacts. "You got a pen?"

"Yes, go ahead." Beth read out the number which Brindle jotted down. *That'll do nicely.*

"Thanks Beth, much appreciated."

"No problem." Brindle left the office, checked the computer that he'd used in CID, to ensure that he had logged out, and left the station. *Time for a pint, then I'll ring Kaur.* Brindle walked away from the station with a spring in his step. His day was improving. He could now photograph the piece of paper and send it into the hub. His instincts told him that Kate was with Forster and Rachel and the hub would get all the information they needed to locate them.

***

Joe had finished work for the day and wandered to the bus stop finishing his recently purchased cheeseburger and chips. His mother was out this evening and wouldn't have left him anything to eat. Work had been fairly busy and with a day off tomorrow he had no concrete plans. Although his lifestyle had settled down, his enforced routine offered him no excitement. The routine was definitely preferential to the life of a drug abuser but just a little bit of fun would be nice. His mind flicked back to Tina, who he'd met in Costa. He walked towards

Costa and walked in. *You never know,* he thought, looking around the tables, but she wasn't there. *Long shot for me but she definitely had something about her.* He left and walked towards the bus stop where his bus had just pulled in. *Oh well, home I go.* Joe climbed on the bus and, scanning around, was relieved to see that his mother's friend was absent and, taking a free seat, placed his bag on the seat next to him. He checked his mobile for messages.

"I'm sorry. Is this seat free?" asked a female drawing Joe's attention from his phone. Joe looked up to see a woman that he'd seen on the bus a couple of times before. She'd always smiled at him. *Maybe my luck's in after all.*

"Of course, let me move this." Joe quickly moved his bag onto the floor and brushed the seat with his hand before she sat down. Joe shuffled to make room and inhaled the scent of her perfume.

"I've seen you before on here haven't I?" asked Joe.

"Yes, a couple of times."

"You work in town?"

"Oh, no. Just been out for some lunch. What about you?"

"I'm a bookseller in Forsetti's."

"Really. How cool, I love reading." *This is going well,* thought Joe.

"I'm Joe."

"Mary. Lovely to speak to you at last." She laughed and watched Joe's eyes twinkle in response. *Men. So, so predictable,* thought Moira. *Now to reel you in.* Twenty minutes later the bus pulled towards Joe's stop.

"This is where I get off," he said, reaching for his bag. Moira checked her watch.

"It's still early and the sun's glorious." She reached a hand up, adjusting her hair and looked him in the eyes. "You fancy going for a quick drink?"

"Me?" asked Joe, surprised at Mary's forwardness.

"Well, I'm not looking at anyone else."

"Well, ehm." He hesitated. "Go on then. I've no plans."

"Great. Let's get off at the next stop and we'll go to the beer garden at The Barn." The bus moved forward, slowly heading to the next stop. Moira pressed the button, the ping notifying the driver of their intention to get off. She stood and walked to the front, Joe following and admiring her body. *Hooked*, Moira thought. The bus stop was next to a local cemetery, the vehicle came to a halt and they both climbed off, Joe too engrossed with his female companion to say thanks to the driver.

"Let's cut through here," indicated Moira, descending some steps to the cemetery pathway. A well-known shortcut to The Barn, it would take five minutes off the walk.

"Sure enough." Joe followed willingly, pleased with himself and with his luck.

* * *

George sat within his vehicle in the small car park to the side of the cemetery with the window down. Adrenaline sharpened his senses as he checked his watch. Moira would be here within two minutes. He climbed out of his car and raised the boot lid. Only one other car occupied the car park and had been here, unoccupied, since George's arrival. He walked around to his passenger door and opened it. Protruding from the driver seat pocket were the cable ties. A strip of gaffa tape hanging from the seat belt mount. Leaving the door open he walked behind the car, flexed his hands and stretched his arms out in front of himself, releasing tension. He was ready and excited. He loved this work, he loved the rush and he loved the risk. Voices could be heard from the footpath. He listened. A male and a female. His breathing slowed. Moira's voice. Dispassionate calm comforted him. He watched. Moira came first.

"Think I'll have a cheeky vodka and coke," she said, seeing the open door of the car and walking towards it.

"Might join you," replied Joe, laughing as he emerged from the path towards the car. "That's weird. Shouldn't leave your car unattended around here, it'll get nicked." Too late his brain registered danger. "Shit!"

George sprang, arm back, and smashed an open hand against Marsden's neck and jaw. The sound cracked the air. Marsden's legs crumpled, temporarily stunned with the trauma to his brachial plexus. George moved. Pinned Marsden down, locking his wrist and arm.

"The tape," he instructed Moira. She took hold of the strip of gaffa tape, in a well-rehearsed movement, and sealed Marsden's mouth. His eyes open, dazed and uncomprehending. George swiftly lifted Marsden and threw him onto the back seat. Face down and head smashed against the opposite door. He crossed Marsden's ankles, bent them towards his back and climbed in behind, pinning Marsden's heels to his back with his bodyweight. The passenger door shut behind him, tinted windows obscuring the view within. Moira climbed into the driver's side.

"Arms." She followed the instruction and locked Marsden's arms behind his back, holding his hands in a wrist lock. Marsden didn't resist, still stunned from the blow. George took the cable ties, securing Marsden's wrists.

"Done. Don't forget the boot." Moira stepped out, closed the door and walked to the boot. The abduction had taken seconds, completed by two consummate professionals who had done this before. She closed the boot and looked around. No persons present. No witnesses. *Easy. Should have paid your debts, Joe.* She climbed in, started the car and drove to their pre-arranged hostage site.

Chapter 13

Joe knelt staring at a stone wall, his legs numb from being stuck in the same position all night. His arms were tied together, above the elbow joints, his wrists were bound tightly, as were his ankles. His shoes had been removed, and around his neck, a collar of some sort, with two lengths of rope pulled horizontally to either side and secured to metal hoops on the wall. He couldn't move his head except to rest his forehead against the wall. His mouth was taped shut and he was terrified. He'd been dragged here last night, punched and kicked and then trussed up. Whomever the bloke was he meant business. Mary had been there but had done nothing. Nothing to help him, but she had helped the bloke. Joe had only got a fleeting glimpse of the man but he had the aches and bruises to prove that he was in real trouble. Nothing had been said. He'd been left here. Wherever here was. He was busting too and having had no option peed into his trousers, disgusted with himself. The ground beneath was compacted soil and the air had the scent of dung and urine. *Some sort of outhouse.* It had been dark but the morning sun was filtering into the building, warming the chilled air. The only sound was morning birdsong as Joe lent his head against the wall, waiting. He had no other choice.

Joe drifted out of sleep as something alerted his senses. He pulled his head from the wall feeling the ache of the pressure on it and listened. *Was that a voice? Definitely someone walking?* He moaned, grunted. Tried to make any noise where he could be heard. The footsteps got closer.

"Help!" he tried to shout behind the tape, an unintelligible noise faintly sounding out. The sound footsteps grew louder as someone walked in. He tried to turn his head. *Footsteps, no voices.* He moved his head frantically side to side but, trapped, saw only the wall. Then a 'thwack', his muffled scream and agony, as a lashing pain assaulted the souls of his feet. A searing second hit to his soles, forcing his head to butt the wall, the scream silenced with his pain. Tears welled in his eyes and merged with blood from his forehead. He was helpless. An animal trapped.

"Right ya little shit. I'm not here to mess about." Joe breathed jerkily through his nose, dealing with the pain. "You get one chance with me or to be honest," the male giggled, "I'll fuckin' gut you." *Shit, it's a bloody Scouser.* Joe's breathing steadied. He listened.

"You owe us, fella. You can't walk away from your debts. Not with us. Two hundred pounds you owe us. Truthfully, it could be ten pounds, we don't give a shit. Whatever it is, you owe us, and we collect our debts." Joe tried to mumble something.

"What's that, son? I can't hear you." Joe could feel warm, heavy breath at his neck. He tried to talk again. A knife was placed against the wall in front of his face. His world shrank to the shiny steel blade, its honed edge focussing his mind.

"I'll tell ya what's gonna happen. We're going to remove this tape." *More than one then.* "And if you shout out I'm gonna slice you. Got that? Nod if you do." A hand cuffed the back of his head, forcing it to hit the wall. Blood from his scalp ran freely, obscuring the vision in his right eye. He heard the man step back. Another hand moved to his mouth and gently teased the edge of the tape away. He recognised the scent. *Mary. You bloody fool, Joe, you bloody fool.* Now holding the edge, the hand ripped the tape away. He yelped with pain.

"Mary. Help me, Mary," he pleaded desperately.

"Shut up, Joe, or he'll hurt you," she spoke ominously into his ear.

"So your debt, Joe boy. What are we gonna do?" asked the male.

"What debt?" he replied, his voice hoarse and shaking.

"Wellbury's debt, Joe. It was passed to you."

"I'll pay it, I'll pay it. I've got the money."

"I know you'll pay it, Joe," said the voice menacingly. "I've got your phone here. I see you've pin locked it. What's your pin number?"

"Why?"

"I need to text your mammy."

"No you bloody don't," replied Joe bravely. The male sprang forward, grabbed Joe's hair, pulling his head backwards against the collar and ropes. "I'll decide that," he shouted, the blade point held directly in front of Joe's eyeball. "I told you," spoken quietly, "one chance. The number." He demanded. Joe provided it. The male stepped back.

"Give him a drink." Joe felt Mary move forward, cupping his chin gently as she poured some water in his mouth. He swallowed desperately, the moisture massaging his dry throat as it passed. The bottle was pulled away, his shirt used to wipe his mouth, and the tape replaced.

"There you go, sweetie. You got to have a drink with me after all." The footsteps walked away from the building and Joe was left with the gentle trill of birdsong and the warm balmy air of a summer's day.

***

Maureen Marsden sat at home worrying. When she got home last night Joe wasn't there and he had left no messages for her. She had spent years worrying about him and was happy that he seemed to have settled down at last. He had religiously stuck to a routine and this was the first time that he had deviated from it. She'd checked his room this morning and found that he had not slept in his bed. Her numerous texts to his phone had not been answered and knowing that he had the day off work knew that she wouldn't find him there.

"He's a grown man. He can look after himself," she said out loud in an attempt to calm herself. She walked to the kitchen to put the kettle on. Her mobile rang and she rushed back to the living room picking it up quickly from the coffee table. Checking the screen she saw that it was Joe.

"Thank God," she spoke aloud and answered the call. "Joe, thank goodness. I've been worried sick. Where are you?" There was no reply. "Joe?" Silence. "Joe, stop being daft."

"Mrs Marsden, listen very carefully," a male's voice stated.

"You're not Joe!"

"I said listen, woman," repeated the voice forcefully. Maureen sat down on her sofa, her free hand raised to her mouth. She recognised a Scouse accent but didn't know the voice.

"Who are you?" she asked. The phone vibrated in her hand. A further message received.

"Do not ring the police. Look at the message. I will ring you back." The phone went dead. Maureen turned the screen, hands shaking, and pressed the button to view the message. She gasped as she looked at an image of her son, mouth taped shut, blood on his face and tethered to a rope like a dog. Tears welled in her eyes.

"Oh son, what mess have you gotten in to?" The phone rang again. Maureen answered, pressing the loud speaker as she viewed the image.

"I have your son. Do you understand?" Maureen nodded, shock silencing her voice. "I said, do you understand?"

"Y-y-yess," she replied hesitantly, her mind bewildered by the situation.

"He owes us money, Mrs Marsden. Money that you are going to bring to me." She sat silently, tears streaming down her face. "If you follow my instructions then he won't get hurt. If you don't then I will slowly bleed him and he will die a lonely death with not a hope of being saved." Fear gripped Maureen, her pulse pounding and her rapid breaths audible on the phone. "I can hear your fear, woman, and believe me you are right to be scared."

"Don't hurt him."

"That's in your hands."

"How much?" Maureen feared the answer.

"Two hundred pounds." She wiped her face. *I've got that hidden in the clothes rail. Joe's housekeeping money.*

"I've got that now."

"Good. Good. Twelve o'clock at the shop."

"What shop?"

"Forsetti's. Take it inside and leave it on the counter." Maureen responded automatically.

"I will."

"Don't think for one minute that I'm not serious. If you are not there then he will pay for his debt with his life."

"I'll be there, I'll be there. Please don't hurt him. Please let him go."

"I'm a fair man, Mrs Marsden. The money gets paid. I let him go."

"I'll be there."

"Good. Mrs Marsden, we are watching you. If you contact the police, he dies." The phone went dead and Maureen was left looking at the horrifying photo of her precious son.

* * *

Maureen climbed out of the bus at the railway station wearing a polo necked jumper and trousers, the first clothes she'd grabbed from the wardrobe in her haste. A blue floral hat perched on her head and a brown leather handbag hung from her shoulder.

Moira checked the image on her phone, which George had sent her thirty minutes ago. He'd watched the woman leave Marsden's house and snapped an image of her from behind. The clothing and hat matched. She was confident it was Marsden. The woman started walking with determination towards the precinct, shadowed by Moira. Moira dialled on her phone.

"She's on her way."

Maureen was trembling with fear, she could not believe that this was happening. The situation was surreal and although Joe had caused her stress in the past this was beyond measure. She watched everyone as she passed, her eyes darting to faces, paranoid that any could be Joe's kidnapper. Her hand moved to her bag, reassuringly patting it, the envelope inside. Sweat ran down her back and she'd not even had time to do her face. *I must look a right state.* Approaching the street where Forsetti's stood she stopped; taking some deep breaths she removed the white envelope from her bag. She had scrawled 'Joe' on the front, her elderly handwriting spidering across the envelope. *Come on, Maureen. You can do it.* She took another deep breath and moved forward, the shop now in sight. Her shoulder collided with another person's.

"Aagh!" she cried out, her body spun to the side.

"Sorry, luv. I'll take dat." The envelope was whipped from her hand. Maureen, confused, never felt it. She looked for the man but it could have been anyone. She recognised the voice though. A female approached her and placed a hand on her arm, reassuringly. She was young and wore a large brimmed sun hat.

"You OK, love? That ignorant bloke."

"Yes, mmm, yes I think so. My envelope has gone though," said Maureen looking at the ground, in case she had dropped it. "Oh no, I need it." Moira leaned in close to Maureen, the brim of her hat touching Maureen's hat.

"We've got it," she said, mimicking a Scouse accent. "Joe will be released soon."

She walked away. Maureen stood dumbfounded, trying to absorb what had just happened. Her phone rang. She answered.

"Well done. I have the money." She recognised the voice. "Go home, Mrs Marsden. Joe will be with you in a while." Maureen walked away, dazed and frightened. She had nowhere to turn and didn't know who to trust. The police had done her no favours in the past and she trusted them about as far as she could throw them. *Go home and wait. What else can I do. What would Joe do? Who would he call?* She walked forlornly away, her shoulders slumped in resignation. *What would you do, Joe?* She could picture his face looking at her, a look of concern on his face. His words echoed in her head. *Ring Matt.*

* * *

Matt walked out into the back garden where Kate was sitting reading a book. The weather was pleasantly warm with the breeze offering a cooling touch to the skin. Rachel sat inside speaking with her team on the phone, harnessing their thoughts about how to progress ensuring the permanent safety of Kate. Matt could only see that happening if her pursuer was apprehended. How that was going to happen he had no idea but with the team's specialisms they may work it out. The main thing was that Kate was safe here. Nobody knew that she was here and the likelihood of her being discovered was small.

"How do you like the house?" he asked Kate.

"It's lovely. You've found a treasure in this place. If it wasn't for the circumstances, I'd feel like I was on holiday."

"Well, hard though it may be, try and treat it as one. Let Rachel and I worry about everything else."

"Have you heard from Gran?"

"Rachel's going to call her this afternoon." His phone rang. "Excuse me." It was Maureen Marsden. *Unusual*, he thought. *What does she want?*

"Hi Maureen. How are you doing?"

"Matthew, Joe's in trouble. Real trouble." He walked into the house heading towards Rachel as she told him what had happened. Rachel sat in the living room talking on the phone as he walked in. He covered his mouthpiece.

"You need to hear this, Rach."

"I'll ring back in thirty, guys." Rachel terminated her group call. Matthew flicked his phone to loudspeaker as the worried voice of Maureen continued.

"Stop there, Maureen," said Matt. "I've got Rachel listening in too now. Let me just tell her what's happening." Matt relayed the story so far. Matt nodded to her and she took the lead in the conversation.

"Maureen. Rachel here. We haven't met but you know who I am."

"Yes, dear. You're that lady from the telly last year."

"Yes, that's me. Have you still got a copy of the photo on your phone?"

"Yes."

"Can you send it to Matt?"

"Yes, I'll try now." They could hear Maureen muttering to herself as she talked her way through forwarding the photo. "Done, I think." Matt's phone pinged as the message came in. They both looked at the image.

"Bastards!" exclaimed Matt, anger sweeping his face. Rachel took his hand and squeezed. Now wasn't the time for anger. A cool, calm head was required. She squeezed his hand again reassuringly letting him know she had this.

"OK, Maureen. Have you rung the police?"

"No, they told me not to or they'll kill him. Joe won't want me to either. He doesn't trust them. That's why I'm ringing Matt."

"It would be best to ring them, Maureen. They've got specialists who deal with kidnaps."

"I'm not ringing them," she replied, her voice determined. "They have the money. They said that they'd release him if I paid." Maureen's house landline rang in the background. "Hang on. That may be him." They heard Maureen's muffled voice as she spoke. Then loud on their handset. "It's Joe. They've released him. I'll ring you back." The line went dead leaving Matthew and Rachel looking at each other.

"What the hell is happening, Rach?"

"Who did he have a debt to?"

"He didn't. Wellbury bloody did, but Joe said that had just gone away when he died." Rachel sighed. *Is that case always going to haunt me?*

"What did Joe say about Wellbury's debt?"

"Bloody hell. It's nearly a year ago, Rach. Some smack dealer slapped Joe and told him he had to pay it. Wellbury died though. Surely the debt died with him?"

"It doesn't work like that, Matt. Debts don't just go away in the drug world. They get enforced. It doesn't matter whether it's ten pounds or ten thousand. It's not about the money. It's about saving face, reputation, and control."

"Why wait so long though?"

"Because it suited them. Maybe they lost track of him when he stopped scoring. More likely that they've just waited until it suits their purposes."

"Why now?" Rachel held her hand up, halting his words.

"The key is Liverpool. Think, Matt." She ticked her fingers off as she spoke. "One, we have a murder, accidental or not in Sterndale, suspected to be connected to a Merseyside OCG. Two, Kate's housemates describe a Scouser making a dubious enquiry, the day after Kate goes missing. Three, the golf club. Bill describes his assailant as having a Liverpudlian accent. Finally, Joe gets kidnapped and Maureen describes the guy on the phone as having a Scouse accent. Too coincidental Matt. It's the same OCG. The murder, the drugs, Joe's kidnap. They have to be connected. They're hunting. Trying to flush Kate out."

"But she's nobody, Rach. She's just an unlucky, unfortunate bystander. Why all this effort?"

"I don't know love, but she seems to have upset their plans and they are determined."

"What do we do?" Matt's phone rang again. "For fu.." He looked at the screen. "It's Joe."

* * *

Joe knelt in his confinement, head aching and a cold sweat covering his skin. Blood had congealed on his face and he was parched. The air in the building was cool though a clammy sweat coated his skin. The combined forces of the assaults and lack of methadone were taking their toll on his body, and his mind circled through the possibilities of what was going to happen to him. He had lost track of time but the sunlight from the doorway behind him indicated that it was daytime as it cast some light to the room. He could hear small feet scurrying nearby and though his hands were numb he felt a nip on his forearm. His arms involuntarily jerked and the pain ceased as he heard the annoyed squeak of a rodent scurrying away. *Rats are the least of my problems.* He heard voices as footsteps approached. *Was that a Scouse accent?* He tensed, his heart beat increasing, muscles tensing as fear took its grip. Too scared to call out, for fear of reprisal, he waited. The footsteps closed in and entered. He held himself rigid, tears welling, heart pounding in his head. A body moved close. Breathing near his ear and from his right side a shiny blade focussed his vision.

"Your debt has been paid," said the male's voice quietly in his ear. "Stay very still." The knife slowly passed across his face and he felt its point against his neck, the blade held flat. This is it. *This is how I'm going to die.* Joe's breathing quickened. His eyes closed. He pleaded, muffled by his gag. A swift movement. The collar round his neck came free as he was pushed, his side hitting the hard earthen floor. Powdered dust covered his face. He breathed. *Still here.*

Hands grabbed him around the shoulders as he was placed in a sitting position, his back against the wall that he had been facing. He looked at his aggressor. Before him stood a tall, slim male, wearing a baseball cap, a dark cloth buff covering his lower face. Mean black eyes looked piercingly at him but Joe's eyes quickly moved to the blade held in the man's hands. He flinched as a hand caressed the left side of his face.

"Joey, Joey. What are we going to do with you?" asked Mary. He turned his head to look but she pushed it away forcing him to look at the male with the knife. "Keep your eyes on him, Joe. He might worry that you are not concentrating. You know, concentrating on what matters." Joe looked forwards.

"Now, we met Mrs Marsden today. A very nice lady who has paid your debt." Joe tensed, anger obvious in his eyes. "Calm yourself, Joe. You are in no position to complain." A phone was put in front of his face showing him an image of his mother within a crowded street. He tried to talk, a muffled noise the only sound. "Shhh. She's fine, for now. Just a picture to let you know that we met her." The phone was pulled away and Joe was again facing the male with the knife, who now stood in the doorway. Though his arms were still locked behind his back, his extended legs now coarsed with blood and pain as the feeling returned to his limbs.

"So," continued Mary. "Part of the debt is paid, but not the interest that you've built up. You are going to sort that out. *What do they want? More money?* "I'm going to show you another picture." The phone displayed an image of a young woman, smiling in what looked like a selfie shot. Joe looked at her, uncertain, but she looked familiar. "Do you know her?" Joe shook his head. "Well, you are going to, because we need you to find her." *How the hell do I do that, you dumb bitch?* "She's a friend of Matthew Forster's." stated Mary. *Well, if you think I'm dragging Matt into this you are wrong.* "If you don't then my mate here is going to visit your mam and he won't be so gentle this time." Joe bucked his legs, pushed with his hands, which only resulted in him falling. A boot kicked him in the stomach, forcing wind through his nose. A hand grabbed him, sat him up and the blade was held against his cheek. He felt the nick of steel, as blood seeped from a clean cut.

"We're not playing games Joe," said the male calmly. "You will do this. Find her, Joe and the debt goes. Use Forster, use his partner, use your friends, we don't care. But use somebody, or your mum's life is forfeit. It's as simple as that." The male stepped back.

"Get the car," he instructed Mary. She walked out and the two men faced each other. No words were exchanged. Joe heard the sound of a car moving. The male stepped forwards and cut the bonds to Joe's feet. He then secreted the knife behind him, grabbed Joe, and lifted him to his feet.

"Move." Joe was manhandled outside, the glare of the light causing him to squint his eyes as he was pushed towards a dark car. *Same car.* He was forced inside face down onto the back seat; he felt the male's arm fold his legs back and felt the man's bodyweight pinning him down. Joe breathed. *They're releasing me.* He heard both the driver's door and boot open. Shortly after the boot was closed, the driver returned and the car manoeuvred. Bumpy at first, the motion smoothed and Joe could tell that the speed had increased. Ten minutes later, following various turns, the vehicle stopped. The male's body pressure ceased as he moved back.

"Your instructions and rules are as follows," started Mary's voice. "If you go to the police we will kill your mum. You have the girl's picture on your mobile phone, she is called Kate. You will find her or you will pay the price. If you don't find her we kill your mum. Then we will find you and kill you." Joe felt himself dragged backwards out of the car, then felt his hands being released.

"Find her," said the male's voice. Shoved forwards, Joe's legs hit a low wall as he tumbled over it into undergrowth, the side of his head skimming stone as he heard the car pull away. His hands shooting out to protect his fall as he instinctively rolled his body, coming to a sudden halt flat on his back, slightly winded. Desperately reaching for his mouth he ripped the tape away, sucking in welcome breaths of fresh air, his hand automatically seeking his right ear.

"Ow! |" *Where am I?* Looking back to the right he saw a headstone, the side of which he had just skimmed. *Graveyard! I need to move.* He checked his body. Though aching, he was alive and could move. *I need to find mum.* He checked his phone, which had been shoved in his pocket. His screensaver had been replaced with the face of Kate. *How am I supposed to contact them?* He saw that he had a message.

This is The Hub

Question answered. He studied Kate's photograph. *I've seen you before.* Searching his mind an image of Tina sitting within Costa came to his mind, and sat next to Tina was this girl. He was sure of it.

***

"Joe, what's happening? Are you OK?"

"I'm fine, Matt. A little bruised and battered but I'll live." Joe sounded tired, his voice hoarse.

"Where are you now?"

"I'm with me mam, at the house. We need to speak, Matt."

"I'm away up north, mate. Away with Rach. I'll be back in a few days. What's it all about? As long as you are safe now."

"It can't wait and no, I'm not safe."

"Ring the police."

"I can't do that." Joe's voice was becoming strained, his hoarse voice rising in pitch. "I'm sorry, Matt, but I need to see you. I can't do this on the phone. It has to be face to face."

"Joe, I can't just break off …." Joe interrupted.

"I need your help, Matt!" His voice now pleading. "It's about Kate. We need to speak. Please!" Matt looked at Rachel who was sitting with a concerned look on her face. She'd clearly heard Joe's tones and had understood the gist of the conversation. She mouthed the word 'Go', silently. He nodded and made his decision. "Hang on tight, mate. I'll head down. I'll ring you when I get near." An audible sigh came from Joe.

"Thanks, Matt. Thanks." The phone went dead.

Matthew stood looking at Rachel. "Did you catch any of that?"

"Not really. Just that he needs you." Matt recounted the conversation.

"So we were right. It's all connected."

"What are we going to do?" He looked at Rachel. "You need me here."

"I have the team, Matt." She clarified. "Joe needs you and we need to know what is going on. You need to go down there and find out exactly what has happened. I'll be fine up here, and so will Kate."

"What about getting around? You'll be stuck here at the house."

"That's not a bad thing." She laughed. "There's worse places to be. If we need to move then I'll pull Ronnie off the team. I can send him to get a hire car in Edinburgh and he can chauffeur us around. I was actually wondering about giving Anne a call to get her up here for a visit, as Kate would benefit from her support, and I think I will now. We'll have her car here too then, so don't worry love, go and sort Joe out." He gave her a cuddle.

"You are terrific, you know."

"Well, don't be telling everyone that, you daft idiot. There's only so much of me to go around." She smiled. "Now, go and pack a bag." Matthew checked his watch and left the room, heading to the bedroom to get his stuff.

Rachel sat down, her mind whirring. Time to start planning. Events were picking up pace and her experience told her that she needed to be ready. She needed plans in place to force this to a head, under her control and under her rules. She walked to the patio window and saw Kate outside still happily reading. *I'll get Matt on his way then make some calls. Anne first, Tom second, I need him as a sounding board, and Jamal Kaur third.*

Chapter 14

In her small flat in Liverpool Paula sat looking at the data that had been provided to her by a person whom she only knew as Al. Paula had been contacted yesterday evening and had been told to ensure that she had the day free for work. She'd managed to get childcare for the day and had picked up the laptop first thing this morning. On arriving home she fired it up and the emails had been continuous since then. Telephone data was being sent to her every couple of hours about three phones, each set of data had been attributed a colour by her. Alongside this she had started receiving a couple of pieces of ANPR data. Her task was to look at it all and to make correlations between each phone and the vehicle data. She'd also received an intelligence profile for a bloke called Forster. Clearly, the boss was still on the hunt, and for Paula this was the first time that she had been given so much to do. She knew that she would get paid well for today and concentrated on the task in hand. *Bugger the consequences to others, I need to look after myself.* She sat back and looked at the screen.

Red and blue followed similar patterns. They had been in Barnston yesterday and had travelled north to the Scottish borders. They hadn't parted company, using the same telephone masts as they travelled north. The ANPR data that she had been given had shown that a car, known to Paula's team, had travelled the same route. When she overlayed the car's movement it was clear that the phones and car had travelled the same route. Paula had thoroughly examined Forster's profile. Realising that he had an open business profile, for his book shop Forsetti's, she had spent some time exploring it. Forster was keen on promoting himself and his travels, with many photographs demonstrating this. After a bit of sifting she was happy she'd found a link, as Forster stood happily on the east coast of Scotland, with the Bass Rock sitting resolutely behind him. The phone data she'd received following her discovery corroborated her findings. Both the phones stopped moving once they hit North Berwick yesterday and hadn't moved overnight. Paula was as happy as she could be that at least two persons of interest were in the vicinity of North Berwick.

The yellow phone showed a different and uncomplicated picture. Yellow had stayed in Barnston throughout the red and blue journey. The yellow phone did not have as much data, as if it hadn't been used much. The most interesting thing was that on a quick glance, Paula could see that yellow had contacted blue today. One call only but a definite link. She checked her watch and stood up, stretching her arms out. It was intense work interrogating the data and she rubbed her tired eyes as she went to her kitchen to grab a glass of water. Her hub phone vibrated and she checked the text.

Situation report?

Paula walked back to her computer and checked her last email. Another ANPR hit on the known car. It was moving south. She picked up her hub phone.

Recommend sending a resource to North Berwick and one to Barnston. Email summary to follow shortly. She received no reply and didn't expect to get one. Her hands moved swiftly as she completed a summary and pressed send. *Now to have a close look at all the phone data to find relevant numbers. This is going to be a long day.*

※ ※ ※

The weather outside was still warm as Rachel slowly walked out to the back garden concentrating intently on a tray which held two glasses of cloudy lemonade.

"Let me help you," said Kate, her chair scraping on the stone flags as she stood up.

"Don't you dare, young lady. I've got this." Rachel moved forwards. "I may be slow but I'm not incompetent." Rachel smiled as she reached the table. "There you go, no spills." Kate took a glass.

"Thank you. Matt should be well on his way now."

"Yes, love. Some good news though." Kate leaned forward expectantly as Rachel sat down. "Your gran is on the way up." Kate's face lit up. "It's all sorted. Bill's sister has arrived at home. She's going to look after him, and Rosie, of course. Debs is bringing Anne up. They're going to share the driving."

"Do they know where to come?"

"I've just told them North Berwick. I didn't want to confuse them with too many directions. I thought that we'd meet them in town tomorrow when they get here."

"Great. I can't wait." They sat chatting for ten minutes before Rachel stood up.

"I just need to make a couple of calls. Are you OK for a while?"

"Yes, thanks. I feel safe here. It's beautiful." Rachel squeezed Kate's shoulder.

"I won't be long." She walked slowly towards the house with an awkward gait. *No stick, Rach. You're getting stronger.*

Her call with Tom went well. She trusted him and he knew his stuff. The team had worked well on the way up the road and with the right coaching he was sure that he could get them up to speed. They had found accommodation in town and at her request he'd sent Jim and Ronnie over to Edinburgh to get a hire car. She'd updated him with Matt and Joe's situation and had agreed with her that there was little planning that they could do until Matt got back in contact. They'd arranged a call later after she had spoken with Matt. The call to Kaur could wait a bit. She had nothing concrete for him yet but felt that she may need his help in the coming days. Whether he would help was the question, but he'd sounded like a good detective so she was hopeful. Rachel reached for her notepad and started writing names and cross referencing with arrows, her chart building as she did so. In the middle, a question mark, for the unknown male hunting Kate. Around it all the people involved and significant locations. Everything she needed was there. The diagram focussed her mind. *How to flush you out, Mr? Go with what you know, Rach.* She drew a diagram of the conflict resolution model on a blank sheet of paper and started covering each area, filling in what she knew, identifying what she didn't, with a view to formulating a plan.

* * *

Matt arrived in Barnston and flicked Rachel a text to let her know that he had arrived and that he would ring her once he knew what was happening. He was tired as he had only taken one quick stop on the way down. He headed towards Maureen's where he knew Joe would be, but being cautious, parked on the outskirts of the estate and walked in. Somehow Joe's assailants had found an opportunity to kidnap him and Matt had to assume that they'd been previously following Joe to achieve the opportunity to do so. He watched everyone closely as he passed them, checking over his shoulder frequently as paranoia seeped into his mind. *What would Tom and Sarah do?* He stopped on the street, looked at his mapping app on his phone and realised that he could take a couple of small alleys to get to Maureen's. *That's what they'd do in the films, use alternate routes to expose anyone who may be following.* Locking the route in his mind he set off, arriving at Maureen's ten minutes later, happy now that he hadn't been followed. Matt knocked on the door and waited, hearing some noises behind the door and a muffled "Thank gawd." The door opened and he was promptly ushered in by Maureen, who held a long handled broom in her right hand.

"Quick, quick," she pushed him into the hall, quickly looked up and down the street and swiftly shut the door. She then secured the door chain, placed a dining chair behind the door, and the broom was placed up against the adjoining wall. On the bottom tread of the stairs stood a short handled axe and a wooden rounders bat. *A scared woman*, thought Matt.

"He's through here," said Maureen, ushering him towards the living room. "I'll stick the kettle on. Coffee?"

"Yes, please." Matt walked further into the room where Joe was standing looking out of the window. He turned around.

"Hi, mate." Matthew was shocked. Joe looked a mess. Bruising covered one side of his face and a scab had formed across his forehead. His colour was poor and he was clearly suffering. "What have they done to you?"

"I'm OK, I'm OK." said Joe, his voice shaking. "I've not had my meth for a couple of days, so that's not helping, but I'm on the lowest dose, so I'll brave it out and quit it."

"Your face though!"

"It's still there. All this will heal." He lifted his hands, indicating his face. "This is the least of our worries. We need to talk." The door opened and Maureen walked in carrying a tray holding three steaming mugs and a plate of Jammie Dodgers.

"Here we go, boys." She placed the tray on a side table and picked up her own mug, selected a biscuit and moved to sit in an armchair.

"Actually, Mum, do you mind if I talk to Matt alone?"

"Oh sorry, no, of course not. She moved to the door, closing it behind her. Joe walked to the door with a finger to his lips indicating for Matt to be silent. He gently turned the handle and opened the door to be faced by Maureen standing outside.

"In private, Mum."

"Oh, sorry, dear. Old habits die hard." Maureen moved away to the kitchen as Joe returned to the lounge, closing the door behind him.

"I'll cut to the chase. They've threatened to hurt my mum, unless I help them find..." Joe produced his mobile phone and showed the front screen to Matt. Matt sat looking at the image of his goddaughter who was looking back at him. *Rachel was right, it was all connected.*

"Do you know her?" he asked.

"No," replied Joe, "but they know that you do. Who is she, Matt?"

"You need to go to the police. They've tortured you and now they are threatening you."

"And what the hell are they going to do?" asked Joe angrily. "They're bloody useless, I don't trust them, and we both know that they'll do bugger all. I've got history with them, Matt. You know that I'm not going to speak to them and that you can't make me. We need to sort this. I don't know how, but we need to." Joe sat down with his head in his hands. "It's all gone to shit. My head's spinning. I need your help." Joe sat there, tears in his eyes, with an imploring and desperate look on his face.

"We will, mate. We will. Yes, I do know her, she's just a young kid who is in a bit of trouble herself. Take a step back and tell me exactly what has happened. I'll tell you my side and we'll go from there."

Joe and Matt spent the next half hour talking, exchanging what they knew, with Matt jotting notes down on a page ripped from a magazine. A knock came on the living room door.

"Come in, Mum." Maureen walked in with two more mugs.

"Everything OK, boys?"

"It will be," replied Matt. "Do you mind if we have a bit longer?"

"Not at all. I'm just going to nip to the corner shop. You two need anything?"

"No, we're fine," replied Joe. He looked at Matt and silently mouthed 'Will she be OK?' Matt nodded his ascent. Now on their own, Matt looked Joe in the eyes.

"I need to speak with Rachel. Get some advice and see where we go from here. You grab a smoke and I'll ring her. That OK?"

"Yep." Joe sat and rolled a cigarette and headed out to the back garden to smoke it. Matt rang Rachel and was still talking on the phone when Joe returned to the room. Joe alternated between pacing and sitting as he listened to one side of the conversation, eventually succumbing to a further cigarette as Matt continued. Time passed slowly as he waited for the outcome of the conversation.

* * *

Rachel finished her phone call with Matt. She needed some time to digest everything that she had been told and now, with copious notes in front of her, she needed to put them in a semblance of order. Kate had rung for a takeaway and delivery was due shortly, so dinner was sorted. They had planned an evening of Netflix but Kate would understand if Rachel got busy. She had given Matt various tasks to do and was happy that he would complete them. Rachel piled her notes together. She could work downstairs at the dining table and keep Kate company whilst she watched television. Rachel grabbed her laptop from the bedroom and set up her workstation at the table. *I'll meet with Tom later this evening but first I need to get this all documented in a situation report. If I have any chance of getting help from Kaur then he will need something tangible to work with.* She set to work.

Later that evening Rachel returned from a quick meeting that she had held with Tom. They had managed to cover most of it on the phone but she had needed some equipment, which he had handed over in person. Jim was primed for tomorrow. The team would now know that there were potentially two antagonists and they had their descriptions. Tom would brief them first thing tomorrow. Rachel was confident they were up to it.

Her conversation with Kaur hadn't gone as well as she had wished. The problem with the police was that they were inherently suspicious of everything and everyone and Kaur was no different. His initial view was that Kate was safe and that Joe Marsden was a criminal. Joe, although having helped the police once previously, was now in trouble. It was Kaur's opinion that Marsden was attempting to use that previous public spiritedness to seek aid in digging himself out of the mire. Kaur said that he would read the report in the morning and give it some thought. Rachel felt alone but at least the seed had been planted with Kaur. Kate had gone to bed a while ago. Rachel now went up the stairs too, tightly grabbing the bannister for support as she climbed. Her whole right side was aching. She needed rest and painkillers as tomorrow was going to be a very busy day.

* * *

"So, your mum can make her own way to her sister's?"

"Yes, she'll be fine with that. She's been meaning to go for a while so it won't be a problem." Joe confirmed

"Good. We have to take the risk that they don't know about your aunt or where she lives. They've clearly been concentrating on us and they have you exactly where they want you."

"They bloody well have."

"Well, now's the time to take a risk. We have to assume that they are capable of following you. Also that they know me and the car, but that's what we want. They need to believe that you are working for them, mate. We need them away from here. Away from where they have become comfortable. Are you ready to text the hub? Then we go."

"Yes." Joe composed his text and pressed send.

With Forster at his house. He's going to see her now. Heading north. They both sat looking at the phone, awaiting a response. The reply came.

Good

The men casually walked out of Matthew's house and climbed in his car. Both tense, paranoid, but strangely excited; thrown back to their risky younger days of imagined adventures. As the engine started the device attached under the car woke up and fired out a message.

* * *

Gently placing his coffee down, George checked his phone where the tracker had messaged him, letting him know that it was moving. He picked up a laptop, ensuring that no one was nearby as he discreetly checked the map displayed on the screen. A flashing green circle indicated that the car was moving. His phone vibrated and he read the confirmation from the hub that Mardsden was with Forster. He smiled, closed the laptop and enjoyed the rest of his drink. He was glad to be leaving Barnston and would be more than happy for this job to finish. It had taken too long and in his opinion the boss was throwing too much at it. Now with Moira well on her way towards North Berwick and Forster, likely to be heading in the same direction, they had a good chance of finishing it, once and for all.

* * *

The car took the slip road from the dual carriageway taking the exit to a small service station. Matt had been driving for a couple of hours and needed a rest break as well as a coffee. Joe and himself had discussed their plans as they travelled, both feeling the tension of danger at their backs, but also buzzing with the thrill of it. Joe was managing to control his cravings with just diazepam and though not looking great, felt as if he was coping. They pulled up into the rear parking area where only a couple of cars sat; further back were some parked lorries where drivers were taking their enforced breaks.

"Just keep your eyes peeled, Joe. They could be anywhere," said Matthew climbing out of the car and heading to the toilet block.

Joe sat scanning the area, but no cars entered the services whilst he waited. Matthew exited the toilets and walked across to the service station shop; here he purchased and returned with two takeout coffees and a couple of sandwiches.

"This will keep us going." He handed Joe his share of the goods. "You heard from them?"

"Nothing, mate. They'll maybe be waiting for contact from me."

"Maybe," replied Matt. "We'll know in a while. I'll check in with Rachel." Matthew gave Rachel a call and updated her on their progress as Joe scanned the area.

"Right, let's go. Rachel's doing fine. Everything is good at her end." He started the car and gently pulled away from the garage onto the carriageway and continued heading north, the device on his car still transmitting its signal.

* * *

Rachel stood in the car park of Tesco having just taken her phone call with Matthew. The lads were both safe; she would move onto the next stage of their plan. She still hadn't heard from Kaur and would consider ringing him again in a while if needed. She looked across at the hire car where Ronnie and Kate sat chatting. Ronnie was a people person and had quickly made Kate feel comfortable, so much so that she was sitting in the back laughing at something he had said. Looking over to the entrance she spotted Anne's car entering the car park. *Right on time.* Rachel raised her hand in greeting and walked over to Ronnie's car. Anne's manoeuvred onto the petrol forecourt, clearly in need of a refuel. She watched Anne climb out of the passenger side and walk towards the shop as Debs went to the petrol pump. She smiled, happy that the women were working in unison. They would be fine taking Kate back. Rachel climbed into the car.

"You OK, Kate?"

"She's doing fine," said Ronnie. "Can't wait to see her family."

"Yes, I'm fine thanks, Rach."

"So, this is where we part, for a while. Probably just a couple of days and then I'll come and see you."

"Thanks, Rach, for keeping me safe." Rachel reached into her bag.

"This is the item we talked about, love." She showed her a metal block and handed it to her. "You just need to put it in your bag." Kate did so. "It will just let me know where you are and as you know, it also records speech. Neither are anything that you need to worry about. They're just there for my reassurance and comfort."

"I understand." Rachel had briefed Kate this morning. Anne was to know nothing except that things were in hand. They didn't want to cause her undue worry following Bill's incident. Rachel would visit and explain everything in a couple of days. Anne's car pulled up in a parking space opposite Ronnie's. Rachel sat as she watched Kate get out and run over to Anne. They both hugged with tears in their eyes. Debs climbed out of the car watching them both fondly, not having been blessed with grandchildren of her own. Rachel climbed out of her car and walked over to them.

"And this is Debs," said Anne to Kate.

"Nice to meet you," said Kate smiling.

"And you, love. I've heard so much about you." She looked over at Rach. "How are you doing, Rachel?" She looked sympathetically at Rachel's leg and walking stick. "Are you getting a restful holiday?"

"You could say that. The leg's improving, thank you."

"Good, now we'd better be off," continued Debs, quickly changing the conversation. "We have a long drive ahead." Deborah immediately took control of the situation, positioning herself as organiser and instructor. "Now, you two sit in the back and catch up with each other. I'll take the first drive and you both relax." Anne took Rachel's hand.

"Thank you so much, love." She squeezed Rachel's hand. "Everything OK?"

"Just fine, Anne. I'll see you in a couple of days." Rachel returned the squeeze and Anne knew not to ask further.

"Let's go then," Deborah's voice called out. "Everyone in." She ushered them both into the car and climbed in herself, starting the engine. Gears engaged she pulled away, the rear passengers waving goodbye. Rachel waved back then slowly climbed in with Ronnie, using her hands to support her sore leg.

"Causing pain?"

"It's squeezing into this car, Ron. We'll get a bigger one next time. Let's get back to the house." Fifteen minutes later they arrived at the cottage. Rachel peeled herself out of the car.

"We'll set up in the dining room." He walked ahead, unlocked the door and entered, leaving the door open for her. Rachel followed slowly behind, stopping in the kitchen and grabbing a glass of water. She took some painkillers out of her bag and swallowed them with the water. Flicking the kettle on she limped to the dining room and sat herself at the table where Ronnie had placed their equipment. Now infront of her sat the radio base station, her laptop and an iPad showing a mapping system. The basics of what she needed.

"Jim says the office set up will be better," said Ronnie.

"This will do for today though, mate. We'll get better at it as we get practice." She leaned towards the radio's microphone and hearing nobody else talking, pressed the transmit button. "Rachel to Tom with a comms check."

"Loud and clear, Rach. We have control of the subject." The team had been tasked to follow Kate covertly. With the tracking device to assist the three operatives, they would accompany her to her end destination, the reassurance of their presence a balm to Rachel.

"Loud and clear. Over to you." Rachel sat back as the operatives started transmitting to each other using abbreviated dialogue on the radio as they worked.

"Coffee, Rach?"

"Yes, please." Ronnie went to the kitchen, no doubt fitting in a swift drag from a cig as he made their drinks. He returned a few minutes later smelling of smoke. She was beginning to know her team better. Rachel sat looking at the iPad, watching the dot as it tracked away from North Berwick, heading south. She checked her email. Nothing from Kaur. *Patience Rach, give him time.*

* * *

Sterndale Police Station was unusually quiet this morning. Kaur walked through the back door and on through its small corridors towards his office, grabbing a coffee from the kitchen before settling in front of his desk. He powered on the computer and entered his passwords, allowing him access to the police systems and his emails. Rachel's conversation had weighed on his mind overnight causing him a restless sleep. Sure enough the email from Rachel sat looking at him. He opened the mail and started reading. Now reading the document for the second time, he made brief notes. *What the hell is happening here?* Rachel's conjecture gave a clear and convincing picture but all based on supposition. *No evidence, Rachel. You know I need evidence to act.* Checking his notes he started interrogating the intelligence system. There were definitely links to Liverpool from the body found in the van, Wellbury, and Marsden, but with no details of anything to go on, except for the name Mary, the two unknowns may as well have been ghosts. He sat back staring at the screen, a custody photograph of Marsden looking back at him. No intelligence about him had been recorded since the Wellbury incident. He'd been keeping his nose clean. *Why pop up now, Marsden?* Kaur checked through categories of address, work, associates and officers. The officers displayed people who had looked at Marsden's record. Only two names were shown within the last nine months, the first being his analyst in the intelligence cell who had looked a couple of weeks ago, the second being Dave Brindle. *Brindle? Why are you looking at him?* Kaur sat back. *Tasked to go and see Forster but looking at Marsden before you went?* Kaur clicked on Forster's name who was shown as an associate of Marsden. Forster was only recorded on the system as a witness; not unsurprising as he wasn't a criminal. He checked who had looked at him. Some of the enquiry team including Brindle, but Brindle had accessed a Barnston terminal to do so. *Why hadn't he checked the system before visiting him across there?* Kaur felt uneasy as well as confused. *Something isn't right.* Instinct led him to check Brindle's activity on ANPR and his alarm bells rang. *He'd only just checked Forster's car out ten minutes ago.* He walked across to Andrea's office, where the door was ajar. He knocked.

"Come in." Andrea stood hanging up her suit jacket.

"Have you got two minutes, Boss?"

"Of course,"

"This way." He held the door open for her, seeing her confusion. "Just go with it." He reassured her. Kaur walked towards the office where he knew Brindle would be. The door was closed. He took the handle and swiftly turned it, walking in, followed by Andrea.

Brindle sat in the office, alone, a look of shock on his face and a small mobile phone in his hand. He dropped the phone on the desk and stood up. His face looked panicked.

"Sarge," swiftly followed by "Boss," as he saw Andrea enter behind Kaur. "I can explain." Kaur swiftly moved forward, grabbing the phone.

"Away from the desk," he said forcibly. Brindle stepped back, knocking the chair over behind him. Kaur smelt the stink of stale booze waft past his nostrils.

"Explain what?" asked Andrea, arms crossed blocking the door.

"Why he has been misusing the police computer and is in possession of a burner phone," stated Kaur. Brindle's face crumbled. "I'm in the shit, Boss. I need help." Tears welled in his eyes as he picked up the chair disconsolately and sat in it. Andrea closed the door as Brindle prepared himself to tell all.

Chapter 15

The outlet stores stood in a small development to the left side of the road. Matthew manoeuvred his car across the dual carriageway taking the exit that would lead him towards the shops and the large integral open air car park. The air in the car was palpable as Matt looked for a suitable parking space for the car. He trusted that 'the enemy' as Joe and he now referred to them, knew where they were and hoped that they did. He parked up in a quieter area with clear views from his car to the surrounding available spaces.

"Right, let's go for a wander and I'll give Rachel a ring." They both climbed out and walked towards the shops. Matthew made his call.

"How's things going, Rach?"

"Nothing from Kaur. Kate's safe with Anne and Debs though. Seen anything suspicious?"

"Nothing at all."

"That doesn't mean that they're not with you."

"I know, I know. Let's hope that they are." Matt walked into Next, Joe alongside him. "We're going to browse a little and then grab a coffee. Then we'll make our move."

"OK. Let me know when you send Joe off. Take your time, Matt. We want them wondering what you are up to."

"Will do." Matt and Joe spent half an hour checking out the shops before settling for a coffee."

"You see Mary, Joe?"

"Not at all, mate. No one is familiar." Across the car park they watched a police car move to park near McDonald's and the occupants exit and move towards the food outlet. Matt quickly got out his phone and texted Rachel the information.

"Not organised by Rach but let's use it to our advantage. Time to move." Joe acted on his cue and sent his preplanned text to the hub.

* * *

George sat in his car becoming increasingly irate. *What was the little sod getting up to?* He had loosely followed both the males around the outlet, was amazed that they were actually browsing, and he'd left them in disgust, having their coffee. *A bloody shopping trip? He was taking the piss.* Now with a view of Forster's car he waited, his anger building and then the text arrived.

Abort. Marsden won't do it.

"Won't do it. He bloody well will!" George hit the steering wheel and threw the phone down. "The little jumped up bastard." He looked across the car park to see Marsden nonchalantly walking back towards Forster's car. George cracked open the door and stood up. Marsden didn't spot him. *Right.* He slowly closed the door and checked the small of his back. *I'll sort this.* He moved.

* * *

Matt walked from the side of the cafe, on his mobile phone, with a view of Joe strolling back to their car.

"He's walking slowly to the car."

"Anything?" replied Rachel's voice.

"Nothing." Matt looked around. "Wait … There's a bloke who's just got out of his car. He's looking at Joe. Can't take his eyes off him. It's him." Matt started moving. Keeping behind the male, now crouched as he moved across the car park, using cars for cover. *I'm too far away.* "I've got to move."

"Ron's on it," he heard as he pulled the phone away from his ear and started to run quietly forwards.

* * *

Joe kept his pace steady. He was sweating and scared. *Seen you,* he thought, clocking a guy in his peripheral vision. He could feel the man's eyes boring into him. The man started moving towards him. *Pick your spot, Joe.* He maintained his pace, trusting his friend. Towards the car. *Don't let me down, Matt.*

* * *

Two police officers ran out of McDonald's, one still stuffing a burger into his mouth and clutching his coke. They looked around. Zone H. They pointed, threw the coke on the ground and ran to their police car. Engine started and moved the car forwards.

* * *

The male was closing. Hand towards the small of his back.

"Oi, you, you little tosser," said the male loudly, his Scouse accent resonating in Joe's ears. Joe turned to look at him, Matt closed, launched his body as Joe watched his high tackle crunch into the back of the Scouser. Years of practice ensured that Matt nailed it. Their bodies flew forward, Matt's full bodyweight smashing the Scouser's head to the concrete. The Scouser's hands flailed out instinctively to save him, a large knife skittering across the ground. A squeal of tyres pierced the air as a marked police vehicle braked sharply, a copper jumping out of the passenger side as it stopped. The cop ploughed into the melee, grabbing hold of Matt and hauling him backwards. His partner now out of the vehicle, took the arm of the male on the floor, pinning him in a wrist lock. The Scouser tried to struggle but the pin held.

"Don't move." the cop shouted. The second cop, still holding Matt, looked at Joe, and nodded to the knife.

"Whose is it?" Joe pointed to the Scouser restrained on the floor. "It's his."

"Dan," the male said to the officer restraining George "be careful. The knife's his". "You are under arrest, mate," said Dan to George. Dan placed a handcuff on the George's wrist and locked it to George's other wrist, before rolling him onto his side.

* * *

"Thank you." Ronnie took the phone from his ear having been on hold with Cleveland Police Control Room. "They've got him." Rachel punched the air.

"Yes." Her face beamed. Ronnie was standing, fists raised in triumph. He put his phone down and pointed to the radio. Rachel, realising what he meant, leaned forward and waited for a gap in the team's transmissions. The gap came.

"Rachel to Tom."

"Go ahead, just approaching Berwick-Upon-Tweed."

"Male subject detained."

"Loud and clear." She could hear the happiness in his voice. Rachel was overjoyed. *Our first success*. The radio commentary continued with the rest of the team continuing to follow Kate in Anne's car.

"Vehicle has pulled to the front of the railway station and halted." Rachel looked at the radio confused, wondering what they were doing. The plan was to travel straight to Anne's.

* * *

Chapter 15

Anne and Rachel sat in the back of the car chatting amiably as Debs continued to drive. They'd all had a cheery yell as they crossed the border into England and it had taken them an hour to get this far.

"I'm just going to pull in here for a quick rest and the loo, ladies, if that's OK with you?" said Debs, parking the car in front of the station. They both gave their assent. But Deborah remained in the car, seemingly waiting. Anne and Kate looked at each other with Anne frowning. Debs noticed her look in the mirror and saw a young lady walking towards them.

"I'll just ask her where it is." said Debs, clarifying her hesitancy to get out. She wound the window down and as the lady drew near called out. "Excuse me, dear." The woman walked to the window and looked in, reached for the door handle, opened the door and climbed in.

"Hi there, Boss. How are you doing?" Anne jumped in surprise, a small squeak exiting her mouth. Kate leaned forward. *Did she just call Debs, Boss?*

"I'm fine dear. Sick to death of these two wittering on though. They haven't shut up the full journey. Let's get going." Debs swiftly pulled away from the kerb, heading out of the town.

* * *

"A female is approaching the car, photo obtained. She talks to the driver, and is in as the passenger. The vehicle is driving away."

"Stay with the car." transmitted Tom. "Jim, get that photo out."

"Received."

"Tom to Jim."

"Go ahead."

"Take over commentary on the vehicle from your iPad."

"Received."

"Rachel is listening." Interjected Ronnie. Rachel sat shocked. A female getting in. *Who the hell is she?* Her phone pinged with a clear image of the woman which had been taken on Jim's iPhone. She showed it to Ronnie. He nodded.

"Photo received in control." He transmitted and continued to listen in on the vehicle's movements. "Await further instructions from Rach." His voice, calm and unflappable. This was why Rachel needed him on the team. *Think, Rachel, think. Matt would have the photo but was probably still with the police. Joe!* She sent the photo to Joe's phone. Within seconds his reply.

Bloody hell, that's Mary!

Her phone rang, her pulse quickened. *Kate is in serious danger.* Rachel automatically answered.

"Rachel Barnes"

"Rachel, it's Jamal. Kate is in danger."

"I know. I have people behind her." Jamal interrupted her.

"You are on speaker, the Super is listening." Andrea spoke.

"What do you mean?"

"Kate has a tracker in her bag. I have two cars following her." Andrea gave Jamal a bewildered look, hands open as if to say 'What the hell?' "I need someone to stop the car, before something happens." Jamal looked at Andrea who gave him the signal to go with it.

"Where is it?"

"Northumbria, A1 south." Andrea picked up her phone and dialled the Northumbria Police control room to request resources.

***

"You've caused me a lot of pain, Kate," said Deborah, her voice hardened. Kate had already tried the door handle and realised that the child locks were on. She sat there meekly. "It's taken me years and years of hard work to get where I am now at the head of my organisation. Years, Kate. You've embarrassed me. Made me look weak. Unable to take care of my own business issues," Deborah hissed from her mouth. A changed woman with the niceties of age vanished. *Insane. Unbalanced,* thought Kate, clutching Anne's hands tightly. They were terrified.

"But I didn't do anything?"

"You rang the police, Kate. You rang the bloody bizzies." Spoken with a Scouse twang. "He owed me money, lots of money. He deserved it. He tried to embarrass me. It's not the money. I don't care about that. It's the harm that he's caused to my reputation. To my team's reputation. That is something that I won't tolerate. You do what you are told or you pay the price. A debt is a debt. You were unfortunate enough to witness that debt being redeemed."

"I can withdraw my statement, say I made it up," said Kate desperately.

"Too late for that dear. It's gone way beyond that. You have exposed my organisation. Even caused me to have one of them killed. Now Moira and I are going to sort that out."

"How?"

"I haven't decided. What do you think, Moira? A fatal driving accident?"

* * *

Tom sat in his car with Sarah and Jim close behind. He awaited further instruction with various scenarios running through his mind. Rachel advised him that support was on the way. With no communication with the Northumberland cops he would have to trust his own instincts. He checked his rear view mirror and could see Sarah's car about four cars behind him with no sign of any police behind her. He continued with his commentary.

"V1 continues A1 south, speed of seventy." *Damn! Just as I feared.* "Left side indication and V1 exits the A1 and turns left. Sarah, have you still got control of it on the iPad?"

"Yes," came the reply.

"Over to you." Tom slowed his vehicle allowing his target vehicle to pull away but took the same exit towards a roundabout. He listened for Sarah's commentary.

"At the roundabout V1 takes the first exit." Tom continued onto the roundabout intending to do the full circuit before taking the same route as V1. He checked his mirrors and saw Sarah's car shadow V1's movements.

"Rachel to Sarah,"

"Go ahead."

"I am monitoring. Northumbria now have the tracking signal too and are making their way towards you."

"Loud and clear, Rachel. V1 continues on this B road, there are fields now on either side of the road." Tom checked his Sat Nav and saw ahead that there was a beauty spot with surrounding woods and further down the road, a disused quarry. *I don't like the feel of this.* Sarah continued.

"V1 is slowing down on the road. Tom, I'm going to close up. See what's happening."

"Received." Tom slowed his own vehicle and stopped in a gated entrance adjacent to the woods.

"Sighting of the vehicle as it slows in the road with a right sided indication. V1 turns right into a small parking area next to some woods." Rachel quickly transmitted.

"Northumbria still on the A1. Deploy the foot team."

"Received," from Tom.

"Received," from Sarah.

"Tell me what you see. Ronnie is relaying everything to Northumbria." Tom got swiftly out of his vehicle, grabbed a pack off the back seat and vaulted the gate, entering the woods.

"Tom's in the woods to the west." he transmitted.

"Jim and Sarah entering woodland to the east," spoke Jim's calm tones.

Tom started moving slowly forwards through the woods, placing a dark cap on his head as he did so. He grabbed a scarf of military scrim from his dark green backpack and placed it around his neck, in preparation to cover his face and hide his profile. He heard voices and dropped to hands and knees. He edged slowly forwards gently pushing himself into the shrubbery before him.

"Tom has control of the subjects," he whispered into his microphone.

"You are loud and clear to us," replied Rachel, speaking quietly, reacting to Tom's voice.

"Jim, Sarah, hold where you are," continued Tom.

"Received," both replied quietly. Tom knew that they would be ready to react to anything he needed. His heart was pounding in his chest. He took a deep breath, calmed himself, and continued.

"Elderly female and a young female, Moira, stand outside of the car. They are talking. There is one other vehicle in the parking area. A black Ford Focus. Moira opens a rear door and reaches in. Handed items by Kate. Two mobile phones. The door is closed." Tom edged forward straining to hear any conversation and watched as Moira dropped the phones on the ground and smashed her boot heel into both. "Phones destroyed by Moira."

"Sarah is obtaining video evidence of this," interrupted Sarah over the radio. *Brilliant,* thought Tom, *and Jim will be nearby too.*

"The females talk to each other and separate. Elderly woman points her hand to the Focus and four way flashers illuminate." *Right, that's their vehicle then.* "Moira moves towards rear passenger door. Door opened. Reaches in. S1 dragged out by her hair thrown to the ground. Kicked. Jim, move in!" Tom got to his feet.

* * *

"You little bitch," shouted Moira. "You should have just kept quiet." She crouched over Kate, her fist drawn back.

"Steady on, what's happening here?" shouted a bald, tall man who had just walked into the car park. Moira looked at the male, who wore a backpack and carried two walker's sticks. She looked around. *Where the hell have you come from?* Debs was moving towards the Focus. Anne screamed from the car. "Help! Help us!" Moira heard something behind her, turned and saw a lean male in dark clothing, baseball cap and scrim tied around his face, running towards her. The walker was also moving in. Her training took over. She spun and ran, straight at the walker. He slowed. She dipped her shoulder and barged him roughly as she ran past. He fell on his backside and was scrabbling to get back up. She ran towards the Focus.

"Keys," she shouted, hands ready to catch, as Debs approached the car. Debs threw them and moved to the passenger side, Moira heading for the driver's side. She jumped in, Debs fractionally behind her, surprisingly nimble for her age. Engine started, the wheel span and Moira turned the vehicle towards the exit, glimpsing the dark-clothed male with Kate and the walker running towards the other car.

"What the hell's going on?" she shouted at Debs.

"Just drive, DRIVE," screamed Debs.

* * *

Tom took hold of Kate who was curled up and terrified on the ground. "Kate, you are safe. I'm Rachel's friend." She looked at him as she moved her face. "You are safe. Have you got the device Rach gave you?" She nodded.

"Tom to Rach. Subject is safe. Moira and the woman are away in the black Focus. Westerly direction."

"Received, traffic units exiting the A1 towards you." Tom could hear their engines approaching, roaring as they sped past.

"Units in pursuit," confirmed Tom.

***

"That's the police behind us," said Moira looking worriedly at Debs.

"Faster then," instructed Deborah looking over her shoulder. "We can get away," she said more confidently. Moira increased the pressure on the accelerator, easing slightly as she approached an S bend. She cornered well but on exiting was confronted by a group of cyclists. She corrected the car. Over-corrected! Braked as she approached a hedge and tree, the resultant skid flipping the car, the driver side smashing into the tree trunk. Debs screamed as she was thrown forward, towards the windscreen, feeling her face hit an airbag. Cyclists fell, toppling into one another, the sound of a siren approaching behind them. A marked police vehicle came slowly around the corner – having heard the collision it had silenced its siren – as uniformed police officers jumped out. An officer ran towards the Focus, transmitting on his radio as he did so.

"Ambulance and Fire Brigade to the scene. Multiple casualties." He looked into the car. "Young female deceased. Elderly female conscious but injured. Direction please." The response came back.

"Arrest her, suspicion of kidnap."

"Received."

***

In a small cottage in North Berwick, Rachel sat at the dining table with a look of both shock and triumph on her face. Ronnie had to go outside for a cigarette to relieve his tension. Rachel's adrenaline was pumping, she was ecstatic and, for the first time in a long time, really proud of herself. *Bloody hell, that was close but we did it.* Her fist hit the table. *We bloody well did it.* It took all her restraint not to yell out.

Chapter 16

One month later the team sat in their new building on the industrial estate, ready to plan ahead. All were committed now. Old, retired or just needing change, they could all see that they could forge new careers for themselves, could be of use, could serve the public. That is why they had joined their various careers. To protect and serve. This was just a different way of doing it. The jobs they pick up might seem menial but they weren't menial to anyone employing them. They would be employed, because those people needed them. Rachel had taken a lot of time to speak to the team individually and as a whole, and Matthew's place was now guaranteed for him too. They couldn't expand too quickly, but when new people's skills became available, they all agreed that they needed to grasp them. The team sat in the garage area chatting.

"I'm not just going to be the bloody tea boy, you know." A man walked in carrying a tray full of mugs of tea and coffee. The team grabbed their drinks jovially stating, "You've got to start somewhere," "You're trained for nowt else," "Just get on with it". Joe sat down with the group, laughing along with them.

Matthew and Rachel looked at each other and smiled. Rachel was proud. This was her team. She had brought them together. Joe? Well, Joe offered another element. He'd lived the hard life that they hadn't, he'd been a criminal, he'd mixed among criminals. He could give an insight to the team that no one else could. Joe stood up from the group and wandered over to Rachel.

"Can I have a private word, darlin'?" She looked at Matt and frowned.

"Of course, Joe." They walked away to one end of the garage.

"I'll cut straight to it, Rach. Now that I'm legit I wondered if you'd do me a favour?"

"Go on," she smiled.

"That lady, you know the one that was looking after Kate in Barnston."

"Tina?"

"Yep, that's her. You reckon you can set me up on a date with her? Give me an introduction?" Rachel laughed.

"You're irrepressible, Joe. I'll see what I can do."

"Thanks. That would mean a lot to me," he replied humbly, but with a twinkle in his eye, walking back to the group and pretending to punch Ronnie in the stomach. Ronnie flinched, spluttering coffee from his mouth.

"You bloomin' idiot," he yelled.

Rachel looked at them all fondly and walked with her stick back to Matt, giving him a hug. He hugged her back and whispered.

"What is it?"

"They're bloody great, Matt. Every single one of them."

The End

Author's Acknowledgements

Thank you to the team at Pen and Sword for supporting me, in particular Charles and Jon. Special thanks to my editor Amy for all her valuable advice and patience in dealing with my queries.

To Sarah, my wonderful wife and first reader, and my family for their continued support.

Glossary of Police Acronyms

ANPR – Automatic Number Plate Recognition

ARV – Armed Response Vehicle

CHIS – Covert Human Intelligence Sources

CID – Criminal Investigation Department

FIO – Field Intelligence Officer

NABIS – National Ballistics Intelligence Service

OCG – Organised Crime Group

PNC – Police National Computer

SIO – Senior Investigating Officer

SOCO – Scenes of Crime Officer

UWSU – Underwater Search Unit

VIN – Vehicle Identification Number